RUN GAME

BOSTON BLIZZARD SERIES
BOOK 2

C.L. ROSE

RUN GAME

Cover Design: C.L. Rose

Editing and Proofreading: Breanne at Breezy Book Edits

Chapter Break Illustrations: Breanne at Breezy Book Art

To all the girls who don't know their worth. Somebody out there thinks you're priceless.

PLAYLIST

1. Shut Up and Look Pretty - ari hicks

2. We Should Get Married - Dan + Shay

3. Marry You - Bruno Mars

4. Aphrodite - Sam Short

5. One Of The Girls (with JENNIE, Lily-Rose Depp) The Weeknd

6. Slayer - Bryce Savage

7. Spin You Around - Morgan Wallen

8. Come My Way - PLVTINUM

9. Unstable (feat. The Kid LAROI) - Justin Bieber

10. They Don't Know About Us - One Direction

11. Beautiful Things - Benson Boone

12. Stuck with U (with Justin Bieber) - Ariana Grande

13. Pretty Little Poison - Warren Zeiders

14. STAY (with Justin Bieber) - The Kid LAROI

15. You Don't Want That Smoke - Bailey Zimmerman

16. The Heart Wants What It Wants - Selena Gomez

17. Heroin - Andru Jamison

18. Wild As Her - Corey Kent

AUTHOR'S NOTE

While most of the laws and processes in this book have been researched for accuracy, some have been embellished to enhance the storyline. Please do not use it as a guide to getting married or divorced. You can, however, use it as a guide to getting railed by a super hot, fictional football player that wants to spank you and always finishes his dessert.

PROLOGUE

DIA

"WHERE THE *FUCK* ARE WE GOING?" I ask, looking around at the swanky neighborhood. Huge houses with expensive cars in the driveways pass by as I rubberneck from the front seat of Dalton's Audi R8.

"Jesus, Dia," he groans. "Would it kill you to let someone surprise you with something just once in your life?" It may seem like I'm one of those people who hates surprises, but the truth is that I'm just not used to good things happening to me. I don't like to trauma dump, but my life has been a series of very unfortunate events, starting with the family I was born into.

Family.

If it weren't for my best friend Mads and her parents, I wouldn't know the meaning of the word. But while they've always made me feel welcome and loved, I never felt like I belonged. Not really. I'm just their daughter's friend that had the bad luck of being born to the two most selfish human beings on the planet.

I roll my eyes, hoping he sees the gesture. "Fine," I reply. That earns me one of his signature fuckboy grins and I'd love to tell you that I'm immune to it, but as soon as those dimples sink into his cheeks, I can't stop the corners of my lips from turning up.

Dalton reaches across the center console and puts his hand on my thigh. I pretend to be annoyed, huffing a breath as I turn to look back out the window. He may be a pain in the ass, but Dalton is a good guy. And for some reason, no matter how much I push back, he wants to be around me. I should be eating this attention up. He is, by far, the most attractive man I've ever seen. I bet every woman in Boston, single or not, would kill to be in my position right now. And to top it all off, he'd give you the Gucci shirt off his back in a heartbeat. Fuck him for *all of that*, because it makes staying flustered with him really fucking hard.

We pull up to a huge, wrought iron gate and Dalton rolls his window down before punching in some numbers on the keypad. "The code is 1123," he tells me.

I furrow my brows. "Ummmmm, okay?" I reply. Why the fuck is he telling me this? I bet whoever owns this house wouldn't be too happy with him telling me their gate code all willy-nilly. For all they know, I could have a fleet of Mini Coopers in a warehouse somewhere for heists and shit.

I don't, but I *could.*

Dalton puts the car in park, whipping off his seatbelt, and is opening my door before I even get a chance to think. He's a gentleman. I'll give him that. "Let's go, Wifey," he says, putting out his hand for me to grab. I do, but only because this car is so low to the ground. Not because I like how his skin feels against mine.

I roll my eyes. "Are you *ever* going to stop calling me

that?" I sass. I'm in a mood today, but I mainly just like giving him a hard time.

"Let me think," he says, pinching his chin as if he's deep in thought. "No."

Dalton has called me Wifey since the moment we met at Mads' birthday party this past winter. It was annoying then, and it's even more annoying now, considering our current situation. Why it still gives me butterflies every single time he says it, even months later, is something I am not willing to unpack. Ever. We're just going to put it in a box, lock that bitch up, and donkey kick it right into the ocean. I'm not a *butterflies* kind of girl.

At least, I didn't used to be.

He keeps a firm hold on my hand as he leads me down the walkway and up the stairs of the massive porch. Stopping at the door, he drops my hand and removes the front cover of a box mounted above the doorknob. He presses his finger to it until we hear a faint *beep*. Reaching for my hand again, he says nothing as he straightens my pointer finger and presses it to the same place he just put his. When it beeps, he lets go of me and replaces the cover of the box. I stand there wordlessly, completely confused as to what the fuck is going on.

"All set," he says with a grin.

I look at my finger as if it can tell me what's happening before realizing it definitely won't. "What was that?" I ask him.

He furrows his brows. "I was programming our finger-prints into the lock," he answers, looking at me like it's the world's most obvious thing.

"Okayyyyyyy," I say, drawing out the word. "Why?"

He doesn't answer my question before he opens the door and ushers me into the house. I stop breathing completely as I take in my surroundings. To the left of the large entryway is a beautiful living room, completely furnished, with the most luxurious sectional I've ever seen. I bet I could sink right into it and sleep for an entire weekend. A huge flat screen television is mounted above the massive white brick fireplace. Directly in front of me is a beautiful marble staircase that leads to the second floor, where the landing overlooks the entire space. And to the right, a state-of-the-art kitchen peeks through another wide archway. This is absolutely the most beautiful house I've ever seen and I'm barely three steps into the door.

"Who lives here?" I whisper, still nearly speechless as my eyes continue to bounce around the room.

I feel him as he presses his body to me from behind, snaking his arms around my waist before dropping his chin to my shoulder. "We do."

ONE
DALTON
EIGHT WEEKS EARLIER

"VEGAS?" my quarterback, Tanner, yells over the commotion. Players and their loved ones are celebrating from one end of the field to the other as blue and white confetti continues to fall around us. The Boston Blizzard just won the Super Bowl, and we're ready to party. "The jet's waiting. Let's fucking go!" he yells loudly.

I push a hand through my dark brown hair, a smirk blooming across my lips. "Fuck yeah, baby!" I answer. "I'll grab Blaze and Mav!"

I turn to find the guys just as an ice blue blur flings itself into my arms. "I'm so proud of you, baby!" my mom yells over the screaming fans and loud music booming through the speakers. She's swimming in an actual game-worn jersey that I gave her, but she insists it's good luck. And I guess maybe she's right. "You played great!"

"Thanks, Mom," I reply on a laugh, squeezing her tiny frame before setting her back onto her feet. She cups my cheeks with her hands and I don't miss the twinkle in her eyes as she tries to hold back her tears.

"That's how you do it, Champ," my dad says with a

big grin stretched across his face. He leans in, wrapping his arms around me and slapping the back of my shoulder pads with his large hand.

I give him a tight nod, trying not to get too emotional. These people have made so many sacrifices to get me here today, and even though I tell them as much as I can, I'm just so grateful for their love and support.

"We'll let you go celebrate, baby," my mom says, stepping back into my dad as he wraps an arm around her waist. "Go have some fun. You deserve it!"

We say our goodbyes and I start walking toward my best friend and star wide receiver, Blaze Beckham, who is definitely not being shy about ramming his tongue down his girlfriend's throat. Mads, who just bagged her first Super Bowl as the official Blizzard sideline reporter for Tailgate Media, is completely wrapped around him as they shamelessly dry hump in front of about sixty thousand fans. I'd remind them of that, but the kinky fuckers would probably just get more turned on.

When they've finally detached themselves from each other, I make my move. "Hey, Becks," I yell, loud enough to catch his attention. "Lake has the jet readied up. Let's go to Vegas!"

He sets Mads back on the ground, not breaking eye contact with her. "What do you say, Baby Doll? Want to go play in Sin City?"

"Definitely," she replies with a mischievous grin before turning to the person behind her. "What about you, Dia? You in?"

I hold my breath, praying that she says yes. Any extra time I get to spend in the presence of Dia Spencer is always something I want. I'm obsessed with the girl and I don't even try to hide it. She may think I'm joking when I hit on her every chance I get, but I'm dead serious. I want her in a way I've never wanted anyone before. Unfortunately, every advance is met with a different colorful insult. Last week, she told me to go fuck a goalpost. She's creative. I'll admit that much.

Her eyes flit to me for a split second before she answers her best friend. "Sure. Why not?"

Fuck yeah.

What better place to finally make her mine than under the bright lights of Las Vegas? A few drinks to loosen up her icy personality toward me, and I'll sweep her off her feet with my charm. I've done it a million times.

But never with her.

When I met Dia a few months ago, I *felt* something shift within me. I tried to cover it up with a joke about how I needed to text my mom and tell her I had just met the girl I was going to marry, but the way my heart was thumping in my chest at the sight of her told me that she wasn't like any of the other women I'd ever met. Unfortunately, Dia warned me away almost immediately. *"You're cute, but I'd break you."* were her exact words. Normally, that would be enough to have me running the other way to avoid the drama, but with her, all it did was make me desperate to break down her walls. I know Dia has had a rough life. Mads has told me as much. But fuck if I don't want to get inside her head and take out every bad memory, replacing them with new ones.

I know what you're thinking. That I only want her because I can't have her. That I like the chase. And you're partially right. When you're an All-American running back that verbally committed to Ohio State University in the tenth grade, you don't really hear the word *no* very often. Every woman I've ever dated has treated me like some kind of a meal ticket, so I swore off relationships the moment I was drafted by the Boston Blizzard almost four years ago. It's been a long string of meaningless one night stands ever since.

I'm not going to pretend like it's been a hardship. I've spent wild nights with the city's most beautiful women. Sometimes with more than one of them at a time. But for some reason, the only one I've wanted more with is *her*. The one girl in this whole world that seems revolted by my existence.

Ain't that a bitch.

I'm no quitter, though. I know Dia secretly loves our back-and-forth. She feels the attraction and tension the same way I do. She has to. I can practically touch it with my hands when we're bantering with each other. But for some reason, she refuses to take it any further than a few perfectly delivered verbal digs every time we're together. That shit ends tonight, no matter what it takes.

The bass of the electronic dance music thumps through the floors as I sit in the VIP section of the hotel bar with the guys. As soon as we arrived, the girls took off to get drinks while we watched from afar. Maverick, our star defensive end, being smitten by his new girlfriend Bella, was the first to leave. I'm sure he's gifting her with a one-way ticket to Pound Town as we speak. So, it's just Blaze, Tanner, and me, watching as Mads makes her way around the dance floor, champagne sloshing over the rim of her glass as she moves.

Suddenly, a man comes up behind her, grabbing her hips and swaying along to the beat. At first, I wait for her to turn around and punch the asshole square in the dick. But she doesn't. She just continues dancing while he keeps his hands planted on her body.

I'm almost afraid to look at Blaze. There's nothing he wouldn't do for Mads. And that includes killing a stranger with his bare hands for even looking at her, let alone daring to touch her. I use my peripheral vision to peek in his direction, expecting to find him fuming, but end up doing a double take when I realize he's just... *watching her*.

I turn, my jaw practically on the floor as he sips his whiskey like his girlfriend isn't being groped on the dance floor twenty yards away. "Uhhh, you okay bro?" I ask, confusion lacing my tone.

"Yep," he replies with a smirk, never taking his eyes off Mads, who has now turned and wrapped her arms around the guy's neck while they dance.

Am I in the fucking Twilight Zone? Why is he letting this happen?

I turn to Tanner, hoping he can provide me with a little bit of clarity, but he's looking at Blaze with his tongue shoved into his cheek. If I'm not mistaken, there's mischief in his eyes as he moves them back and forth between the couple.

"Am I being Punk'd?" I say out loud. "You're seriously just going to let her do—"

Tanner speaks up from beside me. "Three...two..."

Blaze throws back what's left of his drink, slams the

glass down on the table, and heads straight for the dance floor.

"One," Tanner says with a knowing chuckle.

I sit there, gaping like a fish as he pats me on the shoulder before standing up and leaving the VIP area. I look over to find that Blaze and Mads are gone, as well. The douche canoe that had his hands all over her has moved on to the next girl, which means Blaze didn't beat his ass. *Fucking weird.* I wonder where they went. I wonder where *everyone* went.

I'm brought back to reality as a warm body plops down on the leather couch next to me. I smell her minty shampoo before my brain can even process her long raven-colored hair and deep brown eyes with perfectly curled lashes. I try to act like I'm not enthralled by every detail of her face as I angle my head toward her, taking in the slope of her nose that upturns just slightly at the tip like a cute little button. Hand to God, she gets prettier every time I look at her.

No matter how many times we're in close proximity, my heart always skips a beat when Dia's skin touches mine. I'm hyper aware of the way our arms brush against one another when she shifts her body, sending a jolt of electricity straight to my core.

I want her so goddamn bad.

She huffs an annoyed breath before grabbing the beer from my hand and downing it in one long chug. "Thanks," she says, sitting back with her arms crossed over her perfect tits. I try not to stare, but she's unintentionally pushing them together and all I can think about is how good they'd feel as I slowly thrust my cock between them.

"Rough night?" I ask, raising a brow.

She scoffs. "Not yet, but Blaze and Mads are obviously

off to their spank fest and I was supposed to room with them."

I chuckle. I can't imagine the kind of shit that's going on in their suite right now. If he doesn't have her strung up from the ceiling in some sort of harness contraption, I'd be seriously surprised. I saw the look on his face when he left. Dia can't go back there right now, and I know better than to suggest she room with me.

"You hungry?" I ask.

Her pouty lip curves into a smile. "Starving."

I stand, reaching out my hand. I don't expect her to take it, but she does, allowing me to pull her up. I'm not even shocked by the heat that travels down my arm and straight to my chest at the contact. I'm used to it. A couple months ago, I let her paint my nails in Chicago and I all but came in my pants while she held my hand steady. The effect Dia has on my body is unreal. I can't explain any of it, which makes the whole situation even worse. She doesn't want me. She's meaner than a hornet most of the time, but every now and then, she smiles at me, and I forget everything.

I fucking hate it.

I've been with more women than I can count. I don't bother dating because I've never wanted to be tied down or deal with the extra drama. I had a few girlfriends in college and to no fault of their own, I got bored quickly and wanted out. I broke their hearts. I decided then that I'd just enjoy whatever came with my football career. That included all the pussy that was thrown at me because of who I am.

Until the moment I laid eyes on Dia Spencer. She gave me absolutely no reason to think I could change with the snap of a finger, but I felt it. She's the fucking one. And I'm pretty sure she hates me. No idea how I'm going to change that, but I'll think of something.

Unfortunately, she pulls her hand from mine as soon as we hit the exit, the cool air hitting my face as we make our way down The Strip. There are people all around us, but thankfully, they don't recognize me. As much as I love hanging with fans, I don't want any interruptions right now. It isn't often that Dia is this agreeable when it comes to me, and I want to soak up every second of it. I'll take whatever she gives me for now.

I look over at her to find her eyes moving rapidly, like she's trying to see everything at once. Between the people, the lights, the street performers, and the all-around fast-paced action, it's like she can't decide what's most interesting. I can't help but smile while I watch her. "Ever been here before?" I ask. I can tell by her reactions that she hasn't, but I want to get to know her better.

"No," she replies. "I always wanted to, but it's a pretty expensive vacation for someone who lives on their own and has a mountain of bills to pay."

From what Mads has told me, after I begged her relentlessly, I know that Dia has been on her own since she was a teenager. Her parents aren't good people and they never showed her an ounce of love or affection. I don't know the details, but they dragged Dia into their legal problems, and she drained her savings for them.

I can't even imagine what that's like. I grew up in a loving home with two parents who bent over backwards to make sure my brother and I had every opportunity in the world. We had a calendar on the refrigerator that told them which kid needed to be where so they could *'divide and conquer'*, as they called it. My mom would take Benton to hockey practice while my dad drove me to football.

They made it a point to make sure we felt loved and supported, no matter what we chose to do. On the weekends, we'd do pickup games in the backyard with kids from around the neighborhood. My dad always played with us while my mom cheered from the sidelines. I have so many great memories from my childhood. It sucks that Dia probably doesn't have any, other than the ones she made with Mads.

I slow when I find a hot dog stand on the sidewalk. "How about this?" I ask.

She raises a questioning brow. "Street food? Seriously?"

"Hell yeah, Wifey," I reply. "I'm giving you the full Vegas experience tonight. These are the best hot dogs you'll ever have."

She scoffs. "You realize I'm from *Chicago*, right? The city is literally known for its street food. Nothing you show me here will impress me."

Challenge accepted.

I step up to the stand and order two hot dogs, loaded with everything. I lift my chin, directing Dia to an empty bench by a large water fountain before following her and taking a seat. Handing her the hot dog, I wait for her to take a bite.

"Stop watching me," she says.

I grin. "Why should I?"

She forces out an annoyed sigh. "Dalton, I was mean to you in Chicago the night Blaze came to bring Mads home and your dick got half hard. If you think I'm going to sit here and let you stare at me while I eat a hot dog, you're crazy. I'm not about to be held responsible for your ill-timed boner."

"Good point," I say, looking away before taking a bite

of my food. I give her and her wiener a moment of privacy, but when she lets out a soft moan, I can't stop myself. Thankfully for my dick, she's taken a bite and is slowly chewing.

"I told you it was good," I say with a cocky smirk.

Dia rolls her eyes. "Ok, *fine*. It's a little bit good."

I chuckle as we sit in a comfortable silence while we finish our food. When she's done, I grab her garbage and drop it into the trash can before we start leisurely making our way further down The Strip. We have no destination in mind, and I can't say I hate it. The fact that she hasn't told me to go fuck myself yet is a miracle in itself. But having her actually seeming to enjoy being here with me? It feels better than winning the Super Bowl...which I also did tonight, in case anyone forgot.

"Everything here is so beautiful," she says, voice full of wonder as she takes in the twinkling lights around us.

"Yeah, it is," I reply, never taking my eyes off her. I fucking can't. With all the things to look at in this city, she's the most breathtaking sight of them all. Thankfully, she's too entranced to notice that I'm staring, which allows me more time to drink her in. Her olive skin is flawless. Her pouty lips are begging me to taste them even though I know I can't. But *fuck*. I'd give anything to kiss her just once.

Continuing our walk, we fall back into a comfortable silence as we pass by the massive casinos and hotels. Every once in a while, Dia's bare arm brushes mine, eliciting a warm feeling straight toward my chest. I ignore it as best as I can. It'll do for now, but I know eventually, I won't be able to stop myself from throwing her up against the closest building and dropping to my knees for my queen. How I've lasted this long is a true testament to my self-control when it comes to her. If it were any other woman, I'd have either convinced her to fuck me or gotten bored and moved on. Instead, I've stopped thinking about other pussy altogether. In fact, I haven't had sex at all since the night of Mads' birthday party. The night I met *her*.

Yep. The math is mathing and Dalton Davis hasn't been laid in over two months. *Trust me. I'm as shocked as you are.*

All I can think about anymore is how it would be with Dia. How it would feel to sink into her warm heat, turning that bratty attitude into a moaning, writhing mess underneath me. Would she try to take control? Only giving in when she realized there's no fucking way I'd let her be in charge? She may own every piece of me out here in the real world, even if she doesn't know it. But in the bedroom? She'd be mine.

I'm broken from my fantasy as a very familiar neon sign comes into view. I've never been in there, but I've gone by this place a million times, laughing at the sorry sons of bitches that got roped into putting their balls in a jar for their future ex-wives.

Couldn't be me.

Unless…

I look at Dia, a mischievous smirk blooming across my lips.

"No," she says, shaking her head rapidly. "Abso-fuck-ing-lutely not." She starts walking faster, but I grab her hand, yanking her back toward me. This is fucking *genius*.

"C'mon, Wifey," I coax. "I promised you the full Vegas experience. That wouldn't be complete if we didn't get married tonight and divorced tomorrow."

TWO
DIA

IS THIS MOTHERFUCKER ON DRUGS? Seriously, like, is he an LSD user? Can he hear colors right now? Because I refuse to believe that he's not completely zonked, suggesting that we get fucking *married*.

"You can't be serious," I scoff. I look over to see a boyish grin, complete with those goddamn dimples, without an ounce of trepidation in his dark brown eyes. "Dalton, we can't get married just because we're in Vegas. That's unhinged. We don't even like each other," I remind him.

"I like you," he says, raising a brow. "And you can say you don't all you want. But I know you kind of like me, too."

Balls. Am I that transparent?

He's right. I do like him. I knew right from the moment I met him at the birthday party that if I wasn't careful, I'd get caught in his web. I'm normally cool and collected around guys when they introduce themselves, but for some reason, Dalton knocked me off balance just for a moment. I drank in every detail of his flawlessly symmetrical face, not understanding how a human being could look so perfect. I noticed his chiseled jaw with the faint stubble of a five o' clock shadow that screamed '*I woke up like this.*', which made me think of what it would be like to open my eyes in the morning and see that face instead of an empty pillow across the bed. It was so unlike me to have all those thoughts, especially about a guy I just met. I can't really explain it, but I found myself wanting to be on his radar that night, even if it could never be more.

Don't get me wrong, he's cocky and annoying, but he's hot as fuck and he treats me like I'm the only girl in the world. Like I'm special. I've never had that from a guy before. Actually, the last person I dated broke up with me specifically because he didn't think I was capable of being a good wife. His cruel words play over and over in my head every time I consider dating again. I was naive enough to fall for him, thinking he loved me despite my flaws, and he made me feel like such a fool for giving my heart away. I'm transported back to that conversation, remembering it like it happened just yesterday.

"Do you want to get married someday?" I asked Josh as we watched a rerun of Fear Factor. I'd always hated that show, but getting him to spend time with me was difficult sometimes, so I tried to do whatever I could to keep his interest.

He blew out an annoyed breath. "Yeah, someday. I guess," he responded, not taking his eyes off the television, where some stupid moron was in a casket with about a hundred spiders crawling all over him. Gross.

"To me?" I said. I didn't want to seem like some crazy, desperate girlfriend, but we'd been together for almost a year, and we'd never talked about the future. If there even was *one. I'm sure to him, it seemed like the topic was coming out of left field, but it was something I'd been thinking about a lot at the*

time. I loved him and he said that he loved me, so I just figured we should discuss it at some point.

He turned, looking at me with a brow raised. "I, uh...didn't know that's what we were doing here. I thought we were just having a good time."

I swallowed the lump in my throat, trying to act unaffected. "We are," I said with a shrug. "But I want a family of my own someday soon. At this point, I feel like we should at least be able to talk about what our future looks like. I'm not saying you need to propose today, but I want to know that we're on the same page."

The longer he stayed silent, the smaller I began to feel. Seconds felt like hours as he tried to come up with something to say in response. I knew I shouldn't have brought it up. He clearly wasn't there yet, and me pushing wasn't going to make him ready any faster. I wished I could take the words back as I felt tears prick at the backs of my eyes.

He reached forward, picking up the remote and turning off the TV before turning to me. "Dia, I like you. We have fun together and the sex is off the charts. But if you want complete honesty, I don't see you as my wife or the mother of my future kids. The reason I was so drawn to you is because I didn't think you even wanted those things. With all your family and abandonment issues, I assumed you weren't looking for that kind of thing. You seemed like you were cool with just having fun until it was time to move on and be grown-ups."

The words felt like a knife to my heart. Did I really read him wrong the whole time? No, I couldn't have.

"But you tell me all the time that you love me," I said, trying my best to keep my emotions in check. The last thing I needed was to cry in front of him.

He rolled his eyes. "I do. I love how sexy you are and how you're always down for whatever. We have a blast together. But,

Dia," he said, pausing before delivering the final blow. *"You're not wife material."*

"Dalton," I say, trying to ward away the emotions this whole situation is stirring up. "Even if this wasn't the craziest idea I've ever heard, you don't want to marry me. Not even just for a night. I'm not worth wasting your first marriage on."

His smile fades. "Don't tell me what I want, Dia." He must notice my inability to look him straight in the eyes because he steps directly in front of me, bending just enough at the knees so that we're face-to-face. Gripping my chin between his fingers, he forces me to look at him. "Why would you think I wouldn't want to marry you?"

Fuuuuuuuuck.

I hate this. I hate feelings. But from what I know of Dalton, there's no limit to how annoying he can be when he wants something. So, I pull up my big girl panties and rip off the band-aid, if only to shut him the fuck up so we can get out of here.

"I'm not wife material," I tell him, echoing the words that were so carelessly thrown at me like my feelings didn't matter. "I'm just for fun. Not forever."

He stiffens, hands balling into fists at his sides. "Who told you that?" I stand there wordlessly, suddenly very interested in the small rock I'm kicking with the tip of my shoe. Feeling his stare burning into me, I can't help but peek at him. "Who, Dia?"

I blow out a breath. "It was my ex, Josh," I blurt. "Someone I thought cared about me. I let my guard down one time and was reminded who I really am. Never again."

He stares at me for a moment before abruptly picking

me up and throwing me over his shoulder, making a beeline for the entrance of the chapel.

"Dalton, put me down!" I squeal. "People will see my kitty!" I reach back to cover my butt that's surely on display, but he already has his hand there, yanking my dress down. I kick my feet to no avail right as he lands a hard slap to my ass, making me go completely still.

"Did you just...*spank me*?"

"Yep." His voice rumbles against my body. "Talk back to me again and you'll get another one."

I'm in shock. I've never been spanked before. And between you and me...I didn't hate it. Maybe Mads is onto something, although I can never see myself being as submissive as she is with Blaze. That's just not who I am. I have an attitude. When I'm pushed, I push back twice as hard. My therapist would probably say that's a defense mechanism to prevent people from getting too close, but I like to think I'm just a badass bitch who doesn't need anyone. People leave. I need to know I can take care of myself.

With me still hanging over his shoulder like a ragdoll, Dalton comes to a stop before carefully sliding me down his body. As soon as my feet hit the floor, I right my dress before slapping his chest. "What the fuck?" I yell, not caring who hears. This guy is straight up nuts if he thinks we have any business being in here.

Looking past me, clearly unaffected by my outburst, he addresses the woman at the front desk. "You guys sell rings here?" he asks. "We need a big one. I'm rich."

"What a douchebag," I mutter under my breath. I know they both hear me, but neither reacts.

"Right this way, sir," she replies, leading us through an archway. "You're in luck. Our jeweler was supposed to leave early tonight, but you got here just in time." I follow, because what the fuck else am I supposed to do, as she introduces Dalton to a man who looks like he stepped straight out of an Al Pacino movie. They talk for a while before he turns to me.

"What's your ring size, Wifey?"

Is this real life?

"My *ring size*, Dalton?" I whisper-shout. "That shit is the least of your worries. What's my favorite color? My favorite movie? What size shoes do I wear?" I say, throwing up my arms. "All things you should know about a woman before you marry her!"

"One moment, please," he says to the jeweler before turning to me. "Purple. 10 Things I Hate About You." He looks at my feet. "Probably like, a seven and a half." I gasp as his eyes meet mine again. "Now, what's your ring size?"

"Six and a quarter," I whisper, almost inaudibly. Am I doing this? Am I really going to marry Dalton Davis for the night?

Fine. Fuck it. When in Vegas, right? We can be married by midnight and have it annulled by brunch. Maybe the asshole will give me a few good orgasms before I send him on his way. None of this means anything anyway. May as well add some casual sex into the mix.

Maybe if I'm bad, he'll spank me again.

Dalton swipes his credit card for a total of eighty-five thousand dollars, which I hope he can get back in the morning, and drops down to one knee right in the middle of this janky wedding chapel. I allow myself to live in the moment, pretending that this is really forever, not just for tonight, as he takes my hand in his. I hate that my body reacts to such a simple touch as my knees threaten to buckle under me.

"Diamond Spencer," he begins. He almost looks nervous as he thinks about his next words. "From the moment I saw you, I knew I had to make you my wife. Unfortunately, I only get you for tonight. But I'll take whatever you give me. Will you marry me?"

I roll my eyes, but mainly because I feel like if I don't, some other emotion will show on my face. And we can't have that. I have a reputation for being stone-cold and I'd like to preserve it. It's just easier when people think I'm unapproachable. If they never approach me, I can't get attached. "Depends," I sass. "Do I get half your shit?"

"Baby," he replies. "Say yes and you can have *all* my shit."

This man. He's too fucking good for me and he doesn't even realize it.

"Yes," I say with a defeated exhale. I don't know what's happening, but I'm allowing Dalton to talk me into going along with this crazy *'full Vegas experience'* bullshit. And, okay...maybe I'm just a teensy bit excited about it. After the week I've had, and have been trying to forget about, I deserve a night of fun.

Twenty minutes later, I thank the woman from the front desk as she zips the back of my thigh length strapless tulle wedding dress. As she walks out, leaving me alone in the room, I look over the shoe and jewelry options that were included in the full-service wedding package Dalton bought. Everything in here costs more than I pay for rent in a year. I couldn't imagine living this lifestyle. Blaze bought Mads a fucking Mercedes for her birthday...and he's a hell of a lot more financially responsible than Dalton. Case in point, the four-carat emerald cut ice-skating rink I'm wearing on my finger right now.

I hold out my hand, admiring the beautiful engagement ring. He didn't even ask what style I liked, yet he couldn't have nailed it any harder. It's a shame I'll be giving it back in the morning after we hit the courthouse.

I fasten the straps of my white stilettos before choosing a simple pair of diamond studs for my ears. I decide to forgo any other jewelry, opting for a short, fluffy veil with a jeweled clip in my long, black hair. If I ever planned on getting married for real, it would be exactly like this. Well, my best friend would be standing beside me, but other than that, this is like a dream.

Guilt washes over me when I think of Mads. This will for sure be the only wedding I ever have, and I didn't even bother to tell her. It would be as easy as shooting her a quick text and she'd be here in minutes, even if this whole thing isn't real. She'd dress up right beside me, all the while telling me how ridiculous it is that I'm marrying Dalton for a few hours. But when it came time to stand at the altar, she'd be there to hold my bouquet. Or my puke bucket. Whatever.

I'm an asshole.

I guess it's better this way. I can do this to say that I was, if only for a night, *'wife material'*, then move on with my life. Maybe this will help me through the hang-ups I have about dating. Probably not, but a little delusion never hurt anyone.

I look over myself one more time in the mirror before there's a soft knock on the door. Front Desk Lady pops her head in, prompting me to turn toward her. "Look at you," she says, like a proud mother. Not that I know what that is. "Your fiancé is going to lose his mind when he sees you! He's out there, pacing like a caged lion. I don't think I've ever seen a groom so nervous, and I've been here twenty-seven years. He sure does love you," she tacks on.

"Oh," I say. "We're not really—"

"Off you go!" she interrupts, opening the door fully and ushering me into the hallway. "Can't keep a man with an ass like that waiting long. Someone will come and snatch him right out from under you."

I chuckle quietly as I make my way toward my *fiancé*.

Let's. Fucking. Go.

THREE
DALTON

I STAND AT THE ALTAR, wiping my sweaty hands on my tuxedo t-shirt as I wait for the doors to open. I know it hasn't been long, but I feel like I've been waiting for hours.

Fuck. What if she ran? What if she had time to think and realized that this shit *is* fucking crazy?

"This your first marriage?" Elvis asks from beside me. I almost forgot he was here, which is no easy feat since he's wearing a sequined jumpsuit and smells like a ham hoagie.

I give him a tight nod. "First and last," I tell him. "She's it for me." I mean every single word. I don't know how she did it, but Dia has made me want to be a one-woman man. I'm still not sure how I'm going to convince her to stay married to me, but that's a problem for future Dalton. Tonight, I just need to get these rings on our fingers.

I snap back to the moment as the doors swing open. I feel like I got hit by a three-hundred-pound linebacker straight in the chest as all the breath is forced from my body. Dia looks like a fucking angel in a short, fluffy white dress and heels that make every curve in her gorgeous legs stand out. In her hand, she carries a bouquet of pink roses and white daisies. It's all in perfect contrast to her tan skin and black hair. I've never seen a more beautiful creature, and I know with absolute certainty that I never will again.

She walks toward me by herself, and in this moment, I feel a pang of guilt that she doesn't have Mads or any family by her side. I vow to myself that no matter what happens tomorrow, this woman will never face a single thing alone. Even if I can't convince her to give us a shot, I'll always be there. She deserves way more than this life has given her so far.

I can't help but reach out for her when she's close enough, encasing her small, shaky hand in mine and bringing it to my lips. *Is she nervous?* Fuck, maybe I shouldn't have been so pushy. Maybe she doesn't really want to do this. Or maybe she's only doing it because she knows that by this time tomorrow, she can act like this wedding never happened. She schools her expression before looking at me with a cute little eye roll.

There she is.

I stand straight, giving her a cocky wink before turning back to The King as he begins.

"Thank you. Thank you very much," he says to a room full of absolutely nobody. "We are gathered here today to join these two hound dogs in holy matrimony." Dia chokes on a laugh next to me, covering her mouth with a fist. She recovers quickly, disguising it as a cough as he turns to her. "Dia Spencer. Do you promise never to step on Dalton's blue suede shoes? To always love him tender and never make him spend the night at the Heartbreak Hotel?"

She tucks her lips into her mouth, clearly trying to keep her laughter at bay. She almost falters, but manages to keep a straight face before giving her answer. "I do."

He turns to me. "Dalton Davis. Do you promise to be Dia's teddy bear? To never give her a suspicious mind and to always be her hunka hunk of burnin' love?"

That fucking does it. Dia bursts out laughing, taking me with her as I look for the breath to speak. Tears run down both of our faces as we try to reel it in, but every time we look at each other, it just makes it worse. This shit is so fucking ridiculous, I can't help but continue laughing. Finally, she takes a deep breath, exhaling from her plump, pursed lips as she taps at the tears pooling above her cheeks. I pull myself together, looking from her to Elvis before giving him my answer.

"I do."

We're still trying to keep ourselves under control as he hands me the dainty platinum band to slip on her tiny finger. When she slides my ring on, I immediately notice how heavy it feels. I kind of love it. It's a reminder that I'm hers, if only for tonight.

"By the power vested in me by the state of Nevada," Elvis says, "I now pronounce you husband and wife. Dalton, you may kiss your bride."

Holy fuck, I forgot about the kiss.

I look down at my wife, weaving my hand into her hair before slowly leaning in. My heart pounds in my chest with anticipation as I wait for some sign that she wants me to stop. But when she licks her lips, I can't fucking hold back anymore. I close the final few inches between us as I press my mouth to hers. Sparks go off behind my eyes as she opens wider, letting me massage her tongue with mine. The entire world fades away as she moans into my mouth before reaching up, fisting my shirt in her hands so she can pull me closer. The kiss begins to turn frantic as I try to figure out how I'm going to get out of this chapel without fucking her right here with the King of Rock and Roll as a witness. Holy shit. What is she doing to me?

Thankfully, Dia has better self-control than I do as she breaks the kiss, her beautiful brown eyes staring into mine as she slowly backs away. But I don't let her go far, leaning in for another quick peck before grabbing her hand. I never want to let her go.

"Ladies and gentlemen," Elvis says to the empty chairs in the room. "For the first time, Mr. and Mrs. Dalton and Dia Davis!" I hesitate to look over at her, assuming that she probably isn't too happy with him calling her by my last name, but when I catch her eye, she's looking up at me with something really close to adoration on her face. Either she's a really good actress, or she's actually having a good time with me tonight.

I tighten my hold on her hand, and we walk through the door and into the main part of the chapel together. "You good?" I ask. She hasn't said much other than *'I do'* and that little laughing outburst we had back there. I want to make sure that she's okay.

She blows out a forced exhale and furrows her brows. "I probably shouldn't be," she laughs. "But yeah. Actually, I am good." She almost looks surprised by this revelation. And I have to admit that I kind of am, too. Dia is normally so cold and sarcastic toward me. Tonight, she has been anything but. It could be that she's just playing the part of the blushing bride, but you won't hear any complaints from me about that. I'll take whatever she gives me. And the night is young.

The lady from the front desk walks up to us. "Congratulations Mr. and Mrs. Davis!" she says. "Here is the envelope containing the keys to your honeymoon suite."

"Honeymoon suite?" Dia asks as she takes the package.

"Oh, yes!" she replies. "It's all part of the package you purchased. You get a two-night stay at one of the nicest hotels in Vegas. Your suite has everything you'll need for a weekend of debauchery." She waggles her brows. "You won't even have to come up for air until Tuesday."

Dia's eyes go wide. I hope she's thinking about said debauchery right now. I know I am.

"You hear that, Sugar Tits?" I say, grinning down at her. "Two whole days!" I turn back to the lady. "My wife can't keep her hands off me. She's obsessed. Sometimes, she does this thing with her finger, where— *oof!*"

Giving me an elbow to the breadbasket that makes me immediately double over, Dia smiles sweetly at the lady. "You'll have to excuse my *husband*. He's a bit of an over-sharer. We're working on that. Right, babe?"

I groan, still holding my stomach. "Mmhmm."

She smiles at us like we're the cutest couple she's ever seen. Can't say I completely disagree. "Well, all the information is in the envelope. I won't keep you any longer. Just sign your marriage license and you're on your way!"

We move to the desk, and I grab a pen, scribbling my name by the flag that says '*Groom*'. I hand it to Dia, and she hesitates, blowing out a shaky breath before signing on her line. Even though I'm going to try to get her to rethink our initial agreement, I'm not sure why she seems so nervous. We've seen this in a million different movies. A couple gets married in Vegas, then annulled the next day when they sober up. Although, neither of us are drunk, thankfully.

As we walk back out the door toward the hotel, reality settles in. I'm fucking married. To Dia Spencer, the girl of my goddamn wettest dreams. I have to show her what it's like to be my wife. Maybe if I do a good enough job, she'll second guess the annulment. I know it's unlikely, but I have to at least try. This is going to take more than just a few deep backshots. I need to blow her mind *and* find a way to get that connection I'm guessing she doesn't want to give me.

I'm not going to lie. I've never done this before, so I have no clue what I'm doing. Normally, this would be the perfect situation. Do the bare minimum to get a woman to want to sleep with me, blow her back out for a night, and send her on her way the next morning with a smile. But I don't want to send Dia on her way. I want her to stay and agree to be my wife. I want to show her how good I can be to her...how I can treat her the way she deserves. But I have my work cut out for me. I have to figure out a way to undo twenty-two years of being broken down by others so she can see how special she is. And I only have about eight hours to do it.

FOUR
DIA

WHAT THE *FUCK* did I just do?

No. Seriously. Someone tell me, because I literally just walked out of a fucking Vegas wedding chapel as *Mrs. Dalton Davis.*

Dia and Dalton Davis. That's too much alliteration. It's not normal. Just like it's not normal to marry someone you act like you hate, just to get the *'full Vegas experience'*. We could've gone to Cirque du Soleil or lost a few hundred dollars at a blackjack table. But nope, here we are. Fucking hitched.

I open the envelope and pull out the hotel information as we walk back toward The Strip. Just like the lady at the chapel said, we have a honeymoon suite for two nights. Not that we'll need both of them. As soon as the court-house opens in the morning, I'll be first in line to untether myself from this gorgeous piece of man meat before I go and do something stupid like develop feelings for him. That can absolutely not happen.

I can feel Dalton's eyes on me as we move through the crowds of people, his hand resting protectively on my lower back each time someone gets too close. The smell of his spicy cologne makes my head spin every time I inhale it. God, I've really fucking done it this time. I shouldn't have agreed to marry him, and I definitely shouldn't be thinking about letting him rail me so hard I forget my name when we get to the suite, but I *fucking am*. It's been so long since I've had an adequate dicking, and I can tell just by looking at him that my temporary husband is downright dangerous between the sheets. The sheer strength behind his playful slap back at the chapel makes me imagine what he'd feel like as he drove into me.

"Is this it?" Dalton asks, looking up at the giant hotel. There's a beautiful fountain with a musical light show in front of a well-lit valet area full of luxury cars. I can imagine a suite in this place would cost a fortune, but I'm not really surprised that we've been comped our stay here since Dalton spent over a hundred grand at the chapel between my ring and the wedding.

I double check the paperwork. "Yep," I reply. "We don't have to stay here if you don't want to. If you'd rather go celebrate with the guys, we can go back to the other hotel. I'm sure Mads and Blaze are done playing by now."

He reaches out for my hand, yanking me into his hard body. I shouldn't let him, but maybe I'll just allow it for tonight. Once we get this thing annulled, I'll go back to pushing him away with witty insults and my cold demeanor. Just like I do with everyone else who tries getting too close. "What I want," he growls into my ear, "is to celebrate my wedding night inside my wife."

Fuck.

Am I really going to do this? The wetness between my thighs at his words tells me that, yes, I am, in fact going to have sex with Dalton tonight. The weird part that I would absolutely never admit out loud is that I'm kind of nervous about it. He's a literal manwhore. He's been with some of the most beautiful, thin, successful women in the world. My once perfectly toned dancer's body is now soft and full in some places. I have stretch marks from years of fluctuating weights. What if I don't match up to what he's used to? What if I let him down tonight?

But I guess none of that matters since it'll never happen again. So, fuck it.

"Okay," I whisper.

He grins as he interlocks our fingers before leading me into the massive lobby. Everything is trimmed in gold with intricate designs adorning the light fixtures. My heels click loudly on the shiny marble beneath my feet as we approach the desk.

The desk clerk puts on a flirty smile. "Good evening, sir," she says in a sultry tone. "Welcome to Royal Suites. What can I do for you?" The bitch looks right at him in his stupid fucking tuxedo shirt, standing next to me in my wedding dress, and flutters her fake fucking eyelashes. Dalton grabs the envelope from my hand and takes out the paperwork. Does he not notice the way she's looking at him like she wants to swallow him whole?

"Hi," he replies. "My wife and I are checking in." He slides everything across the counter. She takes it, trying her best to brush his hand with hers. But he's oblivious as he quickly returns his hand to mine.

Take that, homewrecker.

"Thanks," she says, changing her tactics by shyly pushing a piece of hair behind her ear, only taking her eyes off of him to type on her computer. When he doesn't react, she goes back to doing her job. "Okay," she says. "It looks like you have a two-night stay in our honeymoon penthouse. Everything is already paid for, and you have a five-hundred-dollar credit for room service. Here's an extra key card in case you need it."

Dalton looks at me. "No need for that. I'm not letting this one out of my sight now that I finally wore her down and got her to agree to marry me."

This guy is too charming for his own good.

Jolene, *not her name, but that's what I'm calling her*, continues to act like I'm not here, trying one last time to get his attention by giggling as she hands the paperwork back to him. But he's still looking at me as he reaches out to take it and pulls me away without a word.

Maybe I accidentally flip her off over my shoulder as we walk away, too. *Whatever.*

Dalton leads me into the elevator, where an attendant awaits. He's an older man, with gray hair and a big, bushy mustache. He looks like someone's adorable grandpa. I always wanted one of those. But my parents burned pretty much every bridge with every family member we had before I was even born, so I never met any of them. I used to make up stories to tell kids at school about how my grandparents were rich and lived outside the country. I'd talk about how they would send me all sorts of exotic gifts and candy from their travels. Truthfully, I never had any of those things. Christmas would come around every year and my parents had blown all of their money on God knows what instead of even attempting to make me believe in the magic of Santa. I learned at a very young age that some people were just dealt a shitty hand in life. And I was one of them.

The only sense of belonging I've ever really felt has been with Mads and her parents. They've always treated me as their own, even though it's not quite the same as having love from my own flesh and blood. Her mom was the one to sign me up for my first dance class when I was in the third grade. I would dance around their house and annoy the crap out of them, until one day, Diane told me I could turn that into a job if I wanted to. Being young and naive, I decided that I wanted to be a dancer when I grew up. I practiced so hard and put all of my energy into achieving my goals. But my parents were quick to tell me that girls like me don't get jobs like that. That I would never be able to achieve such a big dream. It made me want to give up, but I just couldn't. It was my passion. I still gave it my all throughout high school and was offered a scholarship to the New York School of Dance, but I wasn't even able to accept it. It covered tuition and board, but I would've been responsible for any other costs of living. I had no money saved and was denied for student loans because of mistakes I didn't even make on my own.

It wasn't until I had to get a job in order to help my parents with some legal bills that I quit dancing altogether. Work took up most of my free time, and I was constantly too exhausted to even consider going to the studio on my days off. I miss it so much, but it's too late now.

"Where to, folks?" my new pretend grandpa says as the elevator doors slowly close.

Dalton holds up our key card. "The honeymoon penthouse," he says.

"Newlyweds?" The man says, excitedly. "Congratulations!"

Dalton winks at me, making me crack a small smile. I can't fucking help it. He's just so handsome and charming.

"Ahhhhh," the attendant continues as he presses the button to bring us to the top floor. "I remember my wedding day. Seems like just yesterday. My Marsha almost gave me a heart attack when those church doors opened. As she made her way toward me, I couldn't help but think of how lucky I was to get to share my life with her." His eyes begin to water at the memory. "That was almost fifty years ago, and I love her now even more than I did that day."

What would it be like to have someone love me for that long? I can't even imagine it. Everyone that I've let into my heart has let me down by leaving or hurting me. Except for Mads. She's all I have, and that's all I need.

But she has a new someone now.

I'm beyond happy that my best friend has found love. Blaze is absolutely perfect for her in every way. He gives her love and support in ways that most people only dream of from their partner, and I could never be jealous of that. But I do wonder where I'll be once they're married with a family of their own. Will I still fit into her life? Or will I have to figure out how to go it alone?

The elevator dings softly as it comes to a stop. The doors open, revealing the lobby to our suite. Just like downstairs, everything is dark wood with gorgeous gold accents. The floors look like they have never been stepped on before. They're so clean and shiny. This is the most beautiful place I've ever seen.

Dalton puts a hand on my lower back and guides me out of the elevator. Before the doors close, the attendant addresses us again. "I have a good feeling about you guys. I wish you all the happiness marriage has brought me."

"Thank you," I say quietly before the doors close, leaving us alone.

FIVE
DALTON

THIS IS IT.

I've got Dia all to myself in this room for at least the next seven hours, which isn't nearly enough time, but it's all I have to make her see that we could be good together. I know that all won't happen in one night, but if I can even put a seed of doubt in her mind about getting annulled in the morning, that's good enough for me. We've definitely done things ass backward here, getting married before dating or falling in love, but I saw an opportunity and I took it. If she gives me the chance, I can make her fall for me over time. I don't know what it is about this girl, but I want to give her everything. I want her to have the life she deserves.

Dia looks up at me, all traces of her prickly personality faded away. She's so fucking beautiful, it causes a physical pain in my chest as I move closer to her slowly. Obviously, if she doesn't want me to touch her and just wants to sleep until we can go to the courthouse in the morning, I have no choice but to give her that. But I also know that I won't go down without a fight. And that fight starts right now.

"Is it okay if I kiss you again?" I ask, gently gripping her waist with both hands. She nods, which is good enough for me as I close the rest of the space between us.

"Wait!" she shouts, putting her hand in my face right before our lips meet. "Rules. We need them."

"Okayyyyyyy," I say, drawing out the word. I should've known she wouldn't make this shit easy. I take a step back, giving her my full attention. "Lay them on me."

She forces out an exhale. "First of all, this is a one-time thing. After tonight, we go to the courthouse, get the annulment, and this never happens again. No strings, no emotions...just sex. Got it?" she says, putting a hand on her hip. "And secondly, nobody can know. Not your team-mates. Not Mads. This needs to stay between us."

"What?" I ask. "Why?"

"Because," she says. "If they found out that I dropped my guard for even a second, they'll be on me like flies on shit. They'll be trying to get us to stay together so we fit in their cute little friend group. That can't happen."

I want to ask her if it would be so bad for us to stay married, but I don't want to push my luck here. Instead, I make sure she's finished before I give her my counteroffer.

"Fine," I agree. "I'll go along with your stupid rules. But I have one of my own." She lifts a defiant eyebrow but lets me continue. "While we're married, you're mine. I'll kiss you how I want. I'll fuck you how I want. And you drop that bratty little attitude and let me show you what it's like to have me as your husband."

I stand silently while she considers my stipulation, hoping I didn't just blow this whole thing to shreds. After what seems like forever, she finally gives me her answer. "Fine," she sighs. "It's only until morning anyway."

"Fuck yeah," is all I can manage before I crash my lips

to hers. Just like the first kiss, this one is explosive as I bring my hands around and lift her by the ass. She immediately wraps her legs around my waist, shamelessly rubbing herself on my very rapidly hardening erection. Fuck, she feels good. Even with all these layers between us.

Dia moans into my mouth as I lick at her tongue like a madman. I've never felt this frenzied with a woman before. It's like I can't get enough of her taste. She tastes like my fucking *wife*. The thought makes me even harder as I start walking us in the direction of a bedroom, hopefully. I probably should've looked around when we got in here, but honestly, that was the last thing on my mind. I don't remove my lips from hers as I move throughout the suite. I can't. I feel like I might die if I do.

We reach the hallway, but my throbbing cock is telling me it needs more. Immediately. I press Dia against the nearest wall, grinding into her as I move my lips down her jaw and to her neck. She moans as I thrust my hips into her covered core. "That feel good, baby?" I say into her soft skin. "I'm so fucking hard for you, I can barely see straight."

"Bed," she pants. "Get me to a bed."

I chuckle as I reluctantly pull us from the wall, searching for the nearest door. When I reach it, I swing it open to find a bathroom. "Fuck."

I keep going until I reach the next one, which is thankfully a bedroom. I don't bother turning on the lights since the curtains are wide open and the bright lights from the city are illuminating the room. I'll make sure to have them on next time so I can see her face while I make her come.

Dropping her onto the bed, I reach down and quickly rip her underwear from her body. I can smell her arousal immediately. "Jesus fucking Christ, Wifey. I need to taste you," I say with a heavy sigh. I make my way down her body, pulling the top of her wedding dress down before taking a nipple into my mouth. The moan that comes out of her spurs me on as I reach up, pinching the other one between my fingers.

"Dalton, *oh my God*," she breathes.

I smile against her skin. "That's a good fucking girl, baby. Say my name."

All I get is another moan as I continue my descent. Her whole body is quivering with anticipation as I finally settle between her legs, pushing her short, fluffy dress up to her stomach. I can see her arousal leaking from her as I press my nose to her cunt and inhale her scent. She smells so good; I could fucking come in my pants right here.

"Are you going to eat it? Or should I just take care of myself?" she spits. Seems like she's already forgotten our conversation from a few minutes ago. My hand begins to itch with the need to refresh her memory.

I sit up on the bed, pulling her with me. She makes a cute little growling noise, obviously angry with the change of plans I'm making. "Dalton, what the f—"

"Get over my knee," I order.

She scoffs, rolling her eyes. "Yeah, okay," she replies, sarcasm dripping from her tone.

I grab her wrist, pulling her body over my lap, right where I want her. Her mouth is saying this isn't what she wants, but the fact that there's absolutely no resistance as I lay her on her stomach with her ass in the air tells me that I know what she needs right now.

"We had rules, Dia. And you're not following them. There are consequences for that bratty attitude you agreed to drop while my ring is on your finger," I scold. "I'm giving you five swats to start. I want you to count them. If it's too much, tell me and I'll stop. Okay?"

She says nothing, but I can feel her breathing as it quickens, her chest heaving against the bed.

"Okay?" I ask again.

"Yes," she breathes. And I honestly can't believe she's letting me do this.

Before she has a chance to change her mind, I fist the bottom of her dress with one hand, bunching it above her heart-shaped ass before I rear the other back, landing a firm slap to her left cheek. She yelps in surprise but lets out a quiet moan when I rub my palm gently over the red mark that's already decorating her flawless skin.

"One."

"Good girl," I say before giving her another, and another. She counts them all out, moaning as I soothe them with careful fingers until we reach the last one, where I pull her back up and kiss her lips gently. "Now, are you ready to stop being a brat so I can make you feel good? I'm starving."

"Mmhmm," she hums, voice shaking from either nerves or adrenaline. Either way, I'm going to take that all away right now.

I help her to her back, settling down between her thighs again. This time, I take mercy on her when I see that she's swollen and dripping for me, pressing my tongue to her clit, and dragging it down to collect the wetness. She tastes even better than she smells. I don't know how I'll ever let her go after this. She grips my hair with both hands as I push my tongue into her, thrusting it in and out. "You're so fucking wet," I mumble as I move up to flick her sensitive bundle of nerves. I don't stop as I reach down and free myself of my pants and boxers, continuing to give her everything I have while I do. I only stop momentarily to pull my shirt over my head, leaving me completely naked before her.

She sits up on her elbows, taking me in as I wordlessly reach down, swiping the bead of pre-cum from my leaking cock and smearing it across her hard nipples before returning to devour her pussy.

"It feels so good," she whines as she flops back down onto the pillow.

She gasps when I push a thick finger inside her pussy, groaning as she tightens around me. God, I fucking love her like this. No witty comebacks. No cold demeanor. Just Dia, letting me give her what she needs.

I know she's close when her legs begin to shake. My dick is painfully hard as I hump the mattress like a fucking teenager, not getting nearly enough friction. But I'm not worried about that. I only want to blow her mind, over and over. "Be a good little wife and come on my tongue," I tell her as I suck her swollen clit into my mouth. That sends her over the edge, her orgasm making her slam her legs over my ears as her body convulses wildly.

I continue gently licking the rim of her cunt, just barely using pressure as she comes back down. I could eat this girl all night, but I'm desperate to feel her wrapped around me. Making my way slowly up her sated body, I rub my cock against her slit, tempted more than I've ever been to thrust inside. I always wrap up and get tested regularly, so I know I'm clean, but I want to earn Dia's trust. If and when I finally get to slide inside her without anything between us, I want it to be on her terms.

I reach over for my pants, grabbing a condom from my wallet before rolling it down my weeping cock. Even that feels amazing. I hope I don't nut before I make her come again. I settle back on top of her, trying to look for any inkling that she's not into this, but it seems like she's purposely avoiding eye contact with me. Grabbing her chin between my thumb and forefinger, I turn her head, so we're face to face. At first, she tries to pull away, but I tighten my grip slightly and hold her there. "If you're so hell-bent on only giving me this one night, I want to watch your expression as I sink into you. I want to see what I do to you." I tell her.

I can see in her eyes that she wants to say something smart, but she stops herself, nodding her head in silent consent before I slowly push into her. Her mouth drops open as I take my time feeding my long cock into her tight, wet heat. Black dances around the edges of my vision as I bottom out, refusing to blink because she's so goddamn beautiful right now.

"Holy shit," she whispers. "I can barely breathe. You're everywhere." I'm still unmoving, trying to gather my bearings before I embarrass myself. I lean down and kiss her as I slowly test my own self-control, pulling back and pushing my hips forward again. When I'm sure I can handle it, I begin thrusting into her harder. Her tits bounce with every movement, making my mouth water at the sight. I look down to see her wedding dress bunched around her waist and I swear to God I get harder just thinking about the fact that this perfect girl is my wife. I can't help myself as I bring my hand up, resting it loosely on her throat so I can see what my ring looks like against her skin.

Fuck. Me.

I continue moving inside her, picking up my pace when I feel her pussy start to tighten around me. "You going to come again already, baby?" I coo. "I can't wait to feel it."

"Yes! Dalton, fuck!" she screams, and I know she's there. I give her everything I have left in me as she squeezes me like a vice, soaking my cock with her orgasm.

Already hanging by a thread, I'm done for when she wraps her small hand around my wrist that's still resting on her throat. As soon as the light from outside hits the large diamond of her engagement ring and catches my eye, I go off like a rocket, filling the condom inside her with a loud growl.

I stay enveloped in her, even though there's a large chance that the condom is leaking with the intensity of that fucking orgasm. But I'm not ready to leave her warmth yet. I take a moment to rest my head in the crook of her neck, inhaling her scent one last time before grabbing the base of the condom and pulling out.

"Nooooooo," Dia whines, making me laugh.

"Hold on, babe," I tell her. "Let me throw this away then I'll be back." I give her a quick peck on the lips before running to the bathroom and tossing the condom in the trash. When I return to the room, I find Dia struggling to find the zipper of her dress. She's flopping on the bed like a fish, separating the fluffy material to no avail. I watch, leaning on the doorframe with my arms crossed over my chest for several seconds before she notices me.

"Ugh," she scoffs. "Stop doing that."

"Doing what?" I say, the corner of my mouth lifting slightly.

"That…*thing*," She gets up on her knees and waves her hand wildly in the air. "Where you know you're sooooo hot, so you lean on the doorway without clothes on and you smirk with your stupid sexy face."

I give her a cocky grin. "You think my face is sexy?"

"Don't read into it," she says. "I'm dick drunk. And I also called your face 'stupid'. You just hear what you want to because, husband or not, you're still a fuckboy."

I launch myself from the doorway, tackling her into the mattress, earning myself a full-on laugh. "Say it again." I smile.

"What?" she says, goading me. "That you're a fuckboy?"

"No," I reply, tickling her sides, making her laugh even harder. "The other thing." I dig my fingers deeper as she tries to get away from my attack, but it's no use. I'm way stronger than her.

"Ok!" she finally relents. I still my hands, letting her find her breath. "You're my husband."

And, fuck, I want to hear her say it again every day for the rest of our lives.

SIX
DIA

I WAKE SLOWLY, feeling Dalton's soft lips moving across my skin. I know I said I'd go back to being cold toward him this morning, but maybe it won't hurt to play husband and wife a little longer. We're about to be annulled within the next couple of hours, so that's when I can go back to pushing him away. It's the only option I have if I want to protect myself from him breaking my heart. I know that sounds cynical, but I'm just keeping it real. I am a million times better on my own than I would be if I allowed myself to depend on someone else, just to have them leave in the end. I've started over too many times because of that shit.

"Mmmm," he hums as he kisses his way down my back. I expect him to stop and move back up the bed, but instead, he continues moving down, gently pressing his lips to the sensitive spots on my ass cheeks from his spankings. A dull throb blooms between my legs as his hand skate up my thighs. "Are you sore?" he asks.

"A little," I reply. "But I kind of like it."

"That so?" he says, dragging his tongue along the

crease where my cheek meets the back of my thigh. I can feel my arousal as it begins to dampen my inner thighs. We had sex three times last night, yet I feel like I need more of him. The way Dalton knew everything I needed is really going to put a damper on our parting of ways this morning. I'll definitely miss his dick. That's for sure. The only reason we didn't go for round four was because we ran out of condoms. I mean, what kind of honeymoon suite doesn't have boxes of those things laying around? I'm giving them a bad Yelp review for that shit, for sure.

"Mhmm," I murmur as he continues moving lower before rolling me to my back and looking up at me with that stupid, gorgeous face of his. "Maybe I like being spanked. A tiny bit."

He raises a suspicious brow. "A tiny bit?" he teases. "Judging by how wet and ready you were for me when I got done, I'd say you liked it more than a tiny bit."

I roll my eyes. "You're such an asshole."

"And you're a brat who might do well with a little punishment every once in a while. Somebody needs to put you in your place," he says, settling in between my thighs. I can feel myself throbbing for him as he leans forward and blows directly on my aching bundle of nerves.

"Dalton, we're out of condoms. Remember?" I whimper. "We can't have sex again."

"Who said anything about sex?" he says, smirking up at me. "I'm just trying to eat my breakfast." He leans forward, wasting no time as he presses his tongue firmly to my clit. My back arches at the contact, pushing myself further into his face. I should probably be embarrassed by how quickly he has me writhing around, but the man is lethal with his tongue.

"You taste so fucking good," he says into my sensitive

skin. The vibration from his words adds to the pleasure as he eats me like he's actually starving. Like this is the only meal he'll get for the rest of his life. He runs his tongue along my slit, starting at the top and gliding downward. When I expect him to stop, he lifts my thighs from the bed and continues back toward the place no one has ever touched.

Don't get me wrong, I've had sex with a lot of men. It's not a big deal to me. I scratch the itch and pray they don't ask for a second date. But to me, anal play is something that requires a lot of trust. Trust that is built over time. I've never been able to give it to another person. Even with my ex-boyfriend, we just never got there.

So, why am I not stopping Dalton as he continues moving toward my back hole with his tongue?

I should stop him.

Every alarm bell in my head is blaring as I clench my fists at my sides, but my body is winning the battle. I'm fucking stronger than this. Why am I letting this happen?

As if he can read my thoughts, he stops, looking up at me from between my legs. "I've got you, Diamond. I promise."

How does he know me so well?

He waits, rubbing gentle circles on the inside of my thighs with his thumbs while I war with myself, trying to understand why I'm willing to put so much trust in him when I've never been able to do it before with anyone else. Maybe it's because I'm allowing myself this small amount of time to just exist with him, here in our suite, as his wife. Maybe it's because he's down there, looking hot as fuck, practically begging to do this.

Or maybe it's because, in the couple of months that I've

known him, Dalton has already begun to break down the thick wall of ice that protects my heart.

No. It can't be that. It's definitely just the *hot as fuck and between my legs, begging* thing.

I look down at him, giving a tight nod in consent.

A mischievous grin spreads across his face. "Yeah?" he asks. "You gonna let me eat this tight little asshole, baby?"

Jesus, he's so fucking dirty. In another life, one where I'm not completely damaged, I could definitely see myself keeping Dalton around. As obnoxious as he is, I know we'd have a blast together. But for now, at least I have him for a couple more hours before it all goes back to the way it was before he carried me into that chapel. Besides, even if I wanted to keep this thing going longer, I can't bring him into the problems I have waiting for me when I leave Vegas. This has to be it for us.

"Yes," I breathe. I want to tell him that I've never let anyone do this before, but I can't show any signs of weakness. So, I lay there wordlessly as he grabs behind my thighs, pushing my knees to my ears.

"I love how fucking flexible you are," he says before licking my pussy again. My inner walls clench as he dips his tongue inside, lapping up my wetness before pulling out and flicking at the sensitive skin between my holes.

"Holy fuck," I pant. "That feels so good." He hums contentedly as he licks and sucks before sliding his tongue all the way back and pressing it to my asshole. I'd be embarrassed by the moan that comes out of me if I could have rational thoughts. But at the moment, I can't focus on anything other than the pleasure I'm feeling.

"Hold your legs," he orders. I grab under my knees, but as soon as he returns his mouth to my body, I get so lost in the sensations that I let them drop. Dalton sits back on his heels, shoving my legs back up forcefully before grabbing my face with one hand so I'm looking directly at him. "Let them go again and you're getting ten swats."

My instinct is to push back. I'm so used to answering to nobody and I certainly don't allow anyone to tell me what to do. But letting him be in charge in this room feels good. So, I obey, holding tightly to my legs.

"That's a good little wife, doing as you're told," he praises. "I don't want to punish you, Dia. I want to make you feel good. Okay?"

I nod, sighing in relief as he bends back down and resumes moving his tongue along my sensitive skin, which is now completely soaked with my arousal. He uses both hands to spread my legs even wider than I thought possible before diving in completely. My pants and moans mix in the air with his grunts and the sound of my wetness against his face every time he pushes his tongue into my pussy. This whole thing is so filthy, but I want more. He eats me like I'm the best thing he's ever tasted, massaging every inch of me with different patterns and pressures, driving me absolutely wild. I've never felt pleasure this intense in my whole life. When he pushes two thick fingers inside my cunt, curling and scissoring them just right, I feel my release barreling toward me so fast, I couldn't stop it if I wanted to. He thrusts them in and out as he licks my back entrance, making me clench onto him as I grip my legs tightly. I can barely hold onto them as they shake uncontrollably. It takes no time at all before my orgasm hits me like a speeding train. I come, screaming his name so loudly that I'm sure the tourists on the street below us can hear who's making me feel this good.

Slowly, I return to Earth, still clutching onto my knees as Dalton kisses his way back up my body. I'm quivering from the adrenaline, but he takes his time leaving a wet trail all over my skin. He moves my hands, making my legs drop down to the mattress before he settles his weight on top of me, pressing gentle kisses to my neck and cheeks.

I feel safe. Wanted. Cared for.

Son of a bitch.

SEVEN
DALTON

I JUST WANT to lay here, like a husband weighted blanket, for the rest of the day. Actually, fuck that. I never want to leave this room.

Just as I'm trying to figure out if my budget will allow me to buy this whole fucking hotel, a quiet ding breaks the silence of the suite. Dia and I look over to the nightstand, where her phone lights up with a new notification.

"Ugh," she groans, attempting to reach for it, but I'm still pinning her down. "Get off me, you human tank."

I chuckle, moving just enough for her to roll out from under me. "You know, I liked you better when I had my tongue in your pussy. You were a lot nicer then."

"Yeah," she says, rolling her eyes. "Don't get used to it. As soon as we sign those papers, I get to go back to being mean."

Not if I have anything to say about it.

She looks at her phone, eyes widening when she reads the message. "Oh, shit. It's Mads. They're leaving to go back to Boston and want to know where we are." She looks at me, worried. "What do I tell her?"

"That we fell in love, got married, and are busy fucking each other's brains out in our honeymoon suite," I say, wiggling my eyebrows.

She scowls at me, and fuck, I want to put her over my knee again. "We had a deal, remember? They can't know." Worry settles back over her expression. "We were both missing all night. They're going to know something is going on. What am I supposed to tell them?"

I force an exhale. "Just tell them we slept at a different hotel. You were supposed to go home to Chicago anyway, so you can just tell them you're going straight from here. And say I didn't want to leave you alone, so I'll hop on a later plane after you're gone." She says nothing as she chews on her fingernail. Something is definitely up. "What?" I ask. "What's wrong?"

She looks around the room, trying to avoid eye contact. I wait, staring at her, hoping she'll tell me what's going on. After a minute of silence, she finally relents. "I…um…I don't know if I have a home to go back to in Chicago," she says, quietly.

I sit up on the bed so I can be face-to-face with her. "What do you mean?"

She stands, putting some space between us as she pulls a blanket from the chair in the corner of the room and wraps it around her naked body, keeping her back to me. "Fuck," she says. "I only have two dresses to wear. All the rest of my stuff is in Mads' suitcase. What am I going to wear out of here?"

Okay. Cool. Ignore me.

I stand from the bed, walking over to her and gently grabbing her by the arm to spin her around. "Dia, what's going on?" I ask again.

"It's not your problem, Dalton," she says. "I've been on

my own, figuring out my own shit, since I was a kid. That's not going to stop now."

"Like fuck it isn't," I say, firmly, "You're my wife."

Her eyes shoot up to mine. "Yeah, well I won't be for long," she spits. "Leave me alone."

"No," I yell, a lot louder than I mean to. But goddamn, this woman is stubborn. "Tell me what's going on or I'll call Blaze right now and tell him everything." Apparently, blackmail is a new thing I do. In my defense, she's not giving me a choice.

She lifts her chin in defiance. "You wouldn't."

"Try me, sweetheart," I say with a smirk. "You're breaking the deal by not acting as my wife in this room."

Defeated, she backs away, plopping down on the couch. She twists her hands into the blanket, never looking up at me as she speaks. "I got fired on Friday." It's barely a whisper. I want to scoop her up and hold her in my arms, but I know she needs space in order to open up to me. This isn't something she's used to, and I don't want to scare her. "I had put in for vacation time, because there was no way I was missing my best friend's first big gig at the Super Bowl. They called me Thursday night and told me that they would need me to work the whole weekend. I reminded them that I was off, and they told me that if I didn't show up on Friday, I would be fired. Sure enough, they stuck to their word. And since my apartment is also owned by my boss, I can assume I no longer have a place to live, either."

Fuck.

My instinct is to tell her to come home with me, but I'm not sure she would be down with that, especially if we go through with the annulment. I also know that she won't take money from me even though I have more than enough for several lifetimes. I'm at a loss for what to say to her, so instead, I walk over and sit down beside her, pulling her into my arms. "It's okay, baby," I say, kissing the top of her head as she melts into me. "Fuck those people, anyway," I tell her. "Have you ever considered moving to Boston to be closer to Mads? She's just as alone as you are when we're on the road. I'm sure she'd love to have her best friend with her."

She sighs. "I've thought about it a lot," she replies. "But with a job that pays next to nothing, barely any skills, and the fact that it costs so much to move, it just wasn't possible. Even now that I'll have to find a new job somewhere, I still can't afford to pack up all my shit and relocate to a new city."

"Sell your engagement ring," I tell her. I'll buy her another one if she agrees to stay with me. But this is the best way for her to get the money she needs to move to Boston. I'm not technically giving her any money, so hopefully she'll do it.

She holds the ring out, staring at it. My heart skips a beat when the light glints off the large diamond. "Dalton," she says. "We haven't even been married twelve hours. I'm sure you can return this and get your money back."

"No can do," I tell her. "The law states that once we signed that marriage certificate, the jewelry belongs to you. Just like my ring belongs to me."

She rolls her eyes. "Your ring *does* belong to you. You paid for that one, too. Remember?" Such a little smart ass.

I click my tongue before sucking a breath through my teeth. "I don't make the laws, babe. It's just the way it works. That ring is yours to do whatever you want with. I bet you could get a pretty penny for it. Probably enough to move and live off of until you find a new job in Boston."

She looks up at me, her beautiful brown eyes connecting with mine. "I know what you're doing."

I grab my chest, feigning offense. "I have no ulterior motives here, Wifey. I'm just really good at problem solving."

She smiles. "Yeah?" she chides. "Then where are we going to come up with normal clothes so we can get out of here?"

I grab her phone from her hand, opening the DoorDash app. "Lucky for me, my wife is about to come into a large sum of money. So, she can have matching sweatsuits delivered for us."

"Oh my God, you're so annoying," she says, leaning back into me with a laugh.

One hurdle down, a million to go.

"I can't believe you actually ordered these," Dia says, looking at our reflection in the full-length mirror.

"What?" I say, smoothing the non-existent wrinkles from my hoodie. "You don't like our groutfits?"

"What the hell is a *groutfit*?" she sasses.

I scoff, because does she live under a rock? "It's a gray outfit. Get it?"

"Oh, I get it," she replies. "What I don't get is why you got exactly the same thing for both of us. We look like idiots."

"Nonsense," I say. "We look cool."

She rolls her eyes as she walks away, throwing her phone in her small purse. We're having the hotel ship our wedding clothes back to my place in Boston, so we don't have to carry them around. Dia was ready to just leave them behind, but fuck that. What if we want to relive the memories later on?

"Ready?" she says, moving toward the door.

No, I'm not ready to let you go.

"Hold on," I say, closing the space between us in three long strides and crashing my lips to hers. I fist her hair in my hand, afraid that if I let go, she'll disappear into thin air. I can't stop myself from pushing her against the door and pressing my body tightly to hers, connecting us at every possible point. I kiss her like I'll never get to again. The thought alone makes me want to rip my heart out right here and hand it to her. Because if I have to live a life where this woman isn't my wife, I know I'll never need it.

I swallow every little whimper that leaves her as she brings her hands up to fist the soft fabric of my hoodie. She's going to have to be the one to stop this kiss, because I never fucking will. If it means staying here with these rings on our fingers, I'll move in right now.

Unfortunately, Dia pulls back, dropping her hands at her sides. Her head falls back onto the door as she squeezes her eyes shut tightly. If I didn't know any better, I'd say she doesn't want to walk out this door any more than I do. "Are you sure this is what you wa—"

"It has to be this way, Dalton," she whispers, cutting me off. "You promised."

"Okay," I relent. But if she thinks I'm giving up, she couldn't be more wrong.

EIGHT
DIA

WE WALK into the courthouse and head straight to the front desk. The receptionist is an older woman with gray hair pulled up into what looks a lot like a beehive. She's adorable and actually pulls it off pretty well. Her glasses are slightly crooked, and she has some lipstick on her teeth, but still, she's the cutest thing I've ever seen.

Hello, pretend grandma. I saw grandpa back in the hotel elevator. He says he loves you.

"Can I help you?" she says, pushing her red, thick-rimmed glasses up her nose. I look to Dalton, but he's refusing to be a part of this interaction, standing with his hands in his pockets and a scowl on his face.

I turn back to her. "Yes, we'd like to file for an annulment," I say.

"Pam!" she yells, much louder than someone her size should be able to. "Got another annulment for you!"

A middle-aged woman, presumably Pam, pops her head up from her cubicle, waving us back. "You're in luck!" she says. "My eleven-thirty canceled. Come have a seat." I walk over with Dalton dragging his feet behind me like a child. "So, you need an annulment."

"Yes," I reply, sitting down. "We got married last night and we'd like to be," I search for the words, "*not married*."

"Okay," she says as she begins tapping on her keyboard. "I'll just need both of your driver's licenses."

I take mine out of my wallet and slide it across the desk, looking over to Dalton, who hasn't moved an inch. I look at him, widening my eyes as if to say *hurry up* before he finally reaches into his pocket and tosses his wallet into my lap.

This motherfucker is about to catch these hands.

I smile at Pam while I take out his license, placing it next to mine. She picks them up, putting some information into her computer before turning back to us. "Okay," she begins. "Were either of you under the influence or of unsound mind at the time of the marriage?"

"No," I answer.

"Were either of you forced or tricked into entering the marriage?" she asks.

"No," I answer again.

"Okay," she says, looking back at her computer. "And you're both over eighteen. Are either of you married to someone who may or may not be dead?"

I look at Dalton, hoping he'll participate, but he doesn't. "Ummm…no," I reply.

"You related?" she asks, raising a suspicious brow.

"No," I answer, getting annoyed.

Her eyes go wide. "Are either of you," she looks around before whispering her next words, "physically unable to consummate the marriage?"

My husband chooses that moment to enter the exchange. "Oh, we *definitely* did that," he says with a cocky grin. "*Several times.*" I swear, my head turns to him like the fucking Exorcist, giving him a death glare as I grip onto the armrests of my chair, so I don't launch myself out of it and strangle him until he expires right here on this courthouse floor. I'd go to jail, but it would be worth it.

"Hmmm," Pam says. "Unfortunately, your marriage doesn't qualify for an annulment."

"What?" I reply before looking back to Dalton, who gingerly reaches forward and grabs his driver's license before turning to me with a smile.

She explains further. "In Nevada, there are certain criteria a marriage needs to meet in order to be annulled. People come in here every day thinking it's just like the movies, but it's not that easy. You can still get a divorce. If it's uncontested, you can have it done in as little as two weeks."

"Two weeks!?" I shout, standing from my chair. "I need it today! Please, Pam!" I beg.

She gives me a sympathetic look. "My hands are tied. I'm sorry. Your best bet is to go back to your home state and file there."

Holy fuck. I thought for sure I'd be walking out of here a single woman. Now I have to be married to Dalton for two more weeks. I don't know if I can go that long without Mads finding out. And we're supposed to go back to our home state? Where *is* my home state? I can't go back to Illinois. There's nothing there for me. And I don't want to be there. I really do want to be in Boston. But I certainly didn't want to go as Mrs. Dalton Davis.

Fuck. Fuck. *Fuck.*

"You're getting a bad Yelp review, too," I say to Pam before turning on my heel and stomping out of the building with Dalton hot on my heels.

DALTON

Fuck. Yes.

Somehow fate is on my side as we walk out of the courthouse as a still-married couple.

"Dia, slow down," I say, trying to catch up with my wife, who I had no idea was a professional speed-walker. When I finally reach her, I grab her arm, spinning her to me. "Wifey, it's fine," I say.

Her eyes go wide. *"Don't* fucking call me that," she spits. "This is all your fault. Throwing me over your shoulder like a caveman and bringing me into that stupid chapel. *'The full Vegas experience,'"* she says, trying to mimic my voice. It's actually fucking hilarious, but I like my balls being attached to my body, so I hold back my smile. "Now look at us! Married!" Her face falls and tears of frustration fill her eyes.

Goddamn it. I don't want her to cry. If she wants this divorce, I'm not going to make it any harder on her than it already is.

"Hey," I say softly. "It's going to be fine. We'll go back to Boston, file for the divorce, and focus on getting you a new place to stay. The two weeks will be up before you know it." I reach for her, pulling her in and wrapping my arms around her tightly. I hate seeing her upset.

"Yeah," she sighs into my chest. "Okay."

I give her a soft smile as I pull her to a bench and sit down. She plops down next to me, sitting quietly while I arrange for a car to take us to the other hotel so I can get my luggage, then to the airport for our flight home.

I officially have two weeks to make my wife fall in love with me.

Six hours later, we've boarded our plane to Boston. The East Coast got hit with an ice storm earlier today, so we were stuck in Vegas a little longer than expected. But everything is back on track now as Dia and I make our way to our first-class seats.

"Good evening," says the flight attendant. She's a younger girl, maybe in her early twenties, with red hair and bright green eyes. She's okay, but definitely nowhere near the absolute smoke show sitting next to me. "Can I get you something to drink?" She flutters her lashes and gives me what I think is supposed to be a coy smile. I'm pretty used to this sort of thing happening when I'm in public, but all of a sudden, it's like I can't see any of the other women that exist in this world.

"Oh, no than—"

I'm cut off when a small hand with a very flashy diamond resting on it wraps around my bicep. I look over to see Dia glaring at the girl while digging her nails into my skin like I'm the one doing something wrong. *Ouch.*

"Actually," she says, "I'll take a glass of champagne. We're celebrating. We just got married."

This woman makes my head spin. And my dick hard.

The flight attendant pastes on a fake smile. "Oh. Congratulations!" she says, ducking her head as if she's embarrassed at the fact that she was openly flirting with a married man while his wife sat right next to him. "I'll be right back with your drink."

As she walks away, I slowly turn my head, flashing Dia a shit-eating grin. "What was that?" I ask.

She rolls her eyes. "Nothing. I was just saving you from some thirsty bitch hitting on you the whole flight. You could thank me, you know."

I shouldn't poke the bear, but I can't help myself. "What if I *wanted* her to flirt with me? Ever think of that?"

She scoffs. "You don't." She nonchalantly scans the cabin, looking around at the people who are just now boarding. Suddenly, her eyes go wide and her jaw drops, causing me to direct my attention to where she's looking.

Godfuckingdamnit.

"Oh my God," she whispers. "That's Cam Hardy."

"Who?" I ask, pretending like I don't know him at all. With any luck, she'll drop it.

"Cam Hardy," she repeats his name, never taking her eyes off the handsome motherfucker as he reaches up, putting his carry-on into the overhead bin above his seat. And why wouldn't his shirt ride up, giving her an indecent peek at his bare obliques? "He's only the hottest player on the Bruins roster. Like, ever."

I look over at him, shrugging. "He's alright, I guess. If you're into that sort of thing."

"Oh, I can assure you that *I am* into that sort of thing," she says. There's drool. *She's drooling now.* "I'm going to go say hi."

"Dia, he's married. With children. You can't just go over there and—" Before I can stop her, she's out of her seat and moving toward him. *Fuck.* Hopping up, I follow behind her like the little puppy I am. By the time I get there, she's already introduced herself and they're shaking hands.

"I just had to come say hello," she says to him, giggling like a fucking schoolgirl with a crush. "I'm a huge fan." Oh, okay. So, she had absolutely no idea who I was when she met me, but she's this guy's biggest fan? *thumbs up*

"It's very nice to meet you," he says with a smile. Just then, he sees me looming over her shoulder. "Oh, hey, Davis! What's up, man?" He gives me a high-five. "Haven't seen you since the Children's Hospital fundraiser. Congrats on the big win!"

"Yeah, thanks," I reply. "I see you've met my wife."

His eyes go wide as he flashes a genuine smile. "Oh, wow. I didn't know you were married!"

Dia gasps, looking over her shoulder at me with a scowl before returning to him. "We're not. He's kidding. We're just friends."

Like fuck, we are. "That's not what you were saying last night when my tongue was in your—" She slaps a hand over my mouth, silencing me as she drags me back toward our seats, growling in frustration. I wave to Cam as he chuckles before sitting back down.

She lets out an exaggerated huff as she throws herself in her seat, crossing her arms over her chest like a petulant child. "Thanks for ruining that for me," she sasses.

"You're welcome," I reply. I grip her face, turning it toward me as I move my lips to her ear. "And if you ever refer to me as your *friend* to another man again, I'll put you over my knee and show him how very *unfriendly* I am when it comes to you."

Her shaky sigh as I press a barely there kiss on her lips before turning away lets me know that my message was heard, loud and fucking clear.

NINE
DIA

AFTER A LONG, bumpy flight through terrible weather, we finally made it back to Boston. The rest of the group ended up getting their flight re-routed, so I have an extra night to figure out how I'm going to explain any of this to Mads. I never told her that I lost my job and possibly my apartment, because I didn't want her feeling guilty about it. It wasn't her fault, but she will automatically blame herself because I missed work to be with her at the Super Bowl.

As fucked up as the situation is, I have no regrets about going to the game. My job at the club has been a strain on my physical and mental health, but I stayed because I felt like I didn't have another option. Most of the patrons were very nice, but some were completely out of line and disrespectful. I can't tell you how many times I was touched inappropriately by drunk assholes thinking they could do whatever they wanted as long as they left me a good tip. I guess the silver lining here is that I don't have to deal with that anymore. And in two weeks, when the divorce is final and I can pretend like this marriage never existed, I can take the money from my ring and start my life here.

I look over to Dalton, who's sitting next to me in the back seat of our Uber, finding him out cold with his head resting back on the seat. It's been a hell of a long day and we're on our way back to his house to sleep before we head to yet another courthouse in the morning to file more paperwork. His head lolls to the side and I take in his handsome face. He's such a good fucking guy and I hate that this could potentially end up hurting him. I can tell he would stay married if I allowed it. But it's better that we get this over with now before either of us ends up with a broken heart. My hope for him is that one day, he marries a woman that can give him everything he deserves. Someone that hasn't been broken and jaded by her past. Someone he can be proud of. That's not me. He deserves more.

I reach my hand up, running my fingers over Dalton's stubbled jaw as he peacefully sleeps. My eyes catch on my beautiful ring, and a pang of guilt hits me at his selfless act of telling me to sell it so I can build the life that I want here in Boston. I'd give anything to keep it. Even though we aren't staying married, Dalton will always be my first and only husband. And as wild and crazy as our wedding in Vegas was, I'll look back on it fondly as the night that he gave me the chance to know what it was like to be somebody's wife.

The car comes to a stop outside Dalton's building, and I softly shake him. "Hey, Sleeping Beauty," I whisper. "We're home."

"Mmmm," he hums as he leans into me. He's so warm and he smells so good. I hate to wake him, but the driver is just staring at me in the rearview, so I shake him harder. "Dalton, let's go inside."

He opens his eyes, giving me a sleepy smile before sitting up straight. "Sorry," he says, running a hand down his face. "Thanks, man," he says to the driver. "Five stars."

I chuckle at how cute he is as I open the door and slide out, Dalton following closely behind. He settles a hand on my lower back as we head to the door and toward the elevator. I shouldn't let him touch me anymore because I'm obviously very weak when it comes to him, but maybe one more night won't hurt. Technically, we haven't started the divorce process yet. Once we do, we have to cut all of the touching off completely.

Good logic, Dia. Not delusional at all.

As soon as the elevator door closes, Dalton leans into me, wrapping his arms around my waist as he presses his lips gently to my neck. It's not a kiss. It's not sexual at all. He's just...holding me. The feeling is foreign at first. I can't remember the last time a man held me without it being part of foreplay or after we got done having sex. Even those instances are few and far between. My instinct is to pull away, but I allow myself to wrap my arms around his neck and hold him back.

It's just for tonight.

Just as I begin to relax into him, the elevator dings and the doors slide open. Dalton doesn't say a word as he takes me by the hand and leads me down the hall. He stops at a thick mahogany door before tapping a code into the keypad above the handle. When the green light blinks rapidly, he twists the knob and pulls me inside.

His place is exactly what I would expect of a luxury bachelor pad. Everything is dark and modern with silver accents. A large, flat screen TV is mounted on the wall above a sleek electric fireplace. It smells like his cologne and I kind of want to roll around on the carpet, basking in it.

God, who the fuck am I with this sappy shit? Who says that?

"I'm exhausted," Dalton says. "You ready for bed?"

"Yeah, early day tomorrow," I reply. "We should get some real sleep."

He points a thumb over his shoulder. "My room is this way. Do you want to sleep in there with me? If you're not comfortable with it, I have a guest room you can use. You held up your end of the deal in Vegas. You acted as my wife until we left. I'm not going to pressure you into continuing that here."

Honestly, I wish he would. It would make it a hell of a lot easier to act like I hate the idea of being near him if he dragged me kicking and screaming. Instead, I have to figure out how to tell him I want to be in his bed without him thinking I'm softening to the idea of us.

"I mean, technically, we're still married. So, we could sleep in the same bed for tonight. I'll probably get a hotel room tomorrow anyway, since Mads and Blaze will be back. We won't really be able to explain me staying here without telling them everything," I say.

His expression is sullen as he gives me a tight nod before turning down the hall. I follow quietly as he flips on the light switch, revealing his large bedroom. It's literally bigger than my entire apartment back in Chicago. There's a thick black comforter on the king-sized bed. I can see myself falling into it and spending a whole weekend making Dalton bring me snacks while I watch trashy reality TV.

He clears his throat, breaking me from my daydream.

"Why don't you hop in the shower really quick and relax your muscles. I'll bring you some clothes and towels."

"Yeah, okay. Thanks," I say, heading toward the ensuite. I don't bother closing the door as I start the shower before peeling off my hoodie and sweatpants, letting them fall to the floor. I turn to see Dalton standing there, unmoving as he takes in my naked body. I give him a small smile, never breaking eye contact, as I open the shower door and step inside. The pressure from the multiple shower heads feels like heaven on my sore body. Traveling always makes me so tired. And after the events of the last forty-eight hours, I desperately need this.

I take a moment to relax, leaning my head forward onto the wall, allowing the hot water to beat against my neck and back. I don't even register the sound of the door opening and Dalton stepping into the shower behind me until his hands gently run up my arms, stopping on my shoulders. He kneads at the tight muscles, making me moan in relief. He continues massaging me, stepping closer and dropping warm, open-mouth kisses along my jaw. I keep my hands on the wall in front of me, allowing him to continue. I can't help the small moan that leaves me as he digs into a particularly tender spot at the base of my neck, making the tension slowly melt away.

"Relax, sweetheart," he says softly. "I've got you." His tone makes my clit throb with need, but he doesn't lower his hands. He just continues working to loosen the tightness in my body from the long, stressful day. My brain is reeling, unsure of how to act as I realize that he doesn't have any ulterior motives. He didn't come in here for sex. He came in here to take care of me. And all I can think about is how I don't deserve it.

Dalton stops massaging momentarily as he reaches

over me, grabbing the body wash from the shelf. He squeezes it into his hands before rubbing it all over my neck and shoulders. He moves down to my back, reaching around and smoothing his hands up my stomach. When he's done there, he continues upward, massaging the minty soap into my breasts. It smells exactly like the stuff I use, which is kind of a weird coincidence.

Fuck, this feels good. My body, which was wound tight just minutes ago, relaxes back into him as he continues moving his hands, making sure every part of me is clean. His erection pokes against my lower back and I'm wondering when he's going to take this thing further, but he doesn't.

He stops, squirting more body wash into his hands before returning them to my stomach and slowly moving downward. "Do you want me to wash down here? Or do you want to do it?" he says into my ear.

I'm at war in my own head, knowing I shouldn't let him touch me anymore, but I can't help myself. I want him to do this for me tonight. I'm exhausted, physically and emotionally. I want to burn this feeling into my brain because I may never have it again.

"You can," I whisper, not stopping him as he reaches between my legs, making sure no part of my body is left untouched.

Dalton takes his time rinsing me with the detachable shower head before quickly washing himself. He doesn't speak as he turns off the water, grabs me by the hand, opens the shower door, and leads me to the counter where two fluffy towels sit. He quickly wraps one around his waist before grabbing the other and drying my entire body. I watch him, completely speechless as he carefully brings the towel around my shoulders before wrapping me into a tight, warm embrace.

Tears prick at my eyes, so I close them tightly, willing them to go away so he doesn't see the effect all of this is having on me. I can't remember the last time a man touched me like this, yet nothing even remotely sexual has happened. I'm used to letting them use my body while I use theirs, then moving on to someone else before we can hurt each other. And that's always been so easy. This type of intimacy with Dalton feels almost uncomfortable, but at the same time, it's like my head and heart aren't on the same page. I'm starting to understand that the reality of this situation isn't going to be as simple as I thought. He's nothing like I expected him to be. The perpetual playboy is already proving to be more caring and selfless than any of the guys I've ever been with, and I just know that letting go is going to change me.

"Let's get you to bed," he says, walking back into the bedroom and pulling back the covers for me. I lay down, completely exhausted in every sense of the word as he rounds the bed, sliding under the covers and pulling my naked body tightly to his. Even with all the thoughts running wild in my head, I drift off feeling safer and more peaceful than I ever have in my whole life.

TEN
DALTON

"MR. AND MRS. DAVIS," the Clerk of Courts says. "You can come on back."

We arrived at the local courthouse about twenty minutes ago for our appointment. Luckily, we were able to use a private entrance, staying out of view of any fans or paparazzi that may be lurking around. Doing this in Vegas, where people were less likely to notice me, was one thing. But being back in Boston where I'm a public figure, we couldn't risk being seen. I already said I'd shout it from the rooftops that Dia is my wife. But I made a promise to her that we wouldn't tell anyone and I'm not going to break her trust. She's been through that enough.

We follow the blonde-haired man into a small office, where he motions for us to sit opposite him at his desk. Dia has been quiet all morning, barely touching her breakfast, but downing three cups of coffee before we got in my car and drove here to file our divorce papers. I tried asking if she was okay, but she just said she was jetlagged and wanted to get this over with so she could check into a hotel room and sleep.

"So," he begins, "I see that you were married in Las Vegas Sunday night, and they denied your annulment."

"Yes," I answer, looking over to Dia who still hasn't said a word.

"Not a problem," he says. "We can get the divorce paperwork filed here today, and since it's non-contested, you'll be good to go in fourteen business days. I just need your IDs. I have a copy of your marriage certificate on file already."

We both reach into our wallets, handing him our driver's licenses. He takes mine first, entering the information into his computer before taking hers and pausing.

He looks to Dia. "This is an Illinois state ID. Do you have one with your current Massachusetts address on it? I'll need that in order to prove that you're living at the same residence."

"Umm, we don't live together. I am technically still a resident of Chicago, but I'm moving here to Boston this week," she tells him.

Worry clouds his expression. "Unfortunately, you have to prove that you've shared a legal residence for six weeks before you're allowed to file paperwork for a divorce."

"Oh my God," she says, hanging her head in defeat. "So, you're saying we have to stay legally married while living together for six more weeks?"

He nods. "Yes, ma'am. You can head straight to the Registry of Motor Vehicles and apply for a Massachusetts driver's license with Mr. Davis' address. As soon as you have that, the six-week period starts."

I'm scared to look over at her, but I slowly turn my head to find Dia not nearly as feral looking as I expect. I inspect her face for any type of foaming at the mouth or horns growing from her forehead, but there's none of that.

Just her normal expression as she takes her license, stands up, and leaves the room without a word.

"Thank you," I rush out as I reach forward, grab my license, and chase my wife out of yet another courthouse.

By the time I reach the car, which is parked in the building's underground garage, Dia is waiting by the door for me to unlock it. I click the button on my fob and she gets in, slamming the door so hard, I'm surprised it doesn't chip the paint.

Okay, so she is mad.

I choose my words carefully. "I know this is a little speed bump, but we'll get through it," I tell her. When she doesn't reply, I look over to find her eyes full of unshed tears. "Hey," I say softly, reaching over to cup her cheek. "Tell me what you're feeling."

She closes her eyes and surprises me by leaning into my touch. "I can't."

"Yes, you can," I coax. "I know you don't want me as your husband, but let me be your friend right now, Dia. Talk to me."

She sighs, opening her beautiful brown eyes. "I thought it would be easy. I wanted to know that I was capable of being someone's wife, but I wanted it to be over before anyone got hurt."

Fuck. I hate that she feels like every good thing in her life has to end before she gets to the good part. I hate that she doesn't feel worthy of giving or receiving love. I want to kill her parents and ex for burning these thoughts into her head.

"Dia, listen to me," I say. "Nobody's going to get hurt. I get that you've been left and mistreated by people who said they loved you. But I promise I'll never do that. No matter what happens six weeks from now, I'll always be here. Even if you don't want me to be. I'll wait in the wings for your call. And when it comes, I'll get to you as fast as I can. I know you're strong and independent, but it's okay to lean on the people who care about you. You'll always have Mads. And now, you have me, too. Okay?"

She blinks and the tears she's been holding in finally spill over, landing on her pink cheeks. I reach out, wiping them away with my thumbs before leaning in and dropping a firm kiss to her forehead.

"Okay," she says with a watery smile.

"Alright," I say, pressing the ignition button, making the car roar to life. "Let's go make you a true Bostonian."

She raises a brow, "You gonna teach me how to *pahk the cah*?" she asks.

There's my girl.

"Noooooo," I say, drawing out the word. "I was gonna take you to a *wicked awesome pub, ya chucklehead*."

She rolls her eyes, but I can tell she's trying not to smile. "Just take me to get my new license, asshole."

I feign offense. "Is that any way to address your husband after he just poured his heart out to you? You're fucking brutal, Wifey."

She looks over at me with a defiant look. "What are you going to do? Put me over your knee again?"

My brows just about fly off my head, surprised at the fact that she's bringing that up right now, but I school my expression before reaching over to grab her face so I can look her in the eyes. "You'd better watch that smart mouth, bad girl, or you'll find out."

ELEVEN
DIA

MADS: Helllloooooo? Are you alive?

DIA: Nope. *skull emoji*

MADS: Haven't heard from you in 9 million years, so I wasn't sure.

DIA: OK, that's a little dramatic. It's been 2 days.

MADS: Name the last time we went 2 days without at least checking in. I'll wait.

MADS: You can't

DIA: Sorry. Yes, I'm alive. I'm safe. Not dead in a ditch somewhere. Did that ease all of your intrusive thoughts?

MADS: Yep.

I SET my phone down on Dalton's kitchen table, feeling

immediate guilt for omitting the fact that I'm in the same city as Mads, but hiding from her. I don't want to, but I'm not ready to let her know what's going on right now. I'm not sure I want *anybody* knowing what's going on right now. Which is exactly why I've been holed up here since we got back from the RMV.

After we left the courthouse yesterday, Dalton took me to get my new driver's license. He only agreed to stay in the car if I put his last name on it, so I relented. I didn't want to be followed in there by a six foot one, two-hundred-and-twenty-pound man-child who everyone in the place would recognize and flock to. Knowing him, he'd flash his wedding ring to everyone who came close enough. It would only be a matter of time before photos of a married Dalton Davis would be plastered all over the internet. No fucking thanks.

So, I'm officially Diamond Davis in the eyes of the state of Massachusetts. At least for the next six weeks.

We also agreed that I would stay here instead of spending unnecessary money on a hotel room until we can file our divorce papers. That way, I can take all the cash from the sale of my ring and use it to settle into a new place in Boston before I have to find a job. Continuing to hide from Mads will be difficult, but she thinks I'm in Chicago, so as long as I text and call to check in, it shouldn't raise too many red flags.

Dalton left about two hours ago to meet with a jeweler friend who agreed to buy my ring. I would never say it out loud, but it killed me to watch him walk out the door with it. I've never owned a piece of real jewelry before. My parents certainly weren't worried about providing me with anything other than the basic necessities in life, and I've never been able to afford to treat myself beyond the occasional haircut and color or new outfit. But beyond that, it's a memory of our crazy night in Vegas that will now be sitting on someone else's finger. And the worst part of all is that they probably won't even know how special it is.

I shake the thoughts from my head as I walk over to the cupboard and try to find something to eat. I haven't had much of an appetite the last couple of days, but thankfully I'm feeling better now that we have a plan of action. Even though staying married and living here for the next month and a half isn't ideal, it could be worse. The silver lining is that once this is all said and done, I'll be closer to Mads. I won't have to feel so alone anymore.

Even though it's almost bedtime, I'm finally eating for the first time today. My stomach growls and I zero in on a box of cereal on the top shelf. I stretch my arm toward it, realizing that I'm just too short to get my fingers on it. I look around the room, double checking that I'm still alone before planting my hands on the counter in front of me and hoisting myself to my knees. Just as I go to grab the box, a throat clears behind me, making me lose my balance. I brace myself for inevitable impact but am caught by a strong set of hands gripping my waist.

"Holy fuck, Dia!" Dalton says. "You trying to crack your head open?"

I glower at him over my shoulder. "If you didn't sneak in here like a fucking ninja, I wouldn't have slipped."

He lifts me into the air like I weigh nothing before setting me back onto my feet. Reaching over me, he easily grabs the box of cereal, pulling it down. I reach out, expecting him to hand it to me, but instead, he carries it across the kitchen and opens the cupboard that holds his dinnerware. He takes down a large bowl before turning to the stainless-steel refrigerator and grabbing the milk. I watch, confused, as he pours the cereal and milk into the bowl before setting it in front of me with a spoon.

"Eat," he orders, making my jaw drop because *hell no*. He is not about to tell me what to do.

"No," I reply.

He raises a dubious brow. "No?"

"I'm not hungry," I say, shoving away from the counter and storming toward the guest room. I hear Dalton's footsteps behind me as I enter the room, attempting to shut the door. But he's too fast, pushing firmly against me and barging in. "Get out."

He stands there, unmoving as I pull the covers back and climb into the bed with my back to him. I'm hoping that if I ignore him, he'll leave. I just need some time to think about what I'm feeling and *why*. Why I'm so fucked up that something as simple as another person pouring me a bowl of Lucky Charms triggers me to the point where I run away.

"Who did this to you?" he whispers. "I'll fucking end them."

I squeeze my eyes shut, trying to find my strength. But it seems like the more time I spend with Dalton, the more I feel myself giving in to the idea of being taken care of. And that would be great if this were a real marriage that wasn't ending in six weeks. But like every other relationship I've had, this one will be over, and I'll be back on my own. I don't need to fall deeper into this feeling of being cared for, just to have to let it all go again.

"Nobody did anything to me, Dalton," I say, still facing away. "I don't need anything. I can get my own food. I can take care of myself."

I feel his weight as he sits on the bed behind me. "I

know you can, but you shouldn't have to all the time," he says softly. "Look at me."

When I feel like I have my shit together enough not to cry, I roll over. I don't make eye contact, instead choosing to look at his hand, which is resting on his bent knee. I stay silent, giving him a chance to talk, so maybe he says his piece and leaves.

"It's not really a secret that I'm glad we fucked this up the way we did," he begins. "I know it's not what you want, and I know you're going to leave as soon as you can. I've accepted that. I'd spend a fucking lifetime undoing all the shit that people have done to hurt you. Proving to you that you're worth so much more than you think." He pauses, swallowing roughly. "But I don't have that long. Please give me this, Dia. Just let me spend the next six weeks showing you what you deserve."

I exhale a shaky breath. "Then what?" I ask. "Go back to being on my own, but knowing what I'm missing out on? No thanks."

"Do you think you're the only one in this thing?" he asks. "The only one who's struggling? Because I'm being forced to watch my wife unable to accept a bowl of cereal from me because she thinks it makes her weak and dependent. I'm not like *them*. I'm not going to hurt you. Just let me in."

This man is practically begging to take care of me. Even knowing that I'm leaving him as soon as I'm allowed. Why can't I give him this? Am I really that broken that I can't suck it up for a little while and just be here with him after everything he's doing for me?

I want to, so badly. But I just *can't*.

I roll over, giving him my back again. He apparently gets the message that I don't have an answer for him as he stands up and quietly leaves the room, shutting the door behind him and leaving me wishing I was strong enough to give him what he deserves.

I wake abruptly when a severe hunger pain rips me from my not-so-peaceful sleep. I'm reminded quickly that I went to bed without eating a single thing all day. I check my phone to see that it's after midnight, so I quietly open the door and pad down the hallway. Everything in the house is dark, which means Dalton must've gone to bed already.

When I reach the kitchen, the first thing I see is a small, rectangular piece of paper on the counter. I walk over, picking it up, realizing it's the check from the sale of my ring. No idea how he was able to get more for it than he paid, but I don't have time to think about it before my stomach makes a very loud, audible growl. I set the check back down, vowing to go to the bank tomorrow to open an account, and make my way to the cupboard. When I pull it open, my heart squeezes in my chest. The box of cereal has been moved to a lower shelf, obviously so I wouldn't need help getting to it like I did earlier. The protein powder that was previously sitting on the bottom shelf has been moved up, since there's a one-million percent chance I'll never be reaching for that.

Fuck.

I was awful to him. And he didn't deserve any of it. All Dalton wants to do is care for me and I push back every time he tries to.

But the truth of the matter is that I'm starting to crave it. From the moment he washed me in the shower, all I've been thinking about is how much I want to let him in. I know he'd be so good to me, treating me in a way that I've never experienced before...even from my very own parents. He's already given me a taste of it in so many ways.

My biggest fear is that I'll get used to it, and when he inevitably realizes how unlovable I am and leaves me, I won't know how to go back to being alone. It's taken me my whole life to get to a point where I feel like I don't need anybody else. A Dalton Davis sized hole in my heart will surely leave me right back where I started.

But, for some reason, when I'm done eating and have cleaned up my mess, I find myself outside his bedroom door, the war inside me raging on as I quietly twist the knob and enter the dark space. Like a magnet, I'm pulled to the bed. Dalton lays on his side, facing the spot I previously slept in. It's empty, save for his hand that's stretched out, laying on the mattress. If I were there, it would be protectively wrapped around my waist.

That thought propels me forward, making me remove my clothes before carefully lifting his arm and sliding into the bed next to him. Before I even have a chance to settle in, Dalton's arm loops around me, pulling my naked body into his. I exhale a contented breath, melting into him as his breathing evens back out behind me.

I know this is going to hurt in the end, but for some reason, I can't stay away.

TWELVE
DALTON

"THIS ALL FEELS VERY SEXUAL," Dia says from behind me as I sit on the couch, watching the rerun of last night's hockey game. My younger brother, Benton, just got called up to the Texas Thunder and although he didn't see the ice last night, I still want to see what the team looks like. Currently, they're warming up, with several players doing groin stretches on the ice.

I look over my shoulder to where she's standing. I try not to react to the sight of her in only a pair of panties and one of my Blizzard t-shirts. "It's not *sexual*," I say with a scoff. "They're just making sure they're loose." Just then, one of the guys drops down into a frog stretch and begins rocking back and forth. I've seen this a million times, since I grew up watching my brother. But now that I'm really looking at it…okay, it *does* look sexual.

She rounds the couch, settling herself on the floor, much closer to the television than necessary. "Hockey players are so hot," she says with a sigh. "The muscles. The fighting. The *stamina*. I bet you they can go all night lon—"

Before she can even finish her sentence, I'm up out of my seat hurdling the coffee table, and playfully tackling her to the ground. She laughs as I get her to her back, pinning her down with my thigh between her legs. She tries to buck me off, but I'm unmovable. "Is that so?" I ask. "That's what you want? A man that will fuck that sweet pussy all night long?"

"Mhmmm…" she half hums, half moans as I shove my thigh up, wedging it against her core. I feel her hips flex, just slightly, as though she's trying to create some friction against her clit. God, I fucking want her so badly, I can barely restrain myself. But after the other night in the kitchen, I vowed that I wouldn't let my hormones lead me into making her think that's all I'm looking for with her. I want Dia to know there's more to this thing than just sex.

I'm not dumb enough to think we can navigate six weeks of marriage and living together without me needing to make sure she's satisfied, but I can do that without fucking her. At least until she agrees to let me show her how good of a husband I can be.

I know she wants that, deep down. Otherwise, she wouldn't have come into my bed that night…and every other night since. It's been a week since the cereal incident, and neither of us have brought it back up. I didn't want to reopen a fresh wound too soon, but I fully plan on asking her again to give me the next five weeks to prove to her that I can provide the things she deserves.

I lean in brushing my lips against hers, earning an appeased sigh. I trail kisses down her face and jaw, making her squirm underneath me. "I fully plan on making you come in lots of creative ways," I say into her ear. "But if you want this cock again, I'm going to need you to give me what I want, Dia. As soon as you do, I'll fuck you until you beg me to stop."

I don't give her a moment to answer because I don't *want* her to answer right now. I want her to take time to think about what I'm asking for. I also don't want her thinking that she's going to be left completely unsatisfied if she decides that she's not able to agree to let me take care of her. Instead, I kiss her again. This time, I move my thigh against her while I do it.

She moans into my mouth as I add more pressure, making a direct hit with my quad to her clit. She begins grinding her hips into me, taking what she needs. Her eyes are closed as she rides me from below, but we can't have that. Grabbing her face between my thumb and fingers, I squeeze just enough to get her attention. "Eyes on me, Wifey. That's my only rule with this. You look at me when I make you feel good."

Her eyes snap open. Her pupils are completely blown as she locks onto mine, giving me the connection I so desperately need. She's fucking beautiful, with her flushed skin and heaving chest as she sucks in air, letting it out with loud moans. I'm harder than stone as I thrust my thigh forward, simultaneously rubbing my cock on her leg as I do. I refuse to lose it though. I won't come while we do this. I'll wait until I'm alone and jack off in the shower to the memory of her ruining her panties for me right here on our living room floor.

I know how crazy that sounds. Choosing to leave this situation without coming when Dia is completely willing to do everything with no strings attached. But the strings are exactly what I hunger for. And until she understands that I want her for more than what I can get from her body, I'm not taking anything.

"Please don't stop," she whimpers. "I'm so close."

Funny that she thinks I'd ever stop. I live to make Dia Davis come.

I keep thrusting as I reach up her shirt, pleased to find her full tits without the restriction of a bra. I find her nipple, pinching it tightly between my thumb and forefinger. A beautiful scream leaves her lips when I begin rolling it slowly.

"Such a pretty fucking sound, baby," I say. "Come for me. And don't forget how empty your cunt is when it squeezes, desperately searching for your husband's cock."

That's all it takes to make her come undone as her orgasm hits her like a freight train. Her muscles seize as it flows through her, until she finally relaxes with a contented sigh.

"Better?" I ask, leaning down for a quick peck on her open lips.

"Much," she replies on a breathy laugh.

I chuckle, moving off of her. "What are your plans for the week?" I ask, hoping the change of subject will make my dick deflate.

She sits up. "Well, I think I need to go back to Chicago and pack my things. I wouldn't put it past my old boss to throw everything out at the end of the month. I don't have much, but I definitely want to keep it." She looks down. "I need my own clothes. I can't keep walking around here in just your t-shirts and my underwear."

"First of all," I reply, putting one finger into the air, "yes you can. And secondly," I add another finger, "if you'd just let me buy you some new stuff, you wouldn't have to worry about it." I know she deposited the check from her ring into her bank account, but I refuse to suggest that she spend a dime of that. In fact, if she does, I'll just transfer more over. Because if she chooses to leave me in five weeks, I want her life to be as easy as possible.

She rolls her eyes, "That's such a rich person thing to say. I don't need new stuff. I just have to go pack up. My rent is paid for the next two weeks, so it's safe to go back and get it. He isn't a bad guy and he's been a decent landlord. He's just a dick."

"Okay," I relent. "Want me to come with you?"

"No," she says, shaking her head. "Stay here and spend some time with Blaze so he doesn't wonder why you haven't been around as much. I'll go back for a couple days and rent a storage unit in Boston until I get my own place."

I raise a brow. "Now who's talking like a rich person?" I joke. "This place is huge. I have that whole downstairs area where I throw all the PR boxes that I don't feel like opening. There's plenty of extra space down there for your stuff."

She smiles and it makes my heart speed up. She's so goddamn beautiful. "Okay, that makes sense."

"Good girl," I say, reaching to grab my phone from the coffee table and pulling up the airline app. "I'll buy your plane ticket."

She opens her mouth to speak, but I interrupt. "Go ahead and argue with me. I can promise you spankings aren't nearly as fun when you don't get my cock afterward."

She huffs in annoyance, crossing her arms over her chest. I lean forward, kissing her nose before I return to my phone and secure her flight to Chicago.

THIRTEEN
DIA

I TAPE the top of the second full moving box closed before pushing it aside and grabbing an empty one. Sadly, I'm not sure I'll need any more than this. When I moved into this place, I used the furniture that was left by the previous tenant. It was nicer than what I had, so I sold my stuff and used theirs. I had intended on saving the money for myself, but as she always does, whenever I start to build a little nest egg, my mom called saying she needed help.

I carefully slid the last of my shirts into the drawer, proud that I was able to carry all of my boxes into my new apartment and unpack everything by myself. It felt good to know I did it without needing help. At least I knew nobody could throw it in my face later if I couldn't be at their beck and call.

My phone lit up on the dresser, vibrating against the hard wood as my mom's name flashed across the screen. I blew out a breath, preparing myself to answer. She always had a self-serving reason for calling me. It was never just to see how I was doing or to make sure I didn't need anything. It was the exact opposite for as long as I could remember, and I had a feeling that wasn't going to change today.

"Hi, Mom," I said in greeting, trying not to let the annoyance show in my voice. "How are you?"

"Ohhh," she said on an exhale. "Not great, baby. I need a little help."

I knew it before I had even picked up the phone, but it didn't make the fact that she only called because she needed me to bail her out of whatever trouble she managed to get herself into any less disappointing. I didn't even know what having a mom that called just to chat felt like, but I missed it anyway.

I squeezed my eyes shut, trying to keep my voice even so she didn't know how hurt I was. "Help with what?" I asked.

"I wrote a check for some groceries last week and it bounced," she began. "I guess I must've miscalculated when I balanced my checkbook. You know how bad I am at math." I knew she was lying. I was sure she wrote a check for something, *but she never kept track of how much money was in the account. She didn't care. "The bank keeps calling and threatening to take legal action if I don't pay them."*

"How much do you need?" I said through the lump in my throat.

"With fees, the total is four-hundred and twenty-seven dollars. If I don't have it in my account by tomorrow, they're going to call the police."

I knew she hadn't spent four-hundred dollars on groceries. And I also knew she never had that much to spend, so it wasn't just a simple mistake in her math. But I wanted to be a good daughter. I knew I wouldn't have been able to sleep that night, fearing that the police would be knocking on her door and arresting her the next morning when I could've stopped it. I had just enough in the bank to cover the check she had bounced. So, I did what I always did.

"I'll transfer it to your account tonight."

Ever since my mom left my dad a couple of years ago, she has made all of her financial problems *my financial problems*. That wasn't the first bad check she had written, and I doubt it was the last. Thankfully, I haven't heard from her in a while, though. I hope that means she's gotten her life together. As much damage as she's done, she didn't work alone and she's better off without him. My dad gaslit her into thinking she was the only problem when he was just as bad. But by the time she realized it, the damage was already done.

That's probably another reason I struggle to let Dalton help me. I've seen how a man can manipulate his wife into believing that the fault is all hers, ignoring that he had a large hand in their demise. That shit has obviously stuck with me, and Josh didn't ease my worries with it at all, considering he blamed the end of our relationship on me not being worthy of a future as his wife. Maybe he was right, though. It's not like I had a good example of what a healthy marriage was as a kid.

Growing up with parents like mine was not easy. They were addicted to spending money on themselves. Not only did my mother have a shopping addiction, but my father gambled every dollar he could spare. Sometimes, even the ones he couldn't. There were times when he'd drain their joint bank account at the casino, leaving my mom to figure out how to pay the bills. She was no better with money, though. Instead of paying the rent or utilities when she did have it, she'd spend it on designer clothes and bags. I don't know who she thought she was fooling trying to look like she was wealthy, considering she drove an old, rusted out station wagon and moved from trailer park to trailer park every time we'd get evicted for not paying the rent.

When I was barely old enough to write my own name, they figured out that they could use me for extra cash. They signed me up for several credit cards, taking advances from the ATM to pay for their habits. To this day, I still have absolutely no idea how they did it, but by the time I turned eighteen, I had a mountain of debt that I was responsible for.

I gave up on my dream of being a professional dancer for good and got a job as a server at a local club to make money to pay for the bills my parents racked up in my name. Then, when I was twenty, my mom got busted writing bad checks again and ended up in jail. I had enough money to bail her out, but there was still the problem of restitution. She gave me a sob story about how nobody would hire a felon, and I decided I had to help her. I worked my ass off in order to pay that so she wouldn't go back to jail, but I'm still left with all of the credit card bills that they racked up in my name. I've been paying them slowly, but I am nowhere near finished. I know I won't have full freedom until I am.

All of this is part of the reason I agreed to keep my engagement ring and sell it instead of making Dalton return it. I don't want to be rich. I just want to be able to take my paychecks, pay my bills, and have a little something left over each week. I would love to have a savings account for emergencies and maybe be able to take a vacation every once in a while. I've always had hopes of one day owning my own dance studio where I can teach kids the fundamentals of dancing, but at this point, that's all just a pipe dream.

I drag the box over to my dresser, emptying the

contents of the drawers into it. Just as I finish, my phone rings with a Facetime from Mads. I haven't talked to her, besides through text, since we arrived in Vegas, and I miss her. Plus, I've been packing all day and could really use a break. I scoot back, propping my back against my bed before hitting the button to answer the call.

"Oh my God, you really are alive!" she says in greeting. "I was starting to think you were murdered and your killer was texting me as a cover up."

I roll my eyes. "So, you've been watching reruns of Unsolved Mysteries, then? I thought we talked about this, Madison. *The bed-wetting? Remember?*"

She gasps. "I haven't wet my bed since Jenny Bronson's birthday party in the fifth grade."

"Well, that's a lie," Blaze says from somewhere off-camera with a chuckle.

Her cheeks turn red as she shoots him a glare. Like I don't already know what a little deviant my best friend is.

"Anyway," she says, changing the subject. "What's been going on? I feel like we haven't talked in forever."

Shitballs.

I don't want to lie to her, so I need to dance around her question. I just don't think it's smart to tell her everything that has been going on with Dalton. Mads is a romantic. She thinks that everyone has their one true love roaming around in this great big world and that fate always brings them together. I remember how she had her whole wedding planned out on a poster board in her room before she was even old enough to ride a bike. And now, she's living her love story with Blaze.

But that's not for me. There is no soulmate out there waiting to find me. And I'm not saying I won't have a happy life. Because I truly believe that once I pay off my parents' debts and can start living the life I've been working for, I'll be completely fulfilled. But it won't be with my one true love. I'll be doing it all on my own. And that's okay.

"Not much," I answer. "I'm just in my room, organizing clothes." *Not a complete lie. Technically I am organizing clothes…before putting them into a box.*

"What?" she says, perplexed. "Why?"

"Just wanted to make sure everything still fits."

Just then, a loud noise from outside startles me, making my phone slip from my hand. I grab it off the floor, not thinking as I stand and sit on the bed.

Mads squints as she takes in what she's seeing. "Are those *moving boxes* behind you?"

Fuck. Fuck. *Fuuuuuuuuck.*

I look behind me, waving a dismissive hand. "Yeah, I'm just packing some stuff up," I say. I absolutely refuse to outright lie to her. I'm terrible at it. She'll see right through me.

"Packing for what?" she asks. "Are you moving?"

Did I already say *fuck*?

"Yeah," I say with a defeated sigh. "I'm moving."

And because she just can't let anything go, she hammers the final nail in my coffin. "Where to?"

Well, there it is. I'm busted. I have no choice but to tell her.

"Actually," I say, "I'm moving to Boston." Her expression is stoic for several seconds, so I try again. "Surprise?" It's a question because she's honestly freaking me the fuck out with her non-verbal response and frozen face.

Another moment goes by before she covers her mouth and tears fill her eyes. "Please don't mess with me, Dia. Are you serious?" she whispers.

I nod my head. "Yep. I want to be with you. There's nothing here for me anymore," I tell her.

"Oh my God!" she cries. "Blaze, Dia's moving here!"

"About time!" he says, face filling the screen next to Mads. "When are you coming?"

Cue the nervous laughter.

"Ummm, tomorrow?"

They both stare at me like my hair is on fire for a bit until Mads finally decides it's time for the *'rapid fire question'* portion of our evening. "What? Why? How? Where are you going to live? What about the club? How are you getting here?"

Blaze rubs her shoulders soothingly as he laughs. "Relax, Baby Doll."

They're so fucking cute. It makes me want to squeal, kick my feet, and puke all at once. I envy the way they're able to love and support one another so freely. They make it look so easy.

I try to remember everything she asked as I figure out how I'll continue skirting around the fact that I'm fucking married to Blaze's best friend and technically, living with him. "I just decided I want to be in Boston where you are. I hate being so far apart. I'm not working at the club anymore and I have enough in my bank account to make the move. Everything is packed, I've rented a small truck, and I'm leaving in the morning."

Please don't ask where I'm living again.

"Okay, but where are you going to live?" she asks. *Shit.* "I know you didn't just decide to move and find a place in the last week."

"I—" I begin.

"She'll obviously stay with us," Blaze states. I freeze, unable to say anything, because I can't tell them where I was actually going. But I don't want to lie and say I'm staying at a hotel or got an apartment because that's not the case. I was honestly just hoping Mads would be so excited that she'd skim by that detail until I could figure out a plan. But now Blaze is opening his home to me...a pattern he seems to have fallen into...and I'm afraid I won't be able to say no.

"Yes!" Mads shouts. "It's perfect! You can stay here until you find a job and a new place. It'll be just like it used to be! Gossiping during movies, makeovers, junk food..." Tears fill her eyes, spilling over as she smiles. "I'm so happy."

I can't break her heart. Leaving her parents and me behind to move to Boston was so hard on her. In fact, she considered backing out at the last minute, but I promised her we would make it work. Then, she met Blaze and he kept her occupied for a while, but the longer we were apart, the more she voiced her sadness at not being able to see me as often as we used to. And maybe it'll be good to put some space between Dalton and me so I can get a handle on the things I'm feeling. Technically, his address is on my driver's license, so as far as the state is concerned, I'm living with him. I'll just be having sleepovers with my best friend each night. That's all.

"Yeah," I say, nodding my head. "Okay."

FOURTEEN
DALTON

"I DON'T KNOW why you're doing this," I say to Dia as I lug the last of her moving boxes down the stairs to my storage room. I can't believe everything she owns fits into three large boxes. And one of them is clothes. She got back this afternoon and broke the news to me that she's moving out to go stay with Blaze and Mads. I tried arguing, but she seems to be set on this idea.

She reaches the bottom of the staircase and stops, putting her hands on her hips. "What was I supposed to say, Dalton? 'Oh, I married your best friend in Vegas and I need to live with him or we aren't allowed to get divorced.'? I can't do that."

It pisses me off because, yes, she can. The fact that we're hiding something so huge from our best friends is taking a toll on me. Yesterday, I almost word-vomited the entire thing when Blaze asked me where I've been during our workout session at the Blizzard facility. I could really use the guys' advice on how I can convince Dia to stay married to me, but that's kind of hard when I can't even tell them we're married in the first place.

I set the box down with a thud before looking over at her. "Are you really that afraid they won't support your decisions? You're so worried about Mads trying to get you to give this thing a chance, but what about me? What about what I want? I'm a part of this, too. Don't I get a fucking say in how our marriage is going to go? I should! At least until you leave me." The reminder of our inevitable fate hits me like a fucking diesel train. Six weeks was already not enough time for me to spend with Dia. Now I won't even get to see her every day? Hold her at night? We can't create the bond we need as a married couple if we're never together.

"Why does it matter?" she shouts. "You think you can just unfuck my brain into thinking marriage is for me?" She scoffs, throwing her arms up. "It's not, Dalton. This life is something that happens to people like you. People who know how to give their heart away without screwing it all up. But that's not me. I was never meant to be some-one's wife."

She bites the corner of her lip as it begins to wobble and I know if I keep pushing right now, she'll shut down. This conversation isn't over, but I'm pumping the brakes for now so we can talk more when our emotions aren't running so high. I want her to know that I'll be here no matter what, even when we don't see eye to eye. And if in the end, I can manage to get her to stay, I want her to feel secure in our relationship. I was raised in a home with two parents who communicated in a healthy way with each other, as well as us kids. But all Dia knows is manipula-tion, lies, and being left to deal with the aftermath alone. So, for now, we'll shelf this conversation and revisit it after we've had time to cool off.

"Come here," I tell her, closing the distance between us

and wrapping her in a hug. "You're perfect the way you are. And I'm sorry for pushing you on this." I kiss the top of her head and she exhales, sagging into my chest. This, right here, is how I know she's feeling something. Every time she's in my arms, whether she realizes it or not, Dia lets go of some of the tension and worry in her body. It's almost like she feels safe with me. And *that* is exactly why I can't give up on us just yet.

"So," I say, trying to steer the conversation to something not so heavy. "How are you going to explain showing up with only a suitcase when they know you moved out of your apartment?"

She loosens her arms but keeps them resting on my hips as she looks at the small amount of her belongings sitting next to my mountain of PR and endorsement packages. "I told them I was getting a storage locker until I find a place."

It seems she's thought of everything.

I look down at her. "Will you sneak out and come see me sometimes?" I don't want to sound clingy, but I know I'm going to miss her sassy attitude and having her warm body wrapped around me while we sleep.

"Maybe," she says with a coy smile. "Depends on what kind of orgasms you're offering up."

I wink at her before pressing a chaste kiss to her lips. "Ohh, Wifey. You already know."

DIA

I'm in my rental car on my way to Mads' house with one measly suitcase in tow. I have this car for two weeks, but I'll have to figure something out after that. Maybe Blaze will loan me his Audi R8 again. Probably not, since I almost drove it through his garage door the day after Mads' birthday party. It's not my fault the thing goes from zero to a hundred when you barely tap the gas.

Dalton tried to argue with me about the 'stupidity' of paying to rent a car. His solution? To buy me one. Yes, his answer to not spending a thousand dollars was to spend thirty thousand.

My husband, everyone.

I obviously told him no, because there's no way in Hell I'm taking that much money from him when he's already responsible for the one-hundred thousand dollars that's sitting in my bank account. When I find a job and an apartment, I'll see what I can afford with what I have left over after paying my debts and buy something used. It'll be the first car I've owned in my whole life.

I pull down their long driveway and park behind Blaze's truck. Mads' Mercedes is right next to it, so I know they're both home. Just as I start to hoist my suitcase from the backseat, I hear a loud scream from behind me. I barely get a chance to turn around before my best friend leaps into my arms, wrapping herself around me. Staying true to our rituals, I fall to the ground with her on top of me as we laugh and greet each other like a couple of crazy people.

"Jesus, you guys," Blaze says, walking toward us in a black hoodie and gray sweatpants. "I thought we had a couple of pterodactyls fighting in our yard. But, nope. Just you two psychos."

Mads stands up, brushing herself off before turning and holding out a hand to help me up. "Don't mind him. He's just jealous that Dalton doesn't get this excited when they see each other."

I flinch slightly at his name, but reel myself in before either of them notices. *What's that about?*

Blaze scoffs. "That dude walks around bricked up twenty-four seven. Like I want his boner smashed up against my leg every time he greets me. No fucking thanks." He reaches into the back of my rental and pulls out my suitcase, walking toward the door to the house and disappearing inside.

"So," Mads begins. "You're really here. I'm still trying to figure out why, all of a sudden, you decided to come."

I shrug. "Other than your parents, who do I have in Chicago? My parents couldn't give two shits about me. My job was wearing on me and didn't pay nearly enough to be so stressful. And most importantly, you're here. I wanted to be with my real family. So, here I am."

Tears fill her eyes as she leans in, wrapping her arms tightly around me. I hug her, relief flooding me at the feeling of having my person back. Even with everything going on, I know I'm making the right move by staying in Boston. Because in five weeks, when I'm officially divorced and can tell Mads every detail of what happened, I'm going to need her shoulder to lean on while I pick up the pieces and put myself back together like I've done so many times before.

FIFTEEN
DIA

IT'S BEEN five days since I moved in with Blaze and Mads. Thankfully, they've either put their sexual adventures on hold...or these walls are soundproof. Because I haven't heard any moaning or grunting coming from their room at night.

Don't get me wrong. I hope they bang each other's brains out every minute of the day. If I were as hot as they are, I know I would. I just don't want to hear it and then have to look them in the eye while we drink our coffee every morning. Plus, I'd be pretty jealous listening to it when it's just me and my vibrator all alone every night. It's *unfortunate*, to say the least.

I can't even pretend like I don't miss the way Dalton played my body like it was an instrument he'd been mastering his whole life. How he held me like putty in his hands as I willingly gave him things I'd never been able to give anyone else. I want *more*. But I know what that means. He was very clear last week when he told me that if I wanted his dick again, I need to agree to let him take care of me. I don't exactly know what that entails, but I have a feeling it's more than just making me dinner or folding my laundry. My biggest fear is that he'll want to care for me emotionally.

If that's the case, I'm terrified to give in. It's taken me a long time to build this wall around my heart. And it's done a good job protecting me from being hurt. But if I allow Dalton to break it down completely, will I be able to rebuild it again?

I really don't know.

I put on a good front of being strong and confident, but deep down, I'm still that broken little girl that longed for her parents' affection when they were off blowing every dollar we had and ruining my future before I even had a say. They're a big part of the reason I can't let Dalton in. Because a long time ago, I trusted them, and they left me. Over and over again.

I'd run home after school, proud of the graded papers in my hands, only to find a note saying they'd be gone for a few days. I was maybe seven or eight at the time, sitting in the living room with no TV to watch, hungry and scared that someone would find me there alone and take me away from my parents. They'd come back days later, apologizing for being away so long, but never explaining where they were. I'd forgive them and believe it when they said they'd change, just to have them do it again. As I got older, I knew they were on spending or gambling sprees. I still have no idea where they got the money sometimes, and if I'm honest, I don't even want to think about it. They could've been into any number of illegal or immoral money-making activities.

It took me a handful of rebellious teenage years of not letting anyone besides Mads have a piece of my heart. I thought I was healed when I met Josh and slowly allowed myself to fall for him. By the time he let me know his true colors, telling me he never intended on building a future with me in the cruelest and most brutal way, it was too late. The wound was reopened, and it's been hemorrhaging ever since. So, it isn't an easy deal to make, knowing that Dalton may want more than just the Dia that I keep on the surface. He may want parts of me that are too broken to give.

"Dia," Mads says, entering the kitchen as I sit at the counter sipping my coffee. "These just came for you." She hands me a large crystal vase with at least three dozen red roses.

I'm dumbfounded as I reach out taking it from her. "For me?" I ask. "Are you sure?"

"The card says your name on it," she replies. "Who are they from?"

"I, uhhhh…" I stutter. "I'm not sure." I don't say another word as I leave her alone and run up the stairs to the guest room I'm staying in. I lock the door behind me before moving into the ensuite bathroom and locking that one as well. I lower myself to the floor, setting the vase down in front of me as I rip the card from its holder and remove it from the envelope. Inside, there's a handwritten note.

> To my wife,
> I miss you. I hope these flowers brighten your day the way thinking of you brightens mine.
> Love,
> Dalton

Tears fill my eyes at his words. Damn him for this. It

wasn't supposed to be this way. It was supposed to be one crazy night of debauchery followed by a quickie annulment. But here I am, sitting on the bathroom floor, crying because nobody has ever bought me flowers before. Nobody has ever made me feel as special as Dalton does.

I can feel my resolve starting to crumble with every day that I'm away from him, which is the exact opposite of what I expected when I agreed to move in with Blaze and Mads. I thought some space would clear my head of the things I've been feeling. But all it's done is leave me wondering what he's doing all day. Is he sitting alone in his apartment? Is he out with friends? Or other women? The thought makes my stomach turn.

I want so badly to believe that he's different from all the other people who have come in and out of my life, but I've been burned so many times that it's hard not to give in to my knee-jerk reactions. I know I need more time away to think about everything. To sort all these new feelings out and make sense of them.

Standing, I take the flowers with me out of the bathroom and place them on the dresser that sits in front of the bedroom window. I decide to remove the card from the holder and shove it into the drawer under my socks, just in case Mads or Blaze come in here. I stand back, taking one last look at the beautiful bouquet. They really did brighten my day.

I unlock and open the door, making my way back to the kitchen where Mads sits like a little detective, waiting for answers. "Well?" she implores.

Shit. I'm still sorting through my own thoughts on this, and I just don't think I'm ready to bring her into it. So, I tell her my very first lie. "They're a well wish from my old boss," I say. "I'm sorry I gave out the address, but he needed to know where to mail my final check." As soon as the words are out, I want to take them back. I've done plenty of avoiding, subject changing, and omitting. But this is the first outright lie I've told Mads about this situation. Actually, it's the first lie I've told Mads, *ever*.

We've always had that type of friendship that is supportive and non-judgmental. I know if I keep hiding this, the whole thing is going to grow a set of legs and take off on its own, doing irreparable damage to my relationship with my best friend. She's never given me any indication that she wouldn't have my back, no matter what I decide to do with my life. So, what am I really afraid of?

"Mads, I have to tell you—"

"Hey, ladies!" Blaze says, cutting me off as he walks up the basement stairs. He's shirtless and has a white towel hanging over his shoulder, clearly just finishing a workout in his home gym. Mads turns her head just in time for him to run up behind her, pulling her off the barstool and into his arms.

"Ew!" she squeals. "You're sweaty!"

He peppers her cheeks in kisses as she half-heartedly shoves at him. "You love when I'm sweaty," he says, making her giggle.

As I'm watching them be the most disgustingly cute couple to ever exist, movement at the top of the staircase catches my attention. I look over to see Dalton entering the kitchen and, I shit you not, my jaw drops to the floor. He's shirtless as well, with his short, black gym shorts hiked up his deliciously muscled thighs. His abs are completely on display, leading down to the well-defined V that points directly toward what I know is his long, thick cock. This man's body is the fucking gold standard.

"Hey, Dalton!" Mads says in greeting.

"What's up, Shorty?" he replies to her before turning to me. "Looking good today, Dia." Then, the motherfucker winks and *licks his goddamn lips.*

Oh, he wants to play? *Game. Fucking. On.*

I sit up straight. "Nice shorts, Dalton. Do they come in adult sizes?" I quip. "Must be packing a pretty tiny peen if you're able to keep it all contained in those." I squint, looking over the counter at his groin area.

Blaze, who was drinking from his water bottle, almost chokes on it as he laughs. Mads rolls her eyes, patting him on the back while he coughs it up.

He shoots me a cocky grin. "Awww, Wifey. If you want to see my dick, all you have to do is ask. Matter of fact, I bet I could fix that smart mouth of yours by stuffing it full."

"Ooookay!" Blaze yells with a clap as I sit there completely speechless. Neither of us takes our eyes off the other as Dalton is dragged by his arm back down the stairs and I'm left with the mental picture of getting face fucked by my hot-as-sin husband as he tells me what a bad girl I am.

Mads blows out a forced breath. "Too bad you don't like him. Imagine how hot the sex would be with all that tension built up."

Oh, trust me, bestie. I'm imagining, alright.

SIXTEEN
DALTON

I FOLD the throw blanket that's bunched up on the couch and toss it into the basket in the corner of the living room. Turning around, I do a final once-over to make sure the apartment is clean. Tonight is my brother's first actual game with the Texas Thunder, and I've invited the guys and their girlfriends over to watch. I extended the invite to Dia through Blaze, but I doubt she'll come after our little verbal sparring match in their kitchen the other day.

I haven't been able to stop thinking about the look on her face when I told her I wanted to stuff her mouth full of my cock. She wanted to be angry, but it was written all over her face. She was turned on. And *fuck*. So was I. So much so, that I had to jerk off twice that night to thoughts of her taking me down her tight throat. I imagined how her eyes would water and how she'd gag as I pushed as far as I could go while she fought for air. I shot ropes of cum onto the shower wall while her name fell from my lips over and over.

Moving toward the kitchen, I pull out the snacks I bought for tonight. I know better than to invite three professional football players and their significant others over without having the proper food. I take out several bowls and fill them with various kinds of chips. I grab the dips from the refrigerator and pull off the tops, putting them all in the middle of the counter for easy access.

Just as I'm finishing up, the doorbell rings. I hurry to answer it, finding Maverick and his girlfriend, Bella Simon, on the other side. I don't think I'll ever get used to having a global superstar in our friend group, but Bella has to be one of the coolest girls I've ever met. You'd think that because she's one of the most famous people in the world, she'd be hard to talk to, but I swear I could have conversations with her for days. She's so down-to-earth, and it's easy to see why Maverick loves her. She is officially on break from touring, and I'm excited to spend some more time getting to know her.

"What's up, guys?" I greet them, giving Maverick a high-five and hugging Bella. I didn't get to see them much when we were in Vegas because they left the club shortly after we got there.

"Not much," Mav replies as I lead them toward the living room. "Excited to see Benton play tonight. Is he nervous?"

My brother has played hockey since he could walk. We knew almost immediately that he was better than the other kids. As he got older, he put all of his time and focus into it, and it paid off. After playing in the minors for a couple of seasons, he was called up to play for the NHL. I couldn't be prouder of him, although I give him shit for playing the less superior sport.

"I talked to him for a few minutes earlier. He didn't seem too nervous, but he puts on a good front. So, who knows? I'll be able to tell as soon as I see him." Benton has one of those faces that you can read without him saying a word.

I turn to Bella. "How's life as a normal civilian treating you?" After touring for about ten years straight, she's finally taking some time to herself. Her performance at the Super Bowl was the last one she had booked for the next year. She couldn't have met Maverick at a better time. It seemed like their relationship happened so quickly and so easily. I can't even imagine what that would be like. Here I am, married, begging my wife to let me do simple, everyday tasks for her, so she knows the sort of things she deserves in life. And she's fighting me every step of the way.

I get them all settled in just as the doorbell rings again. "That must be Mads and Blaze," I tell them. "I'll be right back. Make yourselves comfortable. There are snacks in the kitchen if you're hungry."

As soon as I twist the knob and pull on the door, I'm stopped in my tracks. I can't believe my eyes when I see Dia standing there, Blaze and Mads both beside her. I really didn't think she would come. I wanted her to, but I refused to get my hopes up about seeing her again. But now that she's here, I realize just how much I missed her.

And, of course, I can't even reach out for her the way I want to because I have to continue keeping this a secret.

"Hey, guys," I say. "Come on in."

Blaze steps in first, pulling Mads by their adjoined hands. Dia follows them, and I sneak a small whiff of her minty hair as she walks by. I want so badly to pull her into my arms, but I can't do that right now. Instead, I turn and close the door, taking a deep breath before following them into the living room. Now, all I can think about is how I'm going to get her alone so I can put my hands all over her. I don't think I'll survive another night here alone if I don't.

About ten minutes later, Tanner arrives. We all fall into an easy conversation, with the girls eventually breaking off into their own little group to talk about God knows what across the room. Tanner tells us about how he's getting ready to go back to his hometown for his best friend's parents' anniversary party, but I can't focus on anything other than my wife. She looks absolutely beautiful in a pair of black leggings and an oversized sweatshirt that hangs off one shoulder, showing the skin that I've tasted so many times. I'm not sure if she's doing it on purpose to get me going, but if she is, *mission accomplished*. Her long, black hair is pulled up into a messy bun and she's wearing minimal make up, but she's still a fucking knockout. I honestly can't believe I got this girl to marry me.

The game broadcast comes on the TV, and we all turn our attention to the Thunder players as they take the ice. I'm full of pride as I watch my little brother skate out as tens of thousands of fans cheer for him and his teammates. When the puck drops, and he comes on for his first shift, I can't take my eyes off of him. He makes everything look so easy, even though I can't skate for shit. He's talented. I'll give him that.

When Benton's shift ends, I see movement out of the corner of my eye. Like a magnet, I watch as Dia gets up and goes down the hall toward the bathroom. I'm at war in my own head about whether or not I should follow her. But I'm obviously a weak man, because my feet carry me across the room, not caring if my brain is on board or not.

"Where you going, man?" Tanner asks as I walk toward the hall.

"Just have to grab something from my room," I say without even slowing down for a second. My dick is obviously running the show here. Who am I to argue?

I make a quick pit stop to my room to grab the thing I've had waiting here for her for the last few days. Thankfully, the bathroom is further down and out of their view, so I quietly pad toward the end of the hall. I wait outside the door for her to finish, and as soon as I hear the lock disengage, I push my way in. I barely even get the door closed and locked again before I'm on her. I roughly press my lips to hers in a searing kiss that steals both of our breath. I turn us, backing her into the wall, and press my body to hers as I move my lips down her neck.

"I fucking missed you so much," I say into her soft skin, making goosebumps rise all over her body. I work my way down, lifting her shirt to find that she's not wearing a bra. Her tits are big and perky, with perfect pink nipples that seem to harden every time I look at them. All I want to do is thrust my cock between them before coming on her face. But, there's no time for that. There is, however, time to punish her for being such a bad girl the other day.

"Turn around and bend over, baby," I tell her, using a low, soothing voice so she doesn't suspect my questionable intentions. It works like a charm as she follows my order, leaning forward and pressing her cheek to the cold wall while she pants with anticipation.

Poor girl has no idea what's coming.

I pull her leggings and panties down before reaching into my pocket and pulling out the small toy. I drop to my knees behind her and flatten my wet tongue on her slit. She muffles her moan with her arm as she wiggles against my face, thinking I'm going to eat her out until she comes. She couldn't be more wrong. I push a finger inside her, finding her soaking wet before replacing it with the remote control vibrator.

"W-what are you doing?" she says on a heavy breath as I stand up, pulling her panties and leggings back up and patting her ass.

"Did you really think I'd let you get away with that cute little attitude you gave me the other day?" I ask. "You want to be a bad girl, you'd better be ready for the consequences. I want you to keep that inside your tight cunt all night or I promise you won't be able to sit for a week. Do you understand?"

She exhales a shaky breath before nodding her head. "Yes."

"There's my good little wife," I say, leaning in to press a soft kiss to her lips. "You go out first. I'll follow shortly after so they don't suspect that I just had my tongue all over your sweet pussy."

She takes a tentative step, testing the feel of the toy inside her before opening the door and slipping back down the hall. I wait for about three minutes before I join everyone back in the living room. Dia is sitting alone in the oversized chair, so I plop down on the side of the sectional that gives me the best view of her face. I don't want to miss a single second of any of this.

"What did I miss?" I ask, focusing on the television.

Mav looks up from his spot next to me where Bella sits on his lap. Dude's hand is definitely up her shirt, but I pretend not to notice because I'm about to do a lot worse. "Texas just scored on a power play. Benton looks good. He's playing strong."

"Nice," I say, pulling my phone from my pocket. At this angle it looks like I'm casually scrolling. Which is why Dia doesn't expect it when I press the circular button in the app, making the toy inside her buzz to life. She lurches forward as her eyes go wide.

Mads turns to her, noticing the abrupt movement. "You okay?" she asks.

"Mmhmm," Dia squeaks out before doing her best to return to her previous position. I press the button to turn the vibrator off, watching with a sly smirk as she relaxes back into the chair. I look back to the TV, cheering out loud as Benton checks one of the opposing players into the boards just before the clock runs out in the first period.

Blaze lifts his girlfriend's legs from his lap before standing up. "I'm going to grab something to eat. Want anything, Baby Doll?" he asks her.

"Yeah, but I don't know what," she replies. "I'll come with you."

He pulls her up and they head toward the kitchen. I look over at Mav, who now has *both* hands up Bella's shirt as he whispers something in her ear, making her giggle. Tanner is sitting on the floor with his back against the ottoman, watching game tape on his phone because, well, that's what he does.

None of them are paying attention when I hit the button in the app again and watch as Dia crosses one leg over the other, her eyes squeezing shut. Just as she sinks her teeth into her lower lip, I cut the toy off. She looks at me with a scowl as I shoot her a cocky wink.

You brought this on yourself, baby.

She uses the moment of relief to stand from the chair, quickly making her way back down the hall toward the bathroom. I chuckle to myself as I tap the button again, this time increasing the intensity of the vibration. If anybody notices the soft moan and the *thud* against the wall from her body leaning into it, they don't say anything. I didn't really get a chance to play with the app much, so I choose now to test how it works, moving my finger up and down the screen to change the pattern of the pulses inside her. There's another, much louder *thud* against the wall before a door slams shut in the distance. Tanner lowers his phone, looking up at me with a raised brow as I stand and walk down the hall behind Dia. I'm expecting to find her in the bathroom, but I can see as soon as I round the corner that the door is open and the light is off. My bedroom door, however, is closed. I know I didn't do that, so I think I've located my wife. Just to be sure, I push the intensity of the toy up another level, hearing a small squeak from inside the room.

I look around to make sure I'm still going unnoticed by our friends before twisting the knob and quietly entering the room, closing the door with a faint *snick*. The lamp on my bedside table illuminates the room as I find Dia on her knees and elbows, on the floor with her hands fisted tightly above her head.

Fuuuuuuck me. What a beautiful sight.

I stand there, knowing the bullet is vibrating against her tight walls, watching as she begins moving her hips on instinct. I can't stop myself from closing the space between us. I need to see her face. I slowly round her trembling body, dropping down to one knee in front of her and lifting her chin with two fingers. "What's wrong, baby?" I coo. "That naughty little pussy having trouble paying the price for that smart mouth of yours?" She looks up at me, her eyes pleading. For more? For me to make it stop? I'm not sure. And I don't fucking care.

"P-please," she begs, hanging her head again as I stand.

"Please, what?" I ask.

"Please make me come," she whines. "Dalton, *please*."

My name on her lips has me hard as stone. I'd give anything to fuck her right now. But I can't give in unless she does. She knows what I want from her.

I lower the vibrations to almost nothing, making her softly cry out in frustration. Thank God for surround sound, otherwise everybody out there would be able to hear this. As it is, I'm sure Tanner is suspicious, at the very least. I back up, sitting on the bed before beckoning her over to me. "Come here." She obeys, standing on shaky legs and walking my way. I don't even have to tell her what I want next as she lays over my lap with her ass in the air. I waste no time pulling her leggings and panties down to her knees, revealing her smooth, tan skin.

"You're being so good for me right now, taking whatever punishment I see fit," I tell her. "Should I turn your beautiful ass red? Or should I edge you with this vibrator until you pass out? I can't decide."

Dia doesn't speak, but her body shakes as she squirms in my lap. I'm feeling like a fucking king with the tables turned this way. I bet you if I offered to fuck her right now in return for her agreement to move back in and let me take care of her, she'd do it in a heartbeat. She's that desperate right now. But I refuse to manipulate her into it. So, instead, I break my other rule because I don't think I can leave this room if I don't.

I grab her hair, lifting the top of her body off of me just enough to pull my sweats and boxers down to my thighs. My dick juts up toward her as I tighten my grip, angling her head so she's looking at it. She moans at the sight and I swear the sound makes me almost blow right onto her face.

"I'll tell you what, bad girl. Suck my cock and *maybe* I'll let you come. But you'd better swallow every fucking drop of me, or you'll leave this room aching worse than you are now."

"Okay," she surrenders before leaning forward and licking the precum off my tip. She teases for just a second before lowering her mouth down as far as it will go. She works her tongue, swirling it around my shaft, while she creates enough saliva to lubricate my entire cock. When she slides all the way down, making me hit the back of her throat, actual stars explode behind my eyes as they roll back into my head. I have to grit my teeth just to keep myself quiet.

Fuck. She's good at this.

She picks up the pace, bobbing her head up and down while massaging me with her hot, wet tongue. I've never felt anything like this in my whole life. When she opens her throat, taking me down even further with a deep moan that vibrates against me, I almost lose it. Instead, I reach down, pulling the vibrator from her body and replacing it with my middle finger. She's so goddamn wet that it drips down my hand after only a couple of thrusts.

"Does this turn you on, baby?" I whisper as she continues sucking the life out of me. "Does choking on my dick turn you into a desperate, needy little whore?"

"Mmhmm," she moans with her mouth full as I bury another finger into her tight cunt.

"Show me," I say. "Come while you swallow me." I pick up my pace, using my free hand to grab the still-vibrating toy from where it lays beside me on the bed, pressing it to her clit as I finger her. Her moans get increasingly louder as she gets closer to her release.

"Shhhh, baby you have to be quiet unless you want everyone to hear how good we are together," I tell her. I couldn't give less of a fuck. I hope they *do* hear us. But I know she's still not on board with that.

She stops moaning, but continues to give me the best blow job of my life as her pussy begins to tighten around my fingers. "That's it, Dia. Give me what I fucking earned. Strangle my fingers with your pussy and my cock with your throat."

That's all it takes for her to go off like a rocket, her cunt sucking my fingers in as it spasms with her orgasm. I follow right after, jerking my hips up one last time as I paint her tongue with my cum. She doesn't spill a drop, even as she's recovering from her release. She somehow swallows it all with me still in her mouth before sliding off of me and giving my tip one last, gentle lick.

"Jesus, fuck," I say on an exhale. "I'd ask you to marry me, but you already did." She wipes her lower lip, hitting me with that gorgeous smile. I don't even give a fuck that she just took my load as I grab her by the back of the neck and haul her to me for a deep kiss. "You okay?" I ask, pressing my forehead to hers. "Was it too much?" Obviously, I wanted to punish her, but I didn't want to take it too far.

"I'm good," she whispers. "Really good."

"Okay," I say, giving her one last peck on the lips and helping her with her pants before pulling up mine. We both stand and I take a moment to pull her into me for a hug, inhaling her shampoo because I have no idea when I'll be able to do it again. I bought the same stuff for my own shower months ago, but it doesn't smell the same on me as it does on her.

"What are we going to tell them?" she says with her face buried into my chest. "We were gone for a long time."

I grab my phone from the bed, checking the clock to

find that we haven't been gone as long as I initially thought. "It's fine," I say. "The second period probably just started. I bet they didn't even notice. Most of them were either in the kitchen or making out on the couch when we left."

"Okay," she says, opening the door. I'm guessing she expects me to wait like I did when we left the bathroom, but I follow her immediately. Everyone is back in the living room, watching the game that's already well into the next period. *Whoops.*

"There you guys are," Mads says. "Where were you? I thought maybe you disappeared and were off killing each other somewhere."

My wife goes to speak, but I cut her off. "We were just talking. Dia was apologizing for having such a bad attitude toward me the other day."

Mads raises a suspicious eyebrow, but thanks to the god of sneaky bedroom blowjobs, she lets it go. "Hmm, okay." She shrugs, cuddling back into Blaze as Dia and I take our previous spots across the room from one another.

I look over, expecting to see her fuming, but I'm surprised when she just shakes her head and gives me a cute little eye roll.

Maybe she's warming up to the idea of us after all.

SEVENTEEN
DIA

I'M SITTING on the couch in Blaze and Mads' theater room when my phone rings. I dig it out from between the cushions and see a vaguely familiar number flashing on the screen. I don't know for sure, but it's a Chicago area code, so I can make a pretty good guess as to who it is. And I'm not interested in talking. I hit the button to send it to voicemail, which I will delete without listening to later.

Just as I toss it back down and reach for my bag of Nerds Clusters, it rings again.

Take a hint and move on.

I ice the call again, putting my phone on vibrate before getting back to my movie. Blaze took Mads on a quick trip to Nantucket so they could enjoy an 'unplugged week-end', as he called it. With all the post-Super Bowl commotion they've both had to deal with, they needed a break. The guys still can't even go to the grocery store without adoring fans stopping to shower them with compliments and congratulations. I know they love it, but it'll be nice for them to enjoy some peace and quiet, just the two of them. Even though it seems like they've been together a lifetime, their relationship is still kind of new.

Maverick is on a guys' trip with his brother, so Bella and I are planning to hang out at some point in the next day or two. I can't believe I'm just going to casually chill with Bella freaking Simon. If you had told me that six months ago, I'd have told you to fuck right off. I'm just a less-than-average girl from a trailer park on the outskirts of Chicago. I grew up eating ramen noodles and showering with watered down body wash. How I have friends that are world-famous and a husband, temporary or not, that is beloved by football fans all over the country, is beyond me. It's like a game of *Which One Doesn't Belong*. I'm the outcast, even though they've all made me feel so welcome.

I'm pulled from my thoughts when my phone vibrates, notifying me of an incoming text. I look to find a new message from Dalton.

DALTON: Hey, Wifey. What are you up to?

DIA: Nothing. Watching a movie.

DALTON: By yourself?

DIA: Yes. It's a normal thing that people do when they're at home alone and bored.

DALTON: Bored, huh? Want me to come keep you company?

DIA: There are cameras all over this house. You don't think Blaze and Mads would think it was weird if you just showed up here when I'm by myself?

DALTON: First of all, Mads only checks the cameras if she thinks Blaze might be naked. Plus, his cabin in Nantucket has no cell service and no WiFi. Only a landline. That's why they went there.

DIA: But what if they decide to look?

DALTON: Don't worry. I'll think of an excuse.

DIA: OK, fine. But only because the house is big and dark. And if a robber comes, I can sacrifice your life for mine.

DALTON: Be right there. I won't be mad if you're naked and waiting for me.

DIA: Dream on.

Twenty minutes later, I see Dalton pull up the driveway. I watch from the window as he rounds the back of his car and pulls a large bag from his trunk, looping the strap over his shoulder. I feel like a teenager sneaking her boyfriend in while her parents are asleep upstairs as I quietly open the door and let him through.

"What's with the golf clubs?" I ask, raising a brow.

"They're Blaze's. I borrowed them last year during our Pro Bowl trip. I figured if they happened to check the cameras and saw me here, I could just say I was returning them. Great cover up, right?" he says with a proud smile.

I huff an annoyed breath. "Uhh, yeah. It's *great*. But don't you think it's going to look a little weird that you're showing up at ten o' clock on a Friday night to return a set of golf clubs that you've had for over a year when he isn't even home? Not to mention, I assume Blaze doesn't do a whole lot of golfing outside in March when it's thirty-five degrees."

He stands there, perplexed for a moment. I almost feel bad, but he sets the bag down and drops a chaste kiss on my lips. "I have the smartest wife in the whole world. Always thinking of everything, aren't you?" He boops my nose before taking off toward the kitchen. *Maybe* I stand there, watching his ass for a minute before I follow.

He opens the pantry door, reaching for the snack shelf and pulling down several boxes of theater candy. Mads and Blaze keep it well stocked, because movie marathons are a way of life around here. He roots around for another minute before popping his head out. "I'm going to have to run back out to the store for your Nerds Clusters before we start the movie. Looks like they're all out."

I stand there, completely dumbfounded and speechless for a moment. "I—I took them downstairs already," I stutter. "How did you know they were my favorite?"

He shrugs his shoulders. "I know everything about you," he says. "Plus, you inhaled two bags of them while we were at Mads' parents' house. It was actually pretty impressive, Wifey. Turned me on a little bit."

I roll my eyes, trying not to crack a smile. "A stiff breeze turns you on."

"My wife is a fucking smoke show," he says with a grin. "You can't blame me for having a rager all the time. I'm a dude."

"Oh my God," I groan, unable to stop the corners of

my lips from tipping up slightly. He follows me with his hands full of snacks as I make my way to the theater room, plopping onto the large couch. Well, it's honestly more like a bed. I think I've slept in here more nights than I have in the guest room since I've been here. I like it because there are no windows and the walls are soundproof. I don't want Mads and Blaze to feel like they have to put their kink-fest on hold while I'm here, so I try to give them space.

"What are we watching?" Dalton asks, taking a seat next to me. His thigh brushes mine and a jolt of electricity runs straight to my core as flashbacks of him coming down my throat the other night hit me like a speeding truck. I seriously need to tamp this shit down. I can't be getting used to him and craving more. This was only supposed to be for one night, but here I am, letting him give me orgasms on multiple occasions and hanging out with him when I'm bored.

"I was watching trashy reality TV, but we can put something else on," I tell him. I know that genre isn't for everyone, so I usually watch it alone when I can sit around in my ratty pajamas and shove snacks into my mouth like a little gremlin.

He tosses a Swedish Fish into the air, catching it in his mouth. "I love reality TV. I binged the new season of Prison Brides in one day."

I raise a brow, "*You* watch Prison Brides?"

"Hell yeah, I watch that train wreck," he says. "One episode and I was hooked. The guys give me shit for it, but whatever. It's like crack. I'm addicted."

I laugh, because *same*. "Okay, then," I say as I grab the remote and start another episode.

I wake up some time later, focusing on the screen as it tells me we've finished the most current season of the show we were watching before we dozed off. Dalton is laying behind me with a heavy arm draped over my midsection. His warm breath puffs against my neck as he sleeps soundly. I take a quiet moment to pretend that this is my real life. That I'm the girl who gets to open her eyes and see this man every morning, forever.

"Mmmm…" Dalton says, his voice deliciously gravelly. "Morning, Mrs. Davis. I missed waking up next to you."

"Morning," I reply, trying to pull away before I do something stupid like snuggle further into him. But he has me pinned down so I can't move. "I have to pee." It's not a lie. We must've been asleep for a while because my bladder is screaming at me. I grab my phone, checking the time to see that it's nine in the morning. We slept all night.

I walk over to the door, pulling it open. I hear faint music coming from the direction of the kitchen and freeze in place. I don't remember leaving the speakers on last night. I listen closely for any indication that we aren't alone. Just then, I hear a muffled male voice and the very familiar sound of my best friend's laugh.

"Fuck!" I whisper-yell, carefully shutting the door. "They're back early."

Dalton sits up, his messy hair and sleepy eyes making him like, fifty million times hotter. My core clenches.

Not now, you horny bitch.

"So, what?" he says. "Just say you were bored and I came over. It's not the end of the world if they think you don't hate me."

"Noooo," I say, drawing out the word. "But it's the end of the world if they think we were in here fucking all night!" I'm starting to spiral, obviously.

He rolls his eyes. "We *weren't* in here fucking all night. As a matter of fact, I poked you with my midnight snack twice and you didn't even move."

"Your *midnight snack*?" I question, raising a brow.

"Yeah," he shrugs. "I get boners in the middle of the night. Wanted to make sure you weren't interested."

I scoff. "Oh my God. What is wrong with you?" I drag my hands down my face, trying not to go into full panic mode. "What are we going to do?"

He walks over, soothingly rubbing his hands up and down my arms to calm me. "My car is out there. They already know I'm here. Let's go up there and act like it's not a big deal. I promise they won't think we were fucking."

I honestly have no idea why he's being so understanding. Or why he hasn't outed this whole situation to our friends yet, seeing as how I know he's perfectly happy telling the whole world for some reason. I've been going back and forth with it and it just feels yucky lying to Mads. I know I need to at least let her in on some of what's going on between Dalton and me. I just have to figure out what details I want to share and which ones I want to stay between him and me. I guess once the conversation happens, I'll just let it go wherever it goes.

"Okay," I relent. I go to turn but he grabs me by the arm, spinning me back around. "What?" I ask.

He cups my face in both hands. "I don't know when I'll get a chance to do this again." He leans forward, dropping his lips to mine in a teasing kiss. As he starts to back away, I fist his shirt and jerk him back to me, needing more. I open my mouth for him when his tongue darts out, letting it tangle with mine. We stand there, making out for several minutes before I break the kiss, barely able to catch my breath.

I try to ignore the ache between my legs as I smooth my hair and clothes before wordlessly opening the door and heading toward the kitchen with Dalton following closely behind. As soon as I round the corner, Mads and Blaze come into view. She's sitting on the counter while he tends to the breakfast food on the stove. When he leans over and kisses her, he catches our movement out of the corner of his eye and turns his full attention to us.

"Well, well, well," he says playfully, making Mads look in our direction. "What do we have here? Is this a double walk of shame?"

"Very funny," Dalton says. "I was cleaning my storage area yesterday and wanted to get your golf clubs out of the way, so I brought them back. Dia was alone, so I annoyed her until she let me stay. We fell asleep in the theater room. That's it."

Blaze raises a suspicious brow, eyeing us both for a moment before shrugging his shoulder. "Oh. Cool."

I stand there, completely flabbergasted as Dalton turns to me with a cocky grin because his dumb story actually worked. *What an asshole.*

Everyone goes about their business, busying themselves with breakfast preparations while my mind is going a million miles a minute. I'm at war with myself, stuck between being relieved that they bought Dalton's excuse and wishing they had grilled us about what's really going on. I don't know what I want anymore, but I know that the longer I stand here, willingly keeping something so big from my best friend, the more I feel like I'm being choked by my own conscience.

"We're married," I blurt, causing all three of them to stop what they're doing and turn to me. I freeze in place, hoping that if I don't move, the floor will swallow me whole and we can pretend this never happened. Unfortunately, thirty seconds later, I'm still here and they're still staring.

"What?" Mads says with an incredulous laugh.

"We're married," I repeat.

"What?" she says again.

"We—"

"We have to stop them or they'll keep going," Blaze interrupts, looking at Dalton. "What's going on?"

Dalton looks at me and I give him a weak smile. He takes a couple steps closer to me in silent support as he explains. "Dia and I ended up alone in Vegas, so we decided to walk along The Strip. We got to talking and she told me how her ex said she wasn't wife material. We were standing right in front of the chapel at the time, and I decided to throw her over my shoulder and talked her into marrying me to prove him wrong. It was just supposed to be for the night, but it turns out that getting married is a hell of a lot easier than getting divorced."

"What does that mean?" Mads asks.

I finally find my voice. "We have to share a legal residence for six weeks before we can file for a divorce. That's why I'm here in Boston. I switched my driver's license to say I live with Dalton right after we got back from Vegas. That's when our six weeks began."

"Wow," Blaze says, blowing out a breath.

Mads looks at me, unshed tears filling her eyes. "Why didn't you tell me?"

Fuck.

I shrug, full of shame for keeping this from her for so long. "I guess I didn't want you to try to change my mind about the divorce. I know you're a romantic. And your relationship with Blaze is what fairytales are made of, so it's fair to assume you'd want that for me. But that's not what I want for my life. After Josh, I decided not to put myself through it again. I've been left too many times to believe that the love you've found is out there for me."

"Josh was a piece of shit," she whispers.

Dalton grabs my hand, interlocking our fingers and squeezing gently, letting me know he's there. Grounding me. It doesn't go unnoticed by the others, but I don't care. They don't have to understand what we're going through.

"So, now what?" Blaze says, eyes locked on our adjoined hands. "Are you guys together?"

"We're whatever Dia wants us to be," Dalton answers. "Right now, she wants to go through with the divorce and stay here with you guys until our six weeks is up. I support that."

"Okay," Mads says, blowing out a breath. "I support that, too." She looks at me, "And I'm sorry that I made you feel like you couldn't come to me."

I round the kitchen island, pulling her into a hug. "I was scared. And confused. I'm sorry I hurt you." I'm relieved when she hugs me back, pulling away after several seconds.

"I forgive you."

EIGHTEEN
DALTON

"SO," Blaze says, stretching his hamstrings. "You're married."

I left his house the other day shortly after we got done explaining to him and Mads what's been going down since Vegas. Dia walked me to the door, where I gave her a hug and kissed her cheek before whispering in her ear to call me if she needed anything. She didn't, of course. But I want her to know that even when I'm not next to her, I'm still there for whatever she needs. Blaze hasn't called or texted either, but now that we're at the Blizzard practice facility for our weekly training meetup, I'm sure he has a lot of questions. It's just the two of us today because Tanner had something else going on. And we don't see Maverick that much during these things because the defensive players have a different time slot.

"Yep," I answer. "Married to the girl of my dreams and already headed toward a divorce."

He walks over to the sideline, grabbing a football and walking about twenty yards away. "How are you feeling about all this?" he asks, passing the ball to me. I catch it before throwing it back.

I shake my head. "I don't know. At first, I was hopeful. That I could convince her to stay and give us a shot. But fuck, man. Her parents and ex did a number on her. She refuses to accept any type of help. I poured her a bowl of cereal the day after we got to Boston, and she lost her shit." I probably shouldn't be discussing all of this with him, but I feel like I have to let it out. Dia has enough going on to worry about how I'm doing. I don't want to add that to her stress. So, I've been holding it all in. But I can't keep doing that. Plus, I trust Blaze. He's my best friend and he's always been there for me. "I keep asking her to just give me the time that we have to show her how she deserves to be treated. I figure even if she doesn't end up with me, she would know that she's capable of receiving love. Because right now, I don't think she's ever truly felt it."

He tosses the ball back to me. "Yeah, Mads hates Dia's parents. She said they used to leave her all the time when she was little, being gone for days without even checking in. She was just a kid. Any time Dia would get money, they'd say they were putting it in a savings account. But really, they'd just gamble it away. Mads said she's been doing really good at standing her ground with not giving them money anymore, but I can't imagine how fucked up it was growing up in a family like that."

My heart twists in my chest. I knew the stuff Mads told me before and the few details Dia has given me, but hearing what kind of childhood she had makes me understand why she won't accept any type of help from anyone else. She's only ever known being on her own. And the few times she's trusted people with her heart, they left her.

I pass him the football. "I just wish I could make her see that I'm not like them. I'm not going to break her heart. I've been doing everything I can to earn her trust, but I'm running out of time."

He forces an exhale. "Do you love her?"

His words catch me off guard. To be honest, I've known since Vegas that I was falling for her, but it's all so fucking complicated, I haven't been able to really sort through all the emotions. I shrug. "How can you love someone if they won't let you?"

He gives me a sympathetic look. "You just have to keep showing her you're there for her. You can't force someone to trust you. They have to give it freely. But don't give up, man. Keep fighting till the clock hits double zeroes." He walks over, giving me a fist bump before dropping the ball on the sideline. "Come on," he says, nodding his head toward the locker room. "Let's go crash our girls' makeover party."

"Baby Doll, I'm home!" Blaze yells from the foyer as we enter the house. Loud music plays from the kitchen speakers, and we can hear both girls laughing hysterically. Exchanging a look before heading their way, we find them dancing around the island, wine glasses in-hand, with several open bottles in front of them on the counter. I'm not sure if they're empty or not, but it's only ten p.m., so they must've started early if they're already this loud. Then again, they're always pretty loud when they're together.

Blaze and I stand in the doorway, watching the girls as they laugh and move to the music. I zero in on Dia. She looks so happy right now. The worry lines that often crease the skin between her eyes are non-existent. Her body is relaxed, and her head is held high as she dances around like she doesn't have a care in the world. This is how it should be. This is the life she deserves.

Blaze can't hold himself back anymore as he walks up behind Mads and spins her around, dropping his lips to hers in a chaste kiss. She gives him a big smile before wrapping her arms around his neck as he dances with her to the upbeat song that's playing. It takes a moment for Dia to notice that they're no longer alone, but when she does, she whips around to me. Whatever reaction I was expecting is blown to smithereens when she runs toward me and jumps into my arms, smiling from ear to ear. I catch her effortlessly with my hands under her ass as she throws her head back in a carefree laugh.

"Ohmygoddddddd," she slurs, clearly very tipsy. "I misssssed you." She's fucking adorable like this. I can't help but grin back at her while she sways from side to side, trusting me not to let her fall.

"That so?" I ask.

She nods her head. "Mmhmmm. I haven't seen my husband in like, twellllllllve daysssss," she says, turning to Blaze and Mads. "Guys. Hey, guys. Stop making out for a sec." They both turn to her. "I haven't seen my husband in twelve days, but look," she points to me. "Here he is. Isn't he so hot?" I breathe a quiet laugh, still holding onto her as she continues her adorable little drunken rant about us being apart for almost two weeks, when it's really only been a couple of days.

"Very hot," Blaze says facetiously.

She looks back to me. "I knowwwww. I want to sit on his face."

Blaze barks a laugh as Mads tips her wine glass back like she isn't surprised in the least by Dia's words. I take it all in for a moment; the normalcy of the whole situation. Blaze and I coming home to our girls, to find them dancing and having a good time. Everybody is happy and acting like the four of us being here together is just no big deal.

I want this forever.

Dia leans her head on my shoulder with a sigh. "I'm sleepy," she says.

I chuckle, bringing one hand from where it's propped under her ass and moving it into her hair. "Alright, Wifey. Let's get you to bed," I say.

We say goodnight to Blaze and Mads before I make my way up the stairs to the guest room with her in my arms. I close the door quietly, trying not to jostle her in case she's asleep. Pulling the covers down, I lower her to the bed and bring the sheet above her chest. I take a minute to look at her beautiful face, all signs of stress and worry smoothed away as she sleeps peacefully. I'm falling for this strong, resilient, fierce woman so hard, and there's absolutely nothing anyone can do to stop it. Not that I'd want them to.

When I met Dia, she joked that she would break me. And now that we're here, married with an impending divorce looming over us, I realize that she was right. If she leaves, I will never be the same. The heart that I promised myself I'd never give away now belongs to Diamond Davis. And I'd let her break it time and time again if it meant that I got the chance to show her what being loved feels like.

I lean down to kiss her forehead, but she reaches out, pulling me closer. "Don't leave me," she whispers. I don't know if she's saying that she doesn't want me to leave her here alone in this room tonight, or if there's a deeper meaning to those words. But I realize it doesn't really matter because regardless of what she decides, I'll be a part of her life until the day I die.

I pull off my shirt and sweats before rounding the bed and sliding in beside her. I wrap my arms tightly around her as she settles into me. "Never, baby. I promise," I vow as her soft snores fill the quiet room. She probably won't remember any of this in the morning, but I mean it with everything I have.

NINETEEN
DIA

I PARK my rental car in the lot behind the dance studio Bella asked me to meet her at. This is the first time we've hung out since Vegas, but when we were texting a few days ago, the subject of dancing came up. Neither of us have been able to do it since the Super Bowl, so we decided to meet up here instead of at Maverick's place in the city. Since she can't really just make a normal trip to a coffee shop for a girls' day without being flocked by fans, we had to find a studio that was willing to let us dance when nobody else was here.

Just as I undo my seatbelt, my phone rings from where it sits in the cupholder. I pick it up to see the same Chicago number that's been calling me since the other night. Eventually, I'm going to have to answer if I want it to stop, but now is not a good time for that conversation. I need to dance, and I know it'll just bring me down.

Not today, Satan.

I grab my bag from the trunk and make my way to the studio entrance, where Bella's bodyguard is standing. "Good afternoon, Miss Spencer," he says in greeting. I almost correct him with my married name on instinct but remember that nobody besides Blaze and Mads knows about it. I've decided to keep it that way for now. Not because I don't trust Bella, but the less people we involve in this whole situation, the better. The fact that the media still hasn't caught on to Dalton Davis getting married in Vegas is a miracle in itself. We're halfway through our six-week period and hopefully we can quietly divorce without having to explain anything to anyone.

"Hey, Carlo!" I say. "I assume my dance partner is inside?"

He nods his head. "Miss Simon is waiting for you." He opens the door, letting me inside before shutting it securely behind me.

The studio is a wide-open space with mirrors along every wall and a ballet barre stretching from one end to the other. Bella is sitting on the floor in the far corner, lacing up her sneakers. Her long, blonde hair is pulled up into space buns on each side of her head and her black leggings and sports bra cling tightly to her toned body. She looks every bit the world-famous pop star she is. But at the same time, she has that *girl next door* vibe. She looks up, a smile covering her face when she sees me.

"Dia!" she says, jumping up. "I'm so glad you're here." She gives me a hug in greeting, which I return. When I lived in Chicago, Mads was the only friend I had. That was kind of by choice. I obviously struggle with letting people get too close, and that has affected my ability to put myself out there with making new friends. Looking back, that probably put a lot of pressure on Mads, knowing she was all I had. But now that I'm here in Boston, I want to do better. This is a fresh start for me, and a way to slowly break out of those old habits. I may still be afraid of love and heartbreak, but I'm hopeful that I can open myself to making new friends out here. Bella couldn't be a more perfect person to start with, because like me, she's struggled to make friends that she felt like she could truly trust.

"Me, too," I reply. "I'm happy to have someone to dance with. I've missed it."

She laughs. "I miss it, too, but I definitely don't miss the hours of practicing to perfect a routine. It'll be nice just to do it for fun." Bella is taking a year off from performing for the first time in a decade, so I can imagine how amazing it must feel to dance for herself. Me, on the other hand? I'd love to do it as a job. It's always been my dream to turn dancing into a career, but once that seed of doubt was put in my head, making it a reality seemed to move further and further out of reach. Then when my parents got busted and needed my help, I couldn't even afford classes at the YMCA. All I had was a broken full-length mirror and the bare floor in the bedroom of our trailer. I'd put on my pointe shoes and do fouetté turns for hours because there was no space for anything else.

I open my bag and grab my sneakers. If Bella wants someone to dance with, that's what I'll give her. I love hip-hop just as much as I love ballet, so it doesn't matter to me what we do. I just want to move.

She stands, connecting her phone to the studio's speaker system. When she queues up Come My Way by PLVTINUM and motions for me to start us off, I walk to the center of the floor. When the lyrics come in, I begin freestyling with absolutely no idea what I even want this to look like. After four sets of eight counts, I start again, waiting for Bella to memorize my steps and fall in with me. When she does, a smile blooms across my face as I look at our reflection in the mirror. We're perfectly in sync.

Bella smiles back, choreographing the next section as I watch, jumping in once the moves are drilled into my memory. When we put them together, it's fucking *magic*. If someone walked in those doors right now, they'd think we've been dancing together for years. I didn't realize how much I needed this until now.

The song ends and I drop to the floor, pretending to faint as Bella follows me, laughing. She probably thinks I'm completely joking, but holy shit. I'm out of breath. I guess not dancing like this for months in a row will do that to you. But even though I feel like I'm dying as I sit here, struggling to catch my breath, I've never felt so alive. I just danced with the biggest pop star in the world.

"Do you mind if we do that again while I record it on my phone?" Bella asks.

I shrug, "Yeah, sure. But I need five. At least," I say with a laugh.

After I catch my breath, we hop back up and repeat the choreography while she takes a video on her phone. The second time through is even more flawless than the first. With all the stuff going on in my life right now, dancing here today has eased some of the anxiety and worry about what the next few weeks hold.

We decide to use the last thirty minutes of our time on ballet, but when I go to pull my pointe shoes out of my bag, I notice one of the ribbons has come off. I'll admit I've never been the most skilled seamstress, so I often have to re-attach ribbons after my weak stitches come undone. But this pair of shoes is particularly old and worn, so I'm not sure if it's worth fixing them.

"I don't have a kit in my bag," I tell her. "Looks like I'm done for the day."

"That's okay," she replies, putting hers away. "I'm not

really that strong of a ballet dancer anyway. I just do it to keep my flexibility and posture where it needs to be."

We sit there for awhile longer, just talking about life. Well, I let her talk because I don't have much I really want to say right now. She tells me how she met Maverick's parents a couple of weeks ago and was shocked that his dad owned all of her albums.

I wonder what it would be like to have a boyfriend whose family welcomed you with open arms. With Josh, it was pretty clear that he never intended on introducing me to his parents. Every time I would bring it up, he'd make some excuse about not wanting them involved in our relationship. But now I realize it's because he never intended to keep me in his life.

When our time is up, Bella and I pack our bags and promise to meet up again soon before heading out the door. I toss my bag into the back of my rental car before getting in the driver's seat and checking my phone. I have eleven missed calls, and as I hold it out in front of me, it rings again.

Fuck it. It's time to end this, once and for all.

"Hello."

TWENTY
DALTON

"COACH WILL HAVE our asses if he sees us doing this. You know that, right?" Maverick says as he lines up on the opposite side of the ball. We had a little disagreement about who's faster, and I'm trying to prove to him that he could never catch me. Tanner isn't with us at the facility today, which is good, because there's no way he'd allow this. Mav isn't technically even supposed to be here. He had a meeting with the Defensive Coordinator, so he dropped down to the practice field, where I started talking shit to him about how our offense carries the team.

I smirk. "If you're scared, just say that. Wouldn't want to embarrass you, Mr. Defensive Player of the Year." I'm goading him. "Wait until I tell your girlfriend you were afraid to go toe-to-toe with me. I'm sure she and I will get a good laugh out of it."

That does the trick. Last thing he wants is for Bella to think he's not the toughest guy on the planet. "Fuck it," he says, going down into a three-point stance. Our backup quarterback, Jamison Sage, holds the ball out in front of him since our offensive line has already taken off for the day and we don't have a center to make the snap. It's just the three of us left on the field, about to do something we definitely shouldn't be doing. These voluntary offseason workouts are pretty relaxed, so we can get away with fucking around for a while after they're over without anyone seeing us.

"Give me a couple seconds to take the handoff since I don't have any blockers," I tell him. "If I get a first down, you have to admit, out loud, that the offense runs this team."

He scoffs. "I could give you ten seconds and it wouldn't matter. You're not making it to the marker." Cocky fucker.

"We'll see," I say, just as Jamison sets up the play.

"Blue, thirty-seven! Blue, thirty-seven! Set, hut!" He pulls the ball back, turning to make the handoff. I take it, tucking it into my arm just as Maverick pushes off the ground and comes my way. I know I can't outsmart him, so I have to outrun him. I take off toward the sideline, moving diagonally toward the first down marker. I can't see how close he is, but I can hear his feet as they pound against the turf, so I know he's hot on my heels. As I approach the marker, I take the ball in one hand, outstretching it to get the first down. But by the time I realize that I'm headed right toward the benches on the sideline, it's too late to slow down. I jump, trying to clear them, but my foot catches and I land head-first on the ground. Pain explodes behind my eyes as I bring my hands up to my pounding forehead.

"Fuck, dude. Are you okay?" Maverick says, kneeling down beside me. "Sage, go grab a medic."

I try to tell him no, that I'm fine, but I'm not completely sure I am. I lay back on the ground, waiting for help, trying to stop the ringing in my ears. It only takes a minute before one of the team trainers comes over and kneels down on the opposite side of Mav.

"What happened?" she asks, shining a light in my eyes. I squeeze them shut on instinct, but when I realize she's checking me for a head injury, I do my best to comply. The last thing I need is Coach Mills finding out we were fucking off and I got hurt. He'll find out eventually, but right now isn't really the best time since I feel like I'm getting hit repeatedly in the skull with a baseball bat.

They help me to one of the motorized carts before we make our way down the tunnel toward the exam rooms. My head is already feeling a little better by the time I get myself situated on one of the tables while I wait for the team neuro consultant to come in. I feel like a fucking idiot because who gets hurt like this during a non-contact offseason workout?

Me, obviously.

"What's going on, Davis?" the doctor asks as he walks through the door. I tell him that I tripped over the benches and hit my head, leaving Mav and Jamison out of it because I don't want them to get an earful. He dims the lights in the room before he sits down at the computer. The darkness helps with the headache as he goes through the list of questions for the concussion screening. I'm able to tell him my name, the date, where we are, and say the months of the year in reverse order without a problem, so that's promising.

We move on to the physical stuff, but when I stand to test my balance, my stomach rolls, making me sit back down. I lay back and bring my arm up over my eyes, trying to breathe through the queasiness. I hate throwing up, so I'll do whatever I can to avoid it.

When I think I can stand without puking, we go through the balance testing, which I fail, but not miserably. He tells me I likely have a mild concussion, and that they want to keep me here for a little while longer for observation, but I'll be able to go home without a hospital visit. All I want to do is sleep, but I know I can't right now. I'm also not allowed to look at my phone, so I just lay in the dimly lit room while I wait for someone to tell me I can go. The league doesn't mess around with head injuries, so if you fail any of the initial tests, they make you jump through all sorts of hoops to make sure you're okay.

I've been by myself in the room for about twenty-five minutes when I hear a very loud, familiar voice coming from the hallway. "Where's my husband? Is he okay?" Dia yells, panic apparent in her tone as she tries to get information. I sit up, ignoring the dull throb in my head as I try to get to her.

"Mrs. Davis, just a moment. They're assessing him now—"

"Dalton!" she yells, ignoring the trainer that's trying to calm her as her voice gets closer. I can hear her quick footsteps as she approaches the room and I call back to her.

"I'm here," I say, loudly enough for her to find me. She stops outside the opened door, relief flooding her expression as soon as her eyes lock on mine. I immediately notice what she's wearing. I could be completely brain dead, but I still wouldn't miss the sight of my wife wearing a Blizzard hoodie with the number thirty-seven embroidered on the sleeve. Without even seeing it, I know it has our last name stretched across the back.

She runs to my side. "Are you okay?" she asks, bringing her hand up to cradle my cheek. "Someone called and said you were hurt. I dropped everything and got here as fast as I could."

I'm still caught off guard by seeing her in my shirt that I don't even register her question. Or the fact that she just called me her husband in the hallway a minute ago to a complete stranger. She wore my clothes when she was staying with me because she hadn't gotten her stuff from Chicago yet. But, she has it now. *And* she's staying with Blaze and Mads, so why does she even have my hoodie? It's all I can focus on.

"Turn around," I tell her.

"What?" she replies, brows pulled together in confusion.

"Turn. Around," I say, and it comes out as more of a growl than a request. But, *fuck.* I need to see it for myself. She spins, putting her back to me, and sure as fuck, it's my hoodie. *'DAVIS'* is printed in large ice blue letters on the back, and it makes me want to beat on my chest like a goddamn caveman that she's out in public wearing it.

"You stole my shirt," I say.

She turns back around, jaw almost hitting the floor in shock. "I was worried sick thinking you were seriously injured, and you're worried about a stupid *shirt*?" She stares at me for a moment before realizing what I just accused her of. Her eyes go wide, looking down at the hoodie that she definitely swiped from my closet before she left and probably didn't want me knowing she had. "It must've fallen into my suitcase when I was packing."

Lie. Her suitcase never even made it into the house that day.

Not that I care. I love that she wanted to take something of mine with her. And the fact that it has my name on it? Even better.

"Alright," the doctor says as he comes through the

door, saving Dia from me making her admit that she misses me. "You're okay to go. No phone or television for twenty-four hours, rest as much as you can, and come see me for Return-to-Play Protocol before your next workout." He turns to Dia. "You must be the emergency contact."

"Ummmm," she says, unsure of what to say.

"Yes," I answer, standing up and taking her hand. I feel weak and exhausted. I just want to get out of here and I know they won't let me leave alone.

He nods before turning to her. "Make sure he gets plenty of rest. You can give him headache medicine for the first couple of days if he needs it, but please call us if it goes beyond that."

"Okay," she says, giving him a tight nod. I lead her from the room, putting a hand above my eyes to shield the bright lights. My headache is almost gone, but I don't want to chance it.

We walk out of the building and I go to give her a kiss goodbye as we get to the door of her rental car, but she stops me. "What are you doing?"

I look around. "There's nobody here to see us kiss. I just didn't want to leave without giving you one."

She gives me a bewildered look. "I'm not letting you drive home, Dalton. You have a head injury."

I want to argue because I'm supposed to be the one taking care of her. I don't want to put pressure on her to do things like this when she already has so much to worry about. I just want her to be able to lean on me. "Dia, I don't even think I have a concussion. I'm sorry they called you. When we had to fill out new paperwork for the team, I put you down as my emergency contact because you're closer than my parents. I really didn't expect to get hurt at a non-contact workout. I'm fine." I give her a reassuring look. I never thought I'd want to watch her get in her car and drive away from me, but it's better than her thinking she has to deal with helping me while I'm weak.

She narrows her eyes. "I'm driving you home, Dalton. Then, I'm getting you to your bed so you can rest while I make dinner. It's not up for debate. So, how'd you say it back in Vegas?" The corners of her mouth turn up in a smug smile. "Be a good little husband and get in the car."

Well, fuck.

DIA

"In you go," I say to Dalton as I pull back the comforter on his bed. I can tell just by looking at him that his body is completely exhausted. Not that it helped much, but I made him throw his arm over my shoulder while we made our way to the elevator from the parking garage. I just feel so helpless right now. I want to do whatever I can to make him feel better. He's always so happy and energetic, so seeing him being taken down like this is heartbreaking.

"I told you, I'm fine," he says. "I'm already feeling a lot better. I just need to take some medicine for this throbbing in my head. I'm sure that will fix me right up. You don't need to do anything for me."

"You're always the first one to remind me that I'm your wife and it's your responsibility to take care of me. So, doesn't that go both ways? You need help right now and I'm here. Let me," I plead.

He sighs, laying back on the pillow. He clearly doesn't like looking vulnerable in front of me, but I really do want to be here for him. I've never been anyone's emergency contact before. And even if it's like he said, and he put me down not expecting to get hurt, it still makes me feel good that someone trusts me enough to make me their first call if something goes wrong. "Okay, fine," he relents, looking completely defeated. But his spirits seem to lift a little when he looks back up at me through his lashes, eyes locking on his shirt that I'm wearing. One corner of his mouth turns up just slightly at the sight.

I'm glad he didn't pry further when I told him it must've fallen into my stuff. I really don't want to tell him the truth. That I took it out of his closet before I left to move in with Blaze and Mads. I can't even really explain why I did it. I guess because going through this whole experience with Dalton has made me feel close to him. I knew I'd be sleeping alone, and I wanted to feel like I was still wrapped up in him, even when I wasn't. So, I grabbed the first hoodie I could find and threw it in my tote bag before I left. I didn't realize until I went to put it on that it has his last name across the back.

When I got dressed this morning, I wasn't expecting to leave the house. I certainly wasn't expecting to get a call from the Blizzard facility telling me that Dalton was injured and I needed to get there right away. I threw on Mads' shoes that were in the closet, grabbed my keys, and flew out the door. They didn't give me any information, so I drove well over the speed limit the entire way, expecting the worst. Thankfully, he's going to be okay. But I still wish I could do more to make him feel better.

"Are you hungry?" I ask. I said I was going to cook for him, but I know his stomach was still upset when we left the exam room.

"Not yet," he says. "Can we just cuddle for a while? I bet that would make my head feel better." He gives me puppy eyes, and how can I say no?

"You're really milking this," I chide, already removing

my leggings. "I'll lay with you, but no hands. You're supposed to be resting. Deal?" I say, waiting for his response with my hands on my hips.

"Whatever it takes to get you in my bed, Wifey," he replies with an adorable grin.

I climb in next to him, pulling the covers over my body. He loops his arm around my waist and slides me across the mattress, into his warm embrace. It takes no time at all for us to fall asleep, where we stay, holding each other until morning.

TWENTY-ONE
DIA

"YOU JUST *LOOK* LIKE A FUCKBOY," I say to Dalton as I sip on my fancy latte in Blaze and Mads' kitchen. They recently upgraded from his old, barely used coffee maker that he had when she moved in. My best friend loves coffee more than anyone, so his little machine was only going to cut it for so long.

The four of us have been sitting here for most of the morning, just talking and making jokes back and forth. Dalton still hasn't been cleared by the team doctors to return to workouts, so Blaze has been skipping them this week to hang out with us. I love these moments. When there's nowhere to be and nobody waiting around the corner to jump out and ruin our day. The guys came up from their light workout about an hour ago and plopped down at the kitchen table, where we've been sitting ever since.

Dalton turns his head, raising a brow. "What does that even mean?" he asks with a scoff.

"Look at you," I reply, waving my hand vaguely. "All

leaned back, manspreading, taking up way too much room at the table. You're...*imposing*."

I'm obviously messing with him. I love our banter. Just because we're married and Blaze and Mads know about it, doesn't mean I'm going to stop picking on Dalton. If I'm being honest, he looks hot as fuck over there, with his short gym shorts, tight t-shirt, and backwards hat. If we weren't in front of our best friends, I'd definitely consider hopping on and taking a ride. But we are, so I'll just hurl some playful insults at him instead. God knows it's like foreplay for him.

"You look like the kind of guy who meets a woman and immediately tells her you have the biggest dick on the team," I say.

"No way," he answers immediately, shaking his head emphatically. "That's Maverick. I have the second biggest dick on the team." He shoots me a cocky wink.

Blaze huffs a sarcastic laugh from the other side of the table, before raising a suspicious eyebrow in Dalton's direction.

"Okay, fine," he says, obviously busted. "I have the *third* biggest dick."

"Good thing Tanner isn't here to check your work," Blaze laughs. "Have you talked to him at all, by the way? I know he's been going back and forth to his hometown for the last couple of weeks, but I've barely spoken with him."

Dalton shakes his head. "Nope. Not a single call or text since the night of Benton's debut. We win the big game and he just forgets about us. Classic QB1," he jokes.

Tanner is probably one of the nicest guys I've ever met, albeit one of the most mysterious. He always seems to pop up when anyone needs help. So, it's weird that we haven't seen him in a while. The guys have been going to the practice facility a few times a week to train, and he hasn't even shown up there, aside from a couple of days. He's the captain of the team, and from what the guys say, he's always the first one there and the last to leave. So, it's a little strange that he's been missing.

"Okay," I say, unable to hold in my thoughts anymore. "Back to Maverick's huge cock."

"Heeeeeere we go," Mads says with an annoyed sigh.

I look at her, raising my brows. "What? Aren't you a little curious? Bella is so small. How does he not rip her to shreds every time they fuck?" I happen to think it's a very valid question, but they all stare back at me like they can't believe I'm saying any of this out loud.

"My wife, everyone," Dalton deadpans. "Talking about another dude's dick right in front of me."

I roll my eyes, sitting back in my seat and crossing my arms over my chest. "I was just wondering," I mumble. "Like, the mechanics of it all."

Dalton reaches over, yanking me by the arm and pulling me onto his lap. "The only Blizzard dick you need to be worrying about is mine," he warns. He leans in, lowering his voice so that even I can barely hear it. "If you think I won't put you over my knee in front of them, you're dead wrong, Wifey. Try me," he whispers, making me immediately rethink my topic of conversation. I know my cheeks are blushing by the way Mads looks back at me with a sly smile stretched across her face.

I'd never say it out loud, but if I *do* have a match in this world, Dalton is one hundred percent it. The way he puts me in my place like no one else can, even surprises me sometimes. But it's also exhilarating. It's nice not having to be in charge all of the time. I know I can't get used to it, but I'm not hating the way it feels when he takes the control like this. An ache forms between my legs, like it always does when he threatens to spank me. I kind of wish we were alone right now, so I could test the waters and see how far he'd let me go before he actually did it.

I've had a lot of time to think about what it might be like if I moved back in with him for the remainder of our marriage, but it always ends up with me talking myself out of it because I already know I'm starting to get attached. The more time I spend with him, the harder it'll be when it's over. The last thing I need when I'm trying to create a new life in a new city, is to fall into another depression caused by missing someone who I let myself have feelings for. I need to remember what it's like to stand on my own two feet. And I am absolutely positive that, if I moved back into Dalton's place, he wouldn't just sit back and let me do that. He really is a perfect husband. He just wants to show me what it's like to have someone who cares for me unconditionally. And I have no doubt that he really, truly does, but I can do it myself. That's the thought that always stops me from giving in, even though in the back of my mind, I want to.

Our six weeks will be up soon. As nervous as I am about whatever my future has in store, I know that I can always count on myself. That's how it's always been, and that's what I want. Let's just hope I can pull it all off without either of us getting our hearts broken beyond repair in the end.

TWENTY-TWO
DALTON

I'M PULLED from a deep sleep by a series of quick, hard knocks on my door, followed by someone laying on the doorbell. I shoot up, confused, until I realize that I'm on the couch and not in my bed. I was watching hockey high-lights and must've dozed off.

The knocks go from a solid fist to a loud, open-handed slap just as I hear my muffled name being yelled from the other side of the door.

Fuck. That's Dia's voice.

I jump off the couch and run as fast as I can to the door, unlocking the deadbolt and ripping it open. I'm not prepared for what stands in front of me. Dia is wearing a pair of shorts and one of her ripped sleep t-shirts. She has no shoes on her feet and her face is tear-stained. She stands there, frozen, her whole body trembling.

Her eyes fill with tears. "I didn't know where else to go," she whispers.

"Baby," I say softly before yanking her into my body and wrapping her tightly in my arms. I carefully pull her through the doorway, managing to close and lock it without letting her go. She continues crying as her knees buckle and she collapses against me. I'm trying not to panic, lifting her from the floor and carrying her straight to my bedroom. It's illuminated only by my dimmed bedside lamp, but I can see as I make my way across the carpeted floor.

I don't put her down. I don't loosen my hold. I just sit on the bed with her in my lap, continuing to comfort her because I have no fucking clue what's going on. All I know is that whoever did this is as good as dead.

"Shhhh," I say in an attempt to console her. "I'm here. You're safe."

Her body continues to shake with her cries as she tries to suck in deep breaths, but she's in the middle of a panic attack and can't calm herself. So, I do the best I can to hold her together as she falls to pieces in my arms. I kiss her hair and steadily rock her back and forth while she lets her emotions out, until she eventually settles into my chest.

I wait several minutes before I speak. "Can you tell me what happened?" I ask.

She sits up, clutching my shirt tightly in her hands as she takes a shaky breath in before exhaling slowly. "Last w-week," she stutters, pausing for a moment before trying again. "Last week, my mom called me. At first, I sent it to voicemail, but she kept doing it, so I finally answered to tell her to stop." I continue rubbing soothing circles between her shoulder blades as she slowly relaxes enough to finish. "She sounded so different. She said she had gotten back together with my dad, and they started outpatient rehab for their spending and gambling addictions. They told me they were with a loan officer at the bank because they were buying a house. They said their credit was approved for the mortgage loan, but they needed collateral. They asked me for help."

"Hey," I say in a soothing tone. "If you gave them some money, it's no big deal. I'll replace it. You can even make payments back to me once you start working if you aren't comfortable taking it outright."

She looks at me, her beautiful eyes filling with tears as she shakes her head. "They put the banker on the phone, and he said they just needed proof of collateral. That I could transfer money from my bank account to theirs so the loan application could be processed, then my parents could wire it back the following day. I told them no at first, but they said the house had an extra room and they wanted me to come stay with them because they missed me and wanted to rebuild our relationship. They wanted to apologize for all the times they had to rely on me."

I'm trying my best not to lose my shit because I know what's coming. They fucking hurt her again. But I stay quiet, letting her say it out loud.

"I sent the money, and they said it would take twenty-four hours to process their application, then they'd send it all right back. It sounded legit to me. But when I hadn't heard from them for a few days, I called my mom's new number and it was disconnected. I finally worked up the nerve to call their bank today, but the person who answered told me that they don't even do mortgage loans there. They have no record of either of my parents having any accounts in their system." She looks up at me with so much sadness in her eyes. "They took all my money and left me. Again."

"It's going to be okay," I say, holding her tightly as she continues to break down.

"Why did I fall for it again, Dalton?" she cries. "I'm so

fucking stupid. Every time, they show me that money will always be more important than me, but I keep helping them, thinking maybe this time it'll be different. Why? Why am I never enough?" She hangs her head, holding me like a lifeline as she starts sobbing again. My heart fucking aches for this woman because she's *more than enough*, but the two people she wants to hear that from the most are too selfish to say it.

"Dia, look at me," I say, gently lifting her chin with my finger. The pain in her eyes makes me want to tear this whole world to shreds with my bare hands, just to find her parents and hurt them the way they've hurt her. "This isn't your fault. You did nothing wrong besides believe in them and love them when they didn't deserve it. And they're missing out on a beautiful, talented, strong woman that became that way *despite them* when it should've been *because of them*. You're worthy of so much more than you've been given, Dia. I need you to believe me when I tell you that."

She grips my shirt tightly, pressing her lips to mine. When I reach up to weave my fingers into my hair, some of the tension in her body eases. I tease at her bottom lip with my tongue, and as soon as she opens for me, I tangle it with hers. If this is what she needs right now to feel like she's not alone, I'll give it to her. I'll give her every piece of me if it'll fill the holes others have left behind.

"Make me forget," she says against my lips, making every rule I had disappear into thin air. I don't care what I said. Even if this is the only time she lets me show her what it's like to be loved and cared for, so be it. I'm not like them. I won't let her go through the hard parts alone.

I kiss her again as I turn us on the bed so I can lower her down to her back. I run my hands up and down her body, never removing my lips from hers as I push her shirt up above her tits. She isn't wearing a bra, and her nipples are pebbled from the cool air in the room. I lower my head slowly, taking one dusty pink bud into my mouth with a gentle suck, before releasing it with a wet *pop*. I slide my tongue across her sweet skin as she writhes under my touch, moving to bring the other nipple into my mouth and teasing it until it's hard enough to be borderline painful. Dia weaves her fingers into my hair, holding me to her. *Like I'd ever go anywhere.* Her moans are the sweetest song I've ever heard as I reach down and press the pad of my finger onto her clit over her shorts, adding enough pressure to make her thrust her hips up for more. I rub firm circles as I move my mouth back to hers, licking and sucking at her tongue.

I can tell that she's not getting enough of what she wants by the sound of her needy whimpers, so I pull her shirt over her head before reaching down for her shorts and panties. I stop for just a moment to take her in. "You're so fucking gorgeous, baby," I whisper, reaching between my shoulders and peeling my shirt over my head. She opens her legs, making room for me to lower my body onto hers. I settle in, rubbing my erection over her bare slit through my boxers as I take her mouth again. She's still trembling as I slowly grind against her.

Her whimpers get louder as she reaches her hands down, attempting to rid me of the final piece of cloth that separates us. I assist by pulling my underwear off and kicking them to the floor. When I fit my body back onto hers, I almost lose it at the feeling of her bare pussy on my hard shaft. She's so wet and warm. Nothing could stop me from being inside her tonight. I'll give her whatever she needs to feel anything other than the pain and heartbreak her parents caused. I reach over to the nightstand for a condom, but Dia grabs my wrist, halting me.

"No condom, please. I want to feel you," she whispers.

We never talked about birth control, but if I'm being completely real, I don't give a fuck. If she was good with it, I'd have a baby with her right now. I'd have ten kids with her if she wanted them. I'll give her the family she's always deserved.

I kiss her again as I lower my hand between her legs, stroking her soaked slit before entering her with two fingers. I pump them in and out, coaxing her swollen flesh as she loosens in preparation for me. When I know the ache is becoming too much, I pull my fingers from her, dipping them into my mouth for a quick taste of her sweetness before lining myself up at her pussy. I can barely see straight as I make sure her attention is solely on me in this moment. I need her to see how I feel about her.

"Look at me while I push in," I tell her. As soon as her big, beautiful eyes connect with mine, I slowly thrust my hips forward, sinking into her tight heat. She's wet and soft and so fucking perfect. She's everything I never knew I was missing.

"Dalton," she whispers, her voice trembling with emotion.

"I'm right here," I reply. "I'm not going anywhere."

She blows out a shaky breath, letting her eyes fall shut as I work to get her toward her release. Every movement of my hips is filled with another promise I can't say out loud.

I'm in this.

I'll never leave you.

I love you.

I loop one arm tightly around her back as I use the

other to pull her knee up higher, opening her further as I pick up my speed. I keep our bodies pressed together as tightly as I can, connecting us at every possible point. I feel her inner walls start to flutter with her impending orgasm and I can't think of anything I want more than to make her feel nothing but euphoria, even if it's only for a few moments.

"Fall apart for me, Dia. I'll put you back together," I say as she explodes around me. Her cunt squeezes so tightly, black dances around the corners of my vision as I try to focus on her face while she comes. As soon as I'm sure she's done, I finally let go, emptying myself into her with a loud groan.

I don't even give her a second to recover before I cup the side of her face and press my lips to hers. We're both still gasping for breath while we kiss, but I don't care. I need her to feel what I'm feeling. I want her to know she's not alone. Not now, not ever.

"Okay," she says quietly, her lips brushing mine.

I pull back so I can look at her. "Okay, what?"

"Okay, I'll move back in and let you take care of me."

TWENTY-THREE
DIA

"WHAT DOES your dream life look like?" Dalton asks as we lay in bed, his fingers running through my mess of black hair.

"I don't know," I say. "Having a steady job that pays enough to go on a vacation every year?" I've honestly never really thought about it. I didn't have the luxury of planning out my perfect life when I was younger, and as I got older, the goals I had seemed to change every time I turned around.

"I don't mean your idea of a comfortable life," he replies. "I mean, if you could have anything you want for your future, what would you choose?"

I lay there, trying to imagine what I would even want if money and circumstances weren't a factor. I've never been into fancy cars and designer clothes. Not that I wouldn't love them. I've just always had a different idea of what success would look like.

"If I could have anything, I would want a white house with a wrought iron gate and a porch big enough for some rocking chairs. It would have to have a fireplace and a big kitchen so I could have friends over on the weekends for wine and makeovers. Mads and Blaze would bring their kids over and I'd be the cool aunt that would wear giant sunglasses and slip them twenty-dollar bills and a boat load of sugar when their parents weren't looking." He laughs, leaning over to kiss the top of my head. But I can't seem to stop myself from falling further into this fantasy. Nobody has ever asked me anything like this before, and now that I'm making up my perfect life in my mind, I just want to keep adding to it. "I would have a big back yard with a pool and a little waterfall that I'd spend hours relaxing at every weekend. I'd just soak up the sun and listen to the sounds of nature. And maybe there would be a dance studio in the basement. A wall full of mirrors with a barre and wood floors for me to dance across, not just to spin around in one spot. I'd replace my worn, old pointe shoes, and do grand jetés until I had blisters, just because I could."

"Can I watch you?" he asks.

I look up at him, my smile fading into a look of confusion. "Watch me what?"

"Do grand jetés," he says. "I don't know what that is, but I already know I could watch you do it all day long."

I breathe a laugh. "This is a fantasy. Not real life, Dalton. You asked me what my dream life looked like. But I will absolutely be working toward the life where I can vacation every now and then. Even that seems unattainable right now, but I'll get there."

"I have no doubt about that," he says, rolling us over so he's on top of me. "My wife is the most beautiful," he kisses my cheek, "strong," he kisses my other cheek, making me giggle, "sexy," *kiss*, "determined woman in the whole world."

With each word of encouragement from Dalton, I feel an imaginary sledgehammer take a whack at the wall I've constructed around my heart. The barrier that once kept me protected from the hurtful words of people I trusted is slowly being obliterated by this man that I still have trouble believing I deserve. Even though I fought him tooth and nail at first, I find myself wanting to know what it would be like to be loved and cared for in a way I'm sure only he can give. And I trust him with my heart. I know he won't hurt me.

Let's just hope I can return the favor.

DALTON

As much as I'd love to lay in this little bubble with Dia, we need to discuss what things are going to look like for the next couple of weeks. Hopefully longer if I do this right. But I know I need to choose my words carefully. She's been burned so many times, I can already tell she's got one foot hovering over the threshold, ready to bolt at the first sign of uneasiness. I have to continue to show her that, no matter what she throws at me, I'm here. I have to show her, without telling her yet, that I love her and want to be the person she runs to when she needs to feel safe and secure. And when she's feeling like she's not enough, I want my words to be the ones that make her realize how special she is.

"So," I say, anxiety clouding my tone, "with the way that things changed tonight, I think we need to talk about what this means for the rest of our time together." I look at her, expecting some inkling of defiance, but she just waits patiently for me to continue.

I keep my arms wrapped loosely around her as we lay

propped up on the pillows in my bed. I want her to feel me here, but I also don't want to make her feel like I'm holding her down while we talk. She's free to move away, leave the room, or tell me to go fuck whatever inanimate object she's feeling like going with today. The more I get to know Dia, the more I understand her. And the last thing she wants is to feel like she's being forced into anything. "I want you to give me one hundred percent free rein to treat you as my wife while we're in private. I understand your hesitation to tell the world about our marriage because I'm in the public eye, and I respect and support that decision. But while we're here in our home, or with Mads and Blaze, I want to be able to do things for you, show you affection, buy you things, and spank that ass raw if you misbehave. Are you sure you're okay with that?" I ask.

She swallows, and I see the rough motion as it moves across her throat. I'm not sure which part of what I just said caused that reaction, but I bet I have a little bit of an idea. My little bad girl likes the idea of getting punished for acting up. And my palm is already tingling at the thought.

"Yes," she whispers. "I mean, I'll try." I can tell she's nervous about all of it. And I understand. Even though Dia has put a lot of trust in me in these last few weeks, that doesn't change the fact that she has yet to experience any type of relationship, besides with Mads, that doesn't end in her being used and heartbroken. But that shit ends here. With us.

"How about this," I say. "Let's come up with a safe word. Not just for sex, although we can use it there, too. Anytime you feel uncomfortable or think I've gone too far, you say the word and we'll take a time out. You can take however long you need to sort through it and decide how you feel, and if whatever it was is an absolute dealbreaker for you, I won't do it again. No questions asked. Sound good?" I ask.

Her smile is so sincere, and I finally feel like we're having a breakthrough. She's going to give me the gift of being her husband for real. "Yeah, that sounds really good," she answers, making my heart do somersaults in my chest.

Fuck yeah, baby.

I lean down, pressing a soft kiss to her lips before exhaling in relief. "Thank you." I want her to know I'm truly grateful for this. I know it's not easy. "Pick a safe word, baby. Something you'd absolutely never say in regular conversation with me." I smirk. "I guess *'Oh my God, Dalton. Your dick is so big and perfect, I can barely stop from ruining my panties whenever you're around'* is out. Pick something else."

She gives me a cute little eye roll. "You're so annoying."

"So I've been told," I reply. "What's your safe word?"

She taps her bottom lip, thinking carefully before looking up at me with a grin. "Elvis."

Jesus fucking Christ, this girl.

"Okay," I say. "'*Elvis*', it is."

TWENTY-FOUR
DIA

"HOW DO YOU LIKE YOUR EGGS?" Dalton asks as I sit at the kitchen table. I tried keeping him in bed by wiggling my ass against him while he spooned me, but he told me that if I wanted more, I needed to eat something. We decided on breakfast food in the middle of the night, agreeing that it should be enjoyed at every hour, not just in the morning. He pulled my naked body from the bed, throwing his worn t-shirt over my head and leading me by my hand into the kitchen. As much as I wanted to stay in his room all night and day, not thinking about the fact that my parents just took off with every dime I had in my bank account, he's right. I can't remember the last time I had food, and my stomach is growling.

"Scrambled," I reply, standing from my seat. "But I can get—"

He raises a brow in my direction, "You'd better sit that cute little ass back down," he warns. I roll my eyes, throwing myself back into the chair and crossing my arms over my chest like a child. Dalton just chuckles before returning to our midnight breakfast. Several minutes later, he walks over with a plate of eggs, bacon, and a piece of toast, setting it down in front of me with a quick kiss to the top of my head. He returns to the stove, plating his own food, which looks to be enough to feed an entire family, and sits down across from me.

I eye his food. "Do you always eat that much?" I ask.

He grins, patting his rock-hard stomach. "I'm a growing boy, Wifey."

I can't help the scowl that mars my expression. "That's so unfair," I mumble, stabbing my fork into my eggs. "Why do boys get the good metabolism *and* the good eyelashes? You should only be able to pick one."

"Eh," he says with a shrug, "But you guys get boobs that you can play with whenever you want. So, I'd say that evens things out."

I scoff, shaking my head. "Why are you like this?" I ask.

"Sorry for being a tit man, babe. It's a damn good thing I don't have a set of my own. I'd never leave the house," he says, shoving a forkful of food into his mouth and chewing while I glower at him. "Eat," he orders, pointing at my plate.

I look down at it, hesitating. I've never had issues with food. Even when I strived to have what society considered the *'perfect dancer's body'*, I ate. Growing up in a house where you weren't sure where your next meal would come from makes you thankful for all the nutrients you can get your hands on. Not to mention, breakfast food is my favorite. When Mads first went to college, we met up every Sunday morning at the diner by my apartment and binged on greasy food until we couldn't take another bite.

So, why am I struggling here right now? It's like the

cereal thing all over again. He made me food because he cares about me. And it's no big deal.

So, just take a bite, Dia.

Sensing my discomfort, Dalton sits back in his chair, a cocky grin tipping up the corners of his lips. "I'll tell you what," he says. *Oh, boy.* "One bite equals one orgasm."

"What?" I say, genuinely confused.

"For every bite you eat, I'll give you an orgasm."

I let out an incredulous laugh. "Dalton, there's an entire plate of food here and I'm starving."

He pops a shoulder. "Cool. Me, too." *Good fucking God.*

I pick up a piece of bacon, eyeing him suspiciously. "There are at least twenty bites here. *At least*," I emphasize. "I'd die."

He smirks. "RIP you, then."

Why is this turning me on? I should be throwing a fit at the fact that he's treating me like a child. Rewarding me for eating my food. And I should be mad at myself for being so jaded and defiant at the thought of him doing something nice for me, that I have to be bribed with sex. But I'm not, and here we are.

I bring the bacon to my mouth, biting off a piece and chewing. He sits forward, smiling, as he stabs his eggs with his fork. "Good girl."

Before I know it, I've taken so many bites that I lost count. My stomach is feeling better as we fall into a comfortable conversation, discussing the plan to tell Mads and Blaze that I'll be spending the rest of our six-week period living here with Dalton. Now that I'm broke again, I'm going to have to go out this week and put in some job applications. It all happened so fast, that I barely had time to consider how I would get the money to move out on my own. I have a few hundred dollars in cash that I had been saving up, but that definitely won't cut it. So, I'll need to take the first job that will hire me. That's nothing I haven't experienced before, though.

I look down to see that my plate is completely empty. A sense of accomplishment washes over me at the fact that I let someone else do something nice for me without running away. And to be honest, it actually felt really good.

"Alright," Dalton says, picking up his plate, moving it to the counter by the sink, returning to his seat, and patting his hand on the table. "Bring me my dessert."

I laugh, rolling my eyes. "I think you've eaten enough, big guy. Let's go back to bed." I walk over, grabbing him by the hand and trying my hardest to yank his massive body up, but he's a lot stronger as he pulls me in, lifting me at the waist and setting my ass on the table in front of him.

"I told you," he says with a wink. "I'm a growing boy." This time, instead of patting his stomach, he grabs ahold of his dick, which I notice is already getting hard under his shorts. "Now, lay back and let me give you the orgasms I promised."

I give him a berating look. "I thought we established that I'd die if you made me come that many times. Plus, I got distracted and lost count, so I don't even know how man—"

"Twenty-three," he interrupts. "Funny that you think I've taken my eyes off those fuckable lips of yours since the day I met you. Now, you have two choices. Lay back on this table and I'll take it easy on you," he pauses for a moment, letting option one sink in, "or you can keep being a brat, I'll carry you to the bed, and rip orgasm after orgasm from your body until you cry. It's your choice, wife."

Well, damn.

As much fun as defying him sounds, I'm not prepared for the consequences right now. That doesn't mean that I won't be poking the bear at some point in the near future, but today is not that day. The corners of my mouth tip up as I slowly lower my back onto the cold wood of Dalton's kitchen table. He grabs around my calves and brings my feet up to rest on his thighs. He takes his time caressing the smooth skin of my legs, starting at my ankles and working his way up. I'm shaking with anticipation as he replaces his hands with his lips, kissing his way upward, slowly. When he darts his wet, hot tongue out and drags it from my knee to the junction of my thigh, I clench them together on instinct. Dalton chuckles as he wrenches my legs back apart, this time lifting my feet and resting them on the table. I'm spread wide in front of him and he's looking directly at my bare pussy like it's the only meal he'll ever need. I can't help myself as I lift to my elbows so I can see him.

I want to say something mouthy, to tell him to hurry up and eat me, but I don't. I just watch him as he leans in, taking a deep breath of me. The first time he did it in Vegas, I was a little confused. But now, I can't get enough of the look on his face as the scent of my arousal hits him. His wide shoulders move up and down rapidly with his deep breaths, and it makes me feel so powerful. His body shakes slightly as he reaches his hands up, and parts my lower lips with his thumbs.

Just when I think I can't take anymore, he shows mercy by leaning forward and dragging his tongue from the bottom of my slit all the way to the top. He groans like he's in pain before diving in fully, pushing inside me as far as he can. I reach down, fisting his hair tightly. I don't know if I'm holding him to me, or if I'm just trying to stop myself from floating right off this table and into outer space.

Dalton licks upward, wrapping his lips around my clit and sucking hard as he slowly enters me with one finger. The varying pressures of what he's doing make me go crazy as I writhe and beg for more.

"Oh God, please. Please. *Please*," I plead.

"Mmmm," he hums. "Not God, baby. Just your husband down here taking what's his."

His words push me to the precipice, and when he adds a second and third finger, I can't hold back anymore. My orgasm hits me as I cry out and shake against him. It seems to go on forever, but when I finally start to float back down to Earth, trying my best to back away from his tongue that is still firmly rubbing all over me, Dalton grabs my hips and pins them down to the table. "There's one," he says. "Only twenty-two more to go."

He can't be fucking serious.

I haven't had very many partners that have given me multiple orgasms. I know from experience that Dalton can, but I don't know how many I can handle. I'm thankful when he reduces the pressure and moves his tongue off of my clit, giving me a moment to recover. But just when I think I have my own body under control, he's back for more.

"Come on, baby," he coos. "I'm gonna need another one of those." This time, he solely uses his fingers, running his lips up and down the goosebumps that are raising along my thighs. He pumps into me, building me up to another orgasm. And because he knows exactly how to work my body, when I'm right there, he curls his fingers forward. The pressure on my G-spot sets me off again as I tense up and explode with my release.

He gives me absolutely no time to recover before going for number three. Dalton lowers his face back down to me and presses his lips to my very sensitive bundle of nerves, swirling his tongue around it in circles. I think I'm screaming, but I can't hear anything besides my heart beating rapidly between my ears. I don't think I can take much more of this. It's painful, but for some reason, I don't tell him to stop. I don't even consider using my safe word. I trust him to know what I can handle.

As I'm making my way back toward another summit, Dalton pulls his head back, looking straight into my eyes as he spits onto my pussy. At first, I think I'm seeing things. But when he does it again, my eyes go wide. Everything about this man is so filthy, but I can't seem to get enough of it.

"I'm going to eat this delicious cunt while I finger your tight asshole. If you don't want me to do that, tell me now," he says. When he licked me there in Vegas, that was different. It was still new to me and something I was unsure about, but I trusted him. But now, he's going to put his fingers inside me. This is something that's so intimate, I don't know if I can do it. But I know that if I want to try it at all, which I do, it has to be with Dalton. There's absolutely no one else in this world that I feel safer with than him. So, I nod my head and lower back down, lying flat on the table.

"You're being such a good girl for me right now," he praises as he gathers his spit and drags it down to my puckered hole. When he pushes against it, I tense up. "Relax for me, Dia," he says in a soothing voice. "You know I'd never hurt you. I only want to make you feel good." His words hit their mark, calming me enough that the tension in my body slowly releases. When he breeches my back entrance, I loosen even more because *fuck, that feels good.* And when he returns his lips back to my clit, sucking and licking gently as he moves his finger in and out, a coil of tightness like I've never felt before starts to twist inside me. The noises that are coming out of my mouth don't even sound human as he brings me toward what I know will be the most intense orgasm of my life. I feel saliva slipping from the corners of my mouth as my head thrashes back and forth. My eyes fill with tears at how overwhelmed with pleasure I am, but I never, ever want him to stop.

"What a fucking sight," he says, looking up from between my legs. "My perfect wife spread across the kitchen table, dripping from every hole while she lets me do whatever depraved things I can think of to her body. You're a fucking dream, Dia."

He's barely touched his tongue to my clit again as I go off, my pussy contracting tightly around nothing. I cry out, my entire body convulsing uncontrollably as I lay there, unable to get a handle on any part of myself. I'm just a passenger on this ride as Dalton makes sure every single ounce of pleasure is wrung from my exhausted body.

I'm completely sure I can't endure another climax. I am utterly spent, lying there nearly unconscious, as he lifts me from the table and holds me close, carrying me back to the bed. He presses a soft kiss to my lips, which I don't even have the energy to reciprocate, making him chuckle.

"Just so you know, I'm not done with you yet," he says. All I can manage is a weak whine at the thought of him putting me through that all over again. Dalton lowers me to the mattress and my limp body sinks into its softness immediately. I snuggle up under the blankets as he pulls them to my chin just the way I like before dropping another sweet kiss to my forehead. "Rest, baby. You're safe here," he whispers as he slides in beside me and wraps me into his warm embrace. I'm asleep instantly, dreaming of a life where I allow myself to be happy and every night is just like this one.

TWENTY-FIVE
DALTON

"I'M DOWN!" I yell into my headset. "Mav, I'm hit behind the wall at the middle of the map. Come revive me!"

"Calm the fuck down, bro. I'm coming," he replies.

Now that it's the offseason, the guys and I get pretty creative with our hangouts. When we get closer to training camp, the team sets up organized team activities, or *OTAs*, for us to build on our relationships before the real work starts. But this early, we make up our own ways to chill. Maverick and I spend a few hours a week playing video games. Blaze joins us when he's not with Mads, but if I'm honest, he's trash at this particular game, so I may have forgotten to mention that we were going to be on this morning. He'll figure it out eventually, yell at us for not telling him, then proceed to punt our chances at a Victory Royale into outer fucking space.

Mav's avatar rounds the wall I'm hiding behind and I wait as he revives me. Once I'm up, I use a med kit to get my health all the way back up to a hundred percent.

"Here," he says into his mic as his character drops

something on the ground in front of mine. "Take this shield potion. You fucking suck today and I don't feel like coming back over to save your ass again. *Might as well be playing with Becks.*" He mumbles the last part like a dick.

My avatar chugs the bottle of potion just as a very sleepy Dia enters the living room. She clearly just woke up. Her eyes are still half-closed, and her hair is wild as she pads over to me wrapped in the king-sized comforter from my bed. She looks at me with a tired smile and I point to my headset, mouthing *'Maverick'* so she knows to stay quiet. I've said it a million times…I'd tell the world about us right now. But I'm respecting the fact that she doesn't want anyone aside from Blaze and Mads knowing.

She keeps moving in my direction, plopping down next to me on the couch and resting her head in my lap. I reach down with one hand and smooth it over her hair as she lets out a contented sigh. This is exactly what I envisioned when I wanted to have her here. Sure, I enjoy the sex-filled nights that we get to have whenever we want now that we're easily accessible to one another, but these are the moments that I was most excited for. Her walking out of the bedroom, still warm and sleepy, as she comes to find me for comfort.

"Dude, what the *fuck?*" Mav's voice blows my eardrum out as I look up and see him getting shot over and over. His avatar drops, crawling on the ground right next to where mine is standing. *Oops.*

I return both hands to my controller and start shooting at the opponent just as Mav dies at my feet. All the items his character was holding surround him as his murderer picks them up then turns his weapon on me. Before I even hit him once, I'm dead.

"You fucking suck!" I yell at the random stranger in my headset.

"I'm fucking twelve!" a high-pitched voice replies, "And a *girl*. You suck!"

I'm stunned silent with my jaw on the floor as Maverick's voice comes back. "That backfired."

"Did you hear the *mouth* on that kid?" I ask.

He laughs. "Yeah, right after she smoked us both. What's with you today? If we lose one more, I'm out."

The next game starts and I'm already sucking as Dia sits up and grabs the controller from my hand. She shrugs the blanket off her shoulders and sits forward, her full focus on the television screen in front of us. I flip the microphone on my headset up so I'm muted. "Babe, what are you doing?" I ask. "Mav will be pissed if we lose again." I go to take the controller back, but she twists her body so I can't reach it. I look to the screen just in time to see her land a perfect headshot to someone, killing them immediately. My eyebrows shoot up to my hairline as I take the headset and put it over her ears so she can hear what's around her in the game. She's doing better than I was, so fuck it.

Dia is stone silent as she moves around the map, building walls to block the bullets when people start shooting in her direction. She picks them off one by one, only stopping when she needs to reload her weapons. She giggles when I hear Mav's muffled voice coming from the headset, no doubt talking about my sudden improvement. I watch the number of kills go up on the screen as she continues owning every single opponent in sight. And when she shoots the last one and the victory message pops up, she turns to me with a smug look, pulling the headset off and putting it back over my ears. I'm still in a state of shock as she kisses my cheek and wraps herself back up like a little burrito, laying her head back in my lap.

"Wow," Maverick says into his microphone. "That was your best game ever. By *a lot*."

I unmute myself, clearing the lump in my throat that I always get before I lie through my teeth. "Uhh, yeah. Thanks," I reply. "I have to go. I…have to wash my hair."

He pauses. "Okayyyy," he says, drawing out the word in confusion. But I'm already gone as I remove my headset and look down at my wife.

"What exactly happened just now?" I ask.

She yawns, closing her eyes. "I just came from a situation where I was always alone, broke enough not to be able to go out, and had a second-hand video game console at my disposal. I got good. You should try it." A small smile tips the corner of her lips up, because she knows she's a fucking brat.

I blow out a breath, leaning back and returning my hand to her head. I massage her scalp with enough pressure to make her sigh with satisfaction. "We have plans tonight, so I want you to take my card and go get something to wear." She looks at me out of the corner of her eye. "And before you argue with me, remember our deal. I get to treat you as my wife and buy you whatever I want while you're here. I don't care what you spend, I just want you to feel as beautiful as I already know you are when I take you out."

She gives me a skeptical look. "I don't want anybody seeing us together in public and going into a frenzy about the new woman on your arm."

"I know," I tell her. "I promise you that no one will see us."

She smiles up at me. She's so fucking gorgeous, I still

can't believe she's mine. "Okay," she relents. "Where are we going?"

I look to the TV, where the stats from her win still fill the screen. "Not to an arcade. I'll tell you that much."

DIA

I look out the car window, getting increasingly nervous as we get closer to the heart of Boston. It's a busy night and there are people everywhere. Dalton promised me that nobody would see us together, so I'm trying to figure out where he's taking me. I can't imagine there's anywhere in this part of the city where fans wouldn't notice one of the Blizzard's most popular players.

My black bodycon dress rides up my thighs as I turn toward him. I spent the afternoon shopping by myself with his credit card. It was weird not buying off the clearance rack, but I made a promise to Dalton and I want to keep it. He's been so amazing, patiently supporting me as I work through a lifetime of baggage. He deserves this experience.

"This doesn't look private," I say. "Looks like you're about to throw me out in front of every Bostonian in existence."

He grins. "I would if you'd let me, Wifey. I'm not breaking any of your rules. We'll be in public, but nobody will recognize me. I'll be incognito."

I already don't like where this is headed. When Dalton uses words like *incognito*, you know he's got something completely fucking weird up his sleeve. I huff an annoyed breath, looking back out the window as he makes a right turn down an alley between two buildings. I've never been to this part of Boston, plus it's way too dark to see where we are.

He pulls into a parking spot, turning off the car. He leans over, and instead of kissing me like I anticipate, he reaches to open the glove compartment. I can feel his warm breath ghosting along my neck right before he moves back just a few inches with something in his hand.

"Put this on," he says, handing me a beautiful black lace masquerade mask. It's not one of the cheap ones you get from a costume shop. It's soft and thick, and when I slide it over my eyes, it fits like it was made for me. "Even with half of your face covered, you're still the most beautiful woman I've ever seen," he says, shaking his head as if he's in disbelief. "How do you do it, baby?" The words are barely a whisper, but he may as well be screaming them from the top of the highest building in the city, because that's how they make me feel.

Even though I'm forcing him to keep this thing private, Dalton finds ways to care for me so loudly. Whether it's holding me in silence when I'm processing things, or the way he always knows how to break me away from my intrusive thoughts and memories, I never have to question that he's here for me. It's getting harder by the day not to just take the leap and see if we can make this marriage work for real. But unlike any of the other relationships that have been broken in my past, I don't know if I'm strong enough to pick myself back up from this one if it ends. And I don't want Mads to have to be put in the middle when she's planning events and has to choose which best friend to invite because it'll be too painful for me to see Dalton with anyone else.

All of this is why I'm going to enjoy this time we have left together. I'll never get to experience this kind of connection again. And as surprised as I am about it, I'm glad he kept pushing until I agreed with what he was asking for. Because even though it's temporary, it feels good to be treated like I'm the most important person in someone's life.

Dalton ties his plain black mask over his eyes. It matches perfectly with his white button up shirt and black dress pants that are snug in all the right places. He steps out of the car and I wait as he rounds the back, coming up to open my door. I take his offered hand and he steals a quick kiss before intertwining our fingers and leading me to the back door of the building. The wind picks up, carrying the scent of his cologne, and my mouth waters in response. Everything about this man turns me on.

He pulls open the door, putting a hand on my lower back as he ushers me inside the dimly lit lobby. A bright blue neon sign with *Liquid* in bold letters stretches across the wall behind a reception desk. We step up as a petite blonde woman wearing a black dress similar to mine greets us. "Welcome to Club Liquid. How can I help you this evening?"

"I'm Dalton Davis. I've arranged for a private booth tonight."

She taps on her keyboard for a few seconds before looking back up at us. "Yes, everything is ready for you. We've given you a corner booth at the very end of the VIP section. You're right above the dance floor. The lights come from fixtures under the mezzanine, so as requested, you'll be able to see everyone below, but they won't be able to see you unless you lean over the railing. It's Masquerade Night, which you already know," she waves a hand between us, gesturing to our masks, "so everyone upstairs will be wearing them, too. We'll send a server for your drink orders shortly."

"Thank you," Dalton says, holding my hand tightly as we walk past her desk, heading straight for a spiral staircase and making our way up to the second floor of the luxury night club. We walk past several booths, all full with groups of people dancing and laughing as they drink. Each one has a blue velvet wrap-around couch and its own private dance floor, illuminated by LED lights.

When we reach the very end of the long walkway, Dalton leads me into our private booth. Unlike the others, ours is separated from the neighbors with a floor-to-ceiling velvet curtain. We're secluded, but as I peer over the railing that overlooks the main part of the club, I see people everywhere. There are hundreds of them on the dance floor, their bodies pressed together as they move to the beat of the music. The layout of the place makes me feel so close to everyone, but we're also safe from being noticed by anyone that may recognize Dalton.

I'm hit with a wave of emotion as I realize what he did for me here tonight. He wanted to take me somewhere where we could enjoy each other outside of his apartment, but he still managed to respect my wishes that we stay out of the public eye. He's always going above and beyond to make me feel special. And bringing me to a club where I get my very own dance floor? *Major* brownie points for that.

He's definitely getting his dick sucked tonight.

As I overlook the club below, a strong set of hands grabs onto my waist from behind. I feel Dalton's body press against mine as he dances, following the rhythm he's moving to. He uses his fingers to gently push my long hair to one side, exposing my neck. He presses his open lips to my already heated flesh, and when his tongue darts out for a taste, I let out an audible moan. But the music is so loud, it may as well be a secret between us.

"You are so fucking sexy," he says into my ear, making goosebumps rise along my skin. "And this tight little body of yours makes my dick so hard." He grinds his erection into my ass, showing me that he's not lying. I bring my hands up, reaching behind me and wrapping them around the back of his neck, desperately trying to keep him pressed against me. His fingertips dig into my hips as I grind right back into him, loving the way his length feels through our clothes. It all feels so forbidden, but from the outside, we're just another couple dancing to the electronic music beating through the speakers.

Out of the corner of my eye, I see our server approaching. I turn, trying to move away from Dalton, but he snakes his arms around me, pulling me back in front of him. I assume he's using me as a shield, considering the hard cock and tight pants, but it's fine because the last thing I want to do is punch this poor girl in the throat for looking at his dick.

"Can I get you some drinks to start off with?" she asks, smiling brightly.

Dalton speaks before I get the chance. "I'll take a whiskey, neat. And my wife will have a vodka cranberry. Right, baby?" he says, looking down at me from above my shoulder.

"Y-yeah," I stutter.

She tells us she'll be back with our drinks before taking off toward the bar. I turn to Dalton. "How did you know what I like?" Other than the night at Blaze and Mads' house with the wine, I haven't really drunk much here. And I only had a chance to drink one glass of champagne and Dalton's beer that I took from him in Vegas. But when I'm out, I strictly go with vodka cranberries.

The corners of his mouth tip up. "I already told you. I know everything about you. Some I've learned from listening and watching. Everything else was dragged out of Mads, mostly against her will. You had me so intrigued right from the second I laid eyes on you. Even if I never saw you again, I still needed to know every detail."

I try to stop my eyes from welling up. I've been so hardened by life that I can usually will myself not to cry in front of anyone. I don't like to look weak or vulnerable, but I know he doesn't see me that way. He sees me as someone who is strong and determined. Someone who feels emotions and deserves to be cared for. And if I didn't know it before, at least somewhere in the corner of my brain, I do now. I'm in love with Dalton Davis. As hard as I've tried not to let myself fall, it was always going to happen.

"I have something for you," he whispers into my ear as he reaches into his pocket. I look down to see what he's holding, but it's too dark up here. So, when he takes my left hand and slides a thin platinum band onto my ring finger, I'm caught off guard. As I look closer, I realize it's the same one he gave me in Vegas after we said our vows. My stomach does somersaults as I stare at it, glad to have it back, but then I'm hit with a pang of sadness when I remember that my beautiful engagement ring is long gone. It's probably on the finger of some random woman who will never love it the way I did. I hope whoever gave it to her treats her the way Dalton treats me.

I look up, my eyes still brimming with unshed tears. When I blink and one escapes, stopping when it hits the lace of my mask, he pulls me into a tight hug before leaning back to look at me.

"Hey," he says softly. "Don't cry. I just," he pauses, furrowing his brows, "couldn't let it go."

I smile, cupping his cheeks before stretching up onto my toes to kiss him. "Thank you," I say. "Did you keep yours, too?"

He grins, holding up his left hand to show me the thick band sitting on his finger. We look like a real-life married couple. I mean, technically we are.

"Let's go down there," I say, nodding my head toward the first floor.

His eyes go wide. "Dia, I'm built like a professional football player. And this mask only covers half of my face. There's a good chance people could recognize me and we're both wearing our rings." As much as I appreciate him for respecting my wishes, I kind of don't really care right now.

I shrug my shoulders, knowing exactly how to get him to go downstairs with me. "Okay. Well, you can stay here. I'll go find someone else to dance with." I turn to walk away, but I don't get far before he brings a heavy arm around my waist, stopping me. I can feel the heat of his breath against the shell of my ear. "You even think about doing that and I'll bend you over that railing and show this whole club how wet your cunt gets when I spank you," he growls. I keep a straight face, smiling on the inside because that worked like a charm. "Let's go," he says, his voice shrouded in jealousy and irritation. Just his tone makes my blood run hot with arousal. He takes my hand, leading me back down the walkway to the stairs. We've all but forgotten about our drinks, although I'm sure the server will leave them at our table.

When we hit the bottom floor, Dalton drops my hand, only to wrap a protective arm around me from behind as we weave through the throng of people until we reach the edge of the dance floor. The music vibrates through my body, starting at my feet and making its way to the tips of my fingers as we move to the beat. He spins me to face him, his hands ghosting down my sides before he reaches around and grips my ass. We're pressed together so tightly, that I can't tell where I end and he begins.

Normally, that feeling alone would make me want to back away. Move on and go find another faceless body to grind against until I start to feel anything other than the meaningless urge to scratch an itch. But with Dalton, I'm starting to feel exhilarated when I think of how things are between us. While I still can't bring myself to completely surrender to this marriage forever, I'm more than willing to embrace it until our time together is up. He's shown me what it's like to be wanted, cherished, and adored. All things I never thought I'd feel, yet he's given them so openly. He deserves all of that, and up until now, I've been scared to give it.

I look up at him, a grateful smile tugging at the corners of my mouth. "Take me home."

TWENTY-SIX
DALTON

WE BARELY MAKE it through the door of my apartment before Dia is clawing at my clothes. Her kisses are desperate and wild as she starts undoing the buttons of my shirt. She's fumbling, blinded by her own arousal as she struggles. I should help her, but I'm having way too much fun watching my wife as she finally fucking snaps in front of me.

"Fuck it," she says against my lips. "You're rich anyway."

Before I can even ask what she means, she curls her fingers around the edges of the placket, yanking as hard as she can. Buttons go flying in every direction as she exposes my muscled torso. She sighs in relief as she shoves my shirt over my shoulders, making it drop to the floor behind me. I walk backwards, further into the living room, while she follows. I only stop when I feel the back of the couch hit my ass.

I stand there as she stares at me for a moment, growing cockier by the second at how needy she is right now. I'm tempted to ask her what changed tonight, but I don't want her to stop. So, I put that on the back burner while she tears wildly at my dress pants. My dick is rock hard, threatening to bust through the zipper, and she hasn't even touched it yet.

"It helps if you undo the belt *before* you try to unbutton the pants," I tease. It's like her brain has stopped working completely. I've never seen Dia like this. Not even on our wedding night when we thought we only had a handful of hours together. She looks up at me, narrowing her eyes as she regroups, taking a shaky breath before reaching for the buckle of my belt. She manages to tamp down her desperation long enough to undo it, along with my pants.

Grabbing under her chin with one hand, I lean down, kissing her passionately as I reach behind her body and lower the zipper of her form-fitting, strapless dress. I feel her shiver, but I don't think it's from the temperature in the room. I pull back, watching the material as it falls to the floor, pooling around her ankles. She's braless, standing in front of me in just a piece of black lace that could barely pass as a pair of panties.

Fuuuuuck. I'm the luckiest son of a bitch in the world.

"Look at you," I say. "You can barely even control yourself right now with how badly you want this cock." I reach into my pants, pulling myself out and giving a few tentative strokes before I take them off completely, along with my boxer briefs. "Get on your knees."

I wonder if she'll push back. If I'll have to resort to using force to get her where I want her, but I'm only half surprised when she wordlessly sinks down in front of me. I can tell by the look in her eyes that this is as submissive as Dia gets, and it makes my dick even harder thinking of what I'm about to get away with right now. She stares at it like a good girl, waiting for direction, but I can tell she's getting antsier by the second.

"Spit on it," I order. "Get it nice and wet before I shove it down that tight little throat."

She never breaks eye contact as she gathers saliva in her mouth before doing exactly as she's told. I've never seen anything hotter in my life as she leans forward, smearing the spit around my shaft with her tongue. And when she pulls back, opening her mouth in invitation, I snap.

"Dirty fucking girl," I grit out, grabbing a fistful of her hair and shoving her down as far as she'll go. Her hands fly up to my thighs, pushing against me as she struggles to breathe. I pull back just enough for her to inhale deeply before surging forward again, cutting off her air. "Look at me." Her eyes, that are filled with tears already, meet mine as I watch her face begin to turn bright red. "You can stop this any time. Just tap my thigh twice. Or you can use your safe word," I say with a smug smile. "If I ever let you breathe long enough to speak." She nods her head rapidly just before I pull out for a moment. She gasps for air as strings of spit hang between my cock and her plump lips.

"You're a fucking goddess, Dia," I praise. "Don't ever let anyone treat you like anything less." The look of trust that she gives me back obliterates the last of my restraint as I take her mouth again, still gripping tightly onto her hair as I thrust wildly, hitting the back of her throat over and over. I watch as tears stream down her cheeks while she gags, but she doesn't back away. She just kneels in submission, letting me use her for my own pleasure. I've never felt this out of control before.

Sex has always been fun for me. A way to blow off steam and get off until I needed it again. But, this? This is different. Right now, I'm claiming my wife in every sense of the word. And we both know it.

"You're fucking *mine*," I growl as I feel my balls start to tighten with my impending orgasm. I can tell that I'm nowhere near finished for the night, but the need to fill her mouth is overwhelming.

"I'm going to come," I tell her as I continue pumping my hips. "And when I do, you'd better not swallow. You're going to hold it in your mouth while I wreck your tiny little cunt. Then I can watch as my cum leaks out of you from both ends. Do you understand?"

She nods her head, struggling to stay upright as I finally unload into her with a loud groan. When I'm finished, I pull out and she closes her lips, but I can tell she's having a hard time not swallowing it down. I grip her cheeks roughly with one hand. "Don't you fucking dare," I grit through my teeth. She calms herself, taking a few breaths through her nose. When I'm sure she's good, I pull her up, spinning her so her elbows can rest against the back of the couch as she leans forward.

I grab the sides of her panties, pulling them down her legs to find that her pussy is already swollen and dripping for me. "Wow," I chide. "Who knew being face fucked like a dirty little whore got you so turned on?" She moans, but keeps her full mouth closed as I drag a finger from her clit to her opening, pushing it inside to the hilt. I can already feel my cock hardening again as I listen to her needy whines paired with the sound of her wetness as I finger her at a slow and agonizing pace.

I'm ready for round two in record time, which comes as

no surprise because nobody has ever made me feel the way Dia does. I stand, pushing her forward so she's leaning over the couch. "Remember, keep that pretty little mouth full for me while I fuck you," I say, slapping the head of my cock onto her wet slit a couple times, making her jump. "Aww," I coo. "Are you needy for your husband, sweetheart? You poor, poor thing."

I don't waste another second before I push inside. I see stars as she tightens around me, a deep moan rumbling through her body as she adjusts. I have to take a second to gather my wits, because I already feel like I could blow again. She's crazy if she thinks this shit is normal...that we weren't made for each other. Because I already know this feeling could never even begin to exist with anyone else.

I start to thrust my hips, running my hands up and down her back, over and over. I don't want to leave a single part of her untouched. The light from the window catches on my wedding ring and I stare at it as it rests against her flawless skin. Drops of sweat run down her spine as I fuck her roughly, and I feel her walls start to flutter around me. She's close.

"You're doing such a good job," I praise. "Come with your mouth full for me." It only takes a few more pumps of my hips until she detonates, screaming in her throat as her legs shake. I pin her to the couch with my body, barely able to hold off until she's done spasming around me. The second I'm sure she's spent, I let go, filling her for the second time tonight.

I pull out slowly, watching as my load drips out of her, falling to the floor between her feet. "That's fucking beautiful," I whisper before reaching up, grabbing her cheeks with one hand and squeezing. "Drool for me, baby. Let me see it," I say as she lets her mouth fall open. A mixture of my cum and her saliva pools into my palm that's resting under her chin. Before I can stop myself, I lower it between her legs, gently pushing as much as I can into her sensitive pussy. As filthy as it is, I can't stop myself from thinking about how much I love this woman. How we've gone from her being scared of me doing something as simple as making her food, to this moment where she's given me complete trust and submission. I was scared that she'd never let me in, and now that I'm here, I'm hers forever. No matter what happens in the future.

I scoop up her exhausted body, kissing her forehead as I head straight for the primary bathroom. She hums contentedly, snuggling into my chest like there's nowhere else in the world she'd rather be. I drop down, setting her on the edge of the bathtub, doing my best to support her while I lean to turn on the tap. When the water is scalding hot, because she's a little demon when it comes to her showers and baths, I help her inside, holding her hand for support as she lowers down.

"Relax while I clean up, then I'll wash your body," I tell her. She nods with a dick drunk smile on her face as she lays back against the spa pillow and closes her eyes. I hurry into the standing shower and rush through washing up so I can get back to her, but by the time I'm dried off and turn to look, she's out like a light. Tiny snores come from her body as she sleeps like an angel, enveloped in the hot water.

I realize then that there's no way I can imagine my life without Diamond Davis. She's mine and I'm hers. I don't know exactly where her head is at, but I'm not dumb enough to think that I've undone a lifetime of trauma in the weeks that we've been married. I don't expect her to just say *'fuck it'* and give up on everything she's ever stood for. But there's *something* here. All I can do is continue to show her how I feel and hope it's enough to make her realize that her heart is safe with me.

Because it is, without a doubt, the most precious thing I've ever held in my hands.

TWENTY-SEVEN
DIA

I PUT my back against the side of the armchair, digging my feet into the floor as I push. It takes a few seconds because Dalton has the heaviest furniture that's ever been built, but it eventually starts sliding over the wall-to-wall textured carpet. I keep my momentum until I've reached the opposite side of the room, where I reposition the chair to face the television that hangs on the wall. I turn up the volume on my headphones as I grab the vacuum, flicking it on before cleaning the blank space where I plan to move the couch.

Bella's debut album plays in my ears, and I move my body to the beat as I vacuum. When I'm done, I turn it off and push it out of the way. I take a moment to stare at the couch, wondering how in the fuck I'm going to get it where I want it. I almost popped a blood vessel in my eye just moving the chair, and it's less than half the size.

But I am a strong, independent woman who has had *three* cups of coffee this morning. I can do this.

I randomly decided an hour ago that I wanted to

rearrange the living room. Dalton is at the Blizzard practice facility, no doubt to grill Tanner for information on
where he's been lately, but I don't think he'll mind me
giving the space a fresh look.

I walk over to the couch, shaking out my arms in
preparation. *Like that'll make a difference.* At first, I try the
same tactic that worked on the chair. I bend at my knees,
bracing my back against the arm before I push with all my
might. It doesn't budge an inch. Changing my plan, I try a
shoulder, but my feet just slide back on the carpet as I
surge forward.

It's fine. No biggie. Let's move on to Plan C.

I walk to the other end, gripping the arm with both
hands and yanking backward. The couch moves just a few
inches, but that spurs me on as a throw my weight back,
over and over, shuffling my feet with each movement of
the heavy piece of furniture.

I'm lost in my determination as I feel a hand touch my
shoulder, making me jump. I yank off my headphones,
smiling sweetly at Dalton, who's looking at me like I'm
crazy.

"What are you doing?" he says. He sounds angry, and I
think maybe I've overstepped. This is his apartment, after
all. I'm just a guest. Josh would always get so mad at me
when I would move things in his apartment, even if I was
only trying to help by tidying up. It's like he was hiding
something. Maybe he was.

I cower slightly. "I'm sorry," I say. "I just had a lot of
energy and thought you might like a change of scenery. I
can put it ba—"

"Dia," he says. "We can put the couch in the bathroom
if that's where you want it. I don't give a fuck about that.

But that thing weighs like, three-hundred pounds. Let me help you. I don't want you getting hurt."

"Oh," I say, quickly remembering how different he is than my ex. "Okay."

"Come here," he says, pulling me into his arms and kissing the top of my head. "You have the zoomies, baby?"

"Mhmm," I mumble into his warm chest. The sound of his heartbeat against my ear calms me a little. "How can you tell?"

He huffs a laugh. "Well, you're rearranging the living room by yourself, and you smell like a coffee factory. That kinda tipped me off."

I giggle as he lifts me from the floor, tossing me onto the soft cushions. I land with a bounce as he leans down, pressing a chaste kiss to my lips. "Where do you want it?"

"On that wall," I say, pointing across the room. I lay back as he picks up one end like it weighs nothing, dragging the couch along the carpet with me on it until it's in the perfect spot. He reaches down, picking out one of the cashmere throw blankets from the basket behind him and covering me up.

"Stay right here, baby. I'll go grab you a yogurt and some water." I look at him adoringly as he leaves the room, heading to the kitchen. I'm pretty sure if he looked at me, I'd strongly resemble the heart-eyes emoji, but I don't care. I'm growing pretty fond of the way he cares for me.

It wasn't long ago that I was completely unable to accept anything from him. But he kept trying; giving me space when I needed it, but never backing away completely. I'm sure there were times when his frustration almost won, and I wouldn't have blamed him. But he never showed it. I'll never be able to fully express to Dalton the way that he's changed my life. Even though I do still fear abandonment, I also have a better idea of what I'm worth. I will no longer fall at my parents' feet every time they show me an ounce of attention. I'll try harder to put myself out there and make more friends. And, most importantly, I'll try to stop blaming myself for the way people have treated me in the past. Because that's what I deserve most of all.

He comes back into the room with a cup of yogurt and a bottle of water. He hands them both to me before lifting my legs and sitting down, placing my feet in his lap. I eat and drink while he mindlessly massages my calves, making my toes curl when he hits all the right spots.

"You were training all morning. Shouldn't I be rubbing your muscles?" I joke.

He wiggles his eyebrows. "Oh, I have a muscle you can rub." He winks like an asshole, and I roll my eyes.

"You really are a douchebag."

He continues rubbing my legs and feet as I finish my yogurt, telling me how Tanner was acting broodier than usual today. They all want to ask him what's going on, but they already know he won't answer. The Blizzard quarter-back is charming, but definitely the quietest of the bunch. He's so private with his personal life, there isn't a single photo of him out with a woman since he was drafted five years ago. I did some sleuthing because I'm a nosey bitch, but I couldn't find anything from before then, either. The only girl I've ever seen him in a photo with was a candid from his last year in college, but the caption said that she was his best friend's sister. Other than that, he's done a phenomenal job hiding his relationships from the public, if he's even had any.

I put my empty cup and bottle on the coffee table as Dalton lays behind me, wrapping a heavy arm around my waist. We put on an old John Hughes movie, but it doesn't last long before we both doze off, wasting the rest of the day away, cuddled up next to each other.

TWENTY-EIGHT
DIA

"I FEEL like I haven't seen you in forever," Mads says, sitting back on the theater room couch. We're both in lounge clothes, just finished our *BFF Makeover Movie Night* skincare routine, and are settling in with our snacks. Bella is in New York because her brother, who's making quite a splash on an Italian soap opera, is back in the states to shoot a movie, so the guys decided to go out for a couple of drinks while Mav was being forced to come up for air. And since it's been a minute since we've done this, here we are. "How's life?"

I think for a moment, because it's been a whirlwind lately and I honestly haven't had a moment to step back and process it all. Mads and I usually tell each other every detail about our days, and it's not that I'm purposely keeping anything from her. I've just been so wrapped up in Dalton that I haven't done much of anything else. We just went through this when she moved in with Blaze, but it's a little weird that the shoe is now on *my foot*.

"Crazy. Confusing. *Amazing*," I say. Desperation melts over my features and she gives a sympathetic smile because she knows how hard this has become for me. She's known me since we were kids and she's seen me go through giving my heart away, only to have it broken over and over. She knows how I feel about relationships and marriage. That I'm absolutely closed off to promising forever to anyone. I'm too scared of failing as a wife. Scared of not being enough.

"You're falling for him, aren't you?" she asks.

"Yes." I cringe. "Fuck him so hard for being perfect. This is all his fault." I lay back, throwing an arm over my eyes in exasperation. "What the hell am I going to do?" I cry.

She laughs because she's an evil shrew who clearly isn't concerned about my current situation. "Oh, I don't know. Maybe don't be such a dumb bitch and realize that Dalton Davis is head-over-heels in love with you. The last thing he wants to do is hurt you."

"First of all, he doesn't *love me*. He cares about me. Just like everyone else that has come and gone from my life did at first." She gives me a look, and I already know what she's going to say, so I respond before she does. "I'm not saying his feelings and intentions aren't sincere. But what happens when I've given him my heart, and five years down the road, he decides that I'm not what he wants? Where would that leave me?" I ask. "It's taken me so long to be okay with being on my own. I can't do it again."

She reaches over, grabbing my hand and squeezing. "I'll support whatever you choose. You know that. But please allow yourself to have some happiness, Dia. If anyone deserves it, it's you."

I squeeze back. "I am. I have you. I've been dancing with Bella. And I've been letting Dalton show me what I'm worth. Even though we won't be married, I know he'll always be in my life." Tears fill my eyes at the thought of how much I've changed in the short time that I've been in Boston. Even though the way I ended up here wasn't exactly ideal, it was the best decision I've ever made. Chicago was holding me back from growing as a person. It was filled with ill-willed people and memories of my past. Everything good is here in Boston and I really feel like I'm finally home.

"How has the job search been going?" Mads asks.

Ugh. The job search. Now that I'm broke, I've been sending out applications and resumes left and right. I wanted to try to get away from serving in gentleman's clubs, so I've been trying for positions at restaurants in the city. Even with all the *'Help Wanted'* signs I've seen, I've gotten zero calls.

"I don't know," I shake my head. "I've put in at least thirty applications. I'm starting to think my old boss is bad-mouthing me when they call to confirm my previous employment. Nobody wants to hire someone who was fired for not showing up," I say with a shrug.

She furrows her brows in confusion. "They *fired you*? Why?"

Oh, fuck. I forgot that I had kept that from her.

I look into my lap, knowing that I can't lie. But she's definitely going to blame herself. "I requested Super Bowl weekend off, but they told me at the last minute that I needed to be there. That if I didn't show up, I'd be fired. I chose what was most important to me." I chance a look at her and, yep, there's the guilt.

"You chose me," she whispers. "And you lost your job and apartment for it."

"Hey," I say firmly. "It's not your fault. I made the decision on my own. And if I hadn't, I'd still be stuck there all alone." I smile, trying my best to reassure her. I really do mean everything I said.

"I'm glad you're here," she says. "And you know that if you can't find anything right away, you can always stay here. Blaze won't mind."

I nod, appreciating her offer, but I really hope it doesn't come to that. Even though I know I'm welcome, I felt like an interloper while I was here before. And there's no doubt there will be a period after the divorce that I'll be missing Dalton. The last thing I'll want is to watch Blaze and Mads living their life, loving each other so openly. Or worse, making them feel like they have to hide their affection from me so my feelings don't get hurt. They deserve their own space where they can show their love as loudly as they want and tie each other to whichever household items will hold their weight. I don't want to stop them from that.

I've always figured it out on my own. I know I'll do it here in my new home.

"We'll cross that bridge when we get there," I say, mainly just to stop this conversation from going any further.

"Okay," she shrugs, grabbing the remote. "We have two choices. There's the new Hemsworth rom-com that came out last week, or we can go old school with Little Giants."

We both look at each other and smile. "Little Giants," we say in unison.

As she flips through the streaming app, finding our favorite childhood movie, the door inches open and Blaze pops his head in. "Can we crash your movie night? Or is it a 'no boys allowed' thing?"

"Come on in," she says, giddy all of a sudden. I love

how happy she is. And I also kind of love the butterflies in my stomach when I realize that he isn't alone.

Dalton shoves Blaze out of the way, making a beeline straight for me. "I missed you," he says, laying down on the massive couch and pulling me with him. "Next time those assholes ask me to go out, I'm telling them my wife said no."

"I'm right here," Blaze says, picking Mads up and setting her on his lap. "And we all know Dia pushed you out the door because it's the only way she can get some peace and quiet."

Dalton scoffs. "Yeah, right. She loves when I'm home. I am *very* useful. And she's gotten pretty good at shutting me up, huh baby?" He kisses my cheek.

"Mhmm," I hum in agreement, snuggling into him.

"Little Giants?" Blaze groans, looking at the movie that's queued up in front of us. "*Again?* Didn't you guys get your fill of Junior Floyd when you were kids? Do you still have to watch this every weekend?"

"Please," I say, fake disgust evident in my tone. "Mads was all googly-eyed over the golden-boy quarterback. But I knew what was up. Spike might've been an asshole, but he could lift a refrigerator."

Dalton gasps. "That what you're into, Wifey? Big muscles? Because guess what?" he says, rolling me on top of him and lifting me up and down like he's bench-pressing. "I can do this all day."

"Put me down, you meathead!" I laugh, trying to slap at his chest. He lowers me, kissing my lips before settling me back on his side with his arm wrapped around me.

We watch the movie, the four of us lounging next to one another. Dalton makes it a point to scoff loudly every time my childhood crush makes an appearance, mumbling about how he's way stronger than the twelve-year-old actor on the screen. I know I've said I'm sticking to the original plan when our time is up; that I'm going to do everything I can to protect my heart...but I can't say that nights like this don't make me a little curious about how it could be if I didn't.

TWENTY-NINE
DALTON

"BACK *UP!*" Dia says, attempting to swat at me with the spatula while I lean over her shoulder. We decided to take turns cooking breakfast, so today, she's making pancakes. And not those shitty Power Cakes the guys love so much. I'm talking, not-from-a-box, homemade flapjacks. She swears it's a secret recipe she got off the internet when she was a kid, but they smell amazing and I'm doing my best to commit the ingredients to memory so I can make them myself in the future.

"Fine," I say, holding my hands up in surrender. I move back, just barely, and take her in. She looks freshly fucked, thanks to me and my very insistent morning wood, wearing a pair of panties under one of my old college football t-shirts. She almost looks as good in scarlet and gray as she does in Blizzard colors. *Almost.* Her hair is up in a messy bun that leans slightly to one side, and she has a pair of my athletic socks pulled up her calves for extra warmth. I know I say it all the time, but she's more beautiful than ever right now.

She turns off the stove, plating the pancakes and

setting them on the island in the middle of the kitchen. I've already set out the maple syrup, butter, and my personal favorite pancake topping, whipped cream. I'll have to bump up the intensity of this afternoon's workout to burn off all this sugar, but it'll be worth it. I reach over, grabbing Dia by the waist and plopping her down on the counter. She swings her feet against the cupboards below as she adds her toppings. When she's finished, I add my butter and syrup. She's too busy cutting her food on the plate that sits beside her to notice the shady look on my face as I spray a mountain of whipped cream onto my stack, *accidentally* angling it just right so that a small amount sputters onto her exposed thigh. She slowly meets my eyes, giving me a suspicious look, but I do my best to look innocent.

"Oops," I say. "Sorry, babe. Let me get that." I give her a guilty smirk as she shakes her head. The corners of her lips are tipped up, and I can tell she's equal parts annoyed and amused. I lean forward, pressing my tongue to her smooth skin, slowly licking at the drops of whipped cream, which have now started melting against her warmth. She tries to hold in her ragged breathing but fails miserably as I move upward. And when she tightens her fingers in my hair, I know I've won the battle.

Before I can fully ascend to the heaven between her legs, the doorbell rings, making us both jump. My building is pretty secure and there are only a handful of people on the list to get up here, none of which I'm expecting, so I assume maybe it's maintenance or the concierge.

"Don't fucking move. I'll be right back," I say, more to her pussy than to her, before hurrying out of the kitchen and to the door. As I look out the peephole, my blood runs cold.

Fuck. She's going to be so pissed.

I swing the door open. "Mom! Dad!" I say, fake excitement masking the underlying fear of how my wife is going to react to this very unexpected visit. "What are you guys doing here?"

They step inside, walking past me like they've done a million times before. I close the door, nervously following, thinking as fast as I can of ways to keep them from going into the kitchen. Dia will freak out if this is how she meets them for the first time.

"Benton has a game against Boston tomorrow, so we thought we'd come a day early and see our other pride and joy. How are you, baby?" my mom asks, giving me a tight hug.

"Good," I say. "I was actually just getting ready for my workout with Blaze. I wish I knew you were coming. I'd have cancelled." *I love you both, but please fucking leave before I get in trouble.*

"No need for that, Champ," my dad says, using my childhood nickname. "We just stopped by on our way to check in to the hotel. Benny said he gave you some extra tickets to the game, and maybe we can grab a bite when you're done at the gym." My dad has always put an emphasis on not slacking off during the offseason, so I knew the workout bit would do the trick.

I nod. "Sounds good," I reply, relieved that I'm almost home free. "I'll call you when I'm on my way home." I start ushering them back toward the door, just as Dia's voice rounds the corner behind us.

"Who was it?" she asks, stopping dead in her tracks when she sees that I'm not alone. Her eyes are wide, and her skin goes pale as she yanks at the hem of my t-shirt that only comes down to her upper thighs.

Please baby Jesus. Help me out of this and I promise I'll never kill another spider as long as I live. Not even the big, hairy ones that could murder me in my sleep.

I look from her to my parents, who are standing expectantly, waiting for an introduction. "Mom. Dad. This is Dia," I say, leaving out her last name because all three of them will need to be eased into this conversation. But fuck it. They're here, so we might as well have it.

"Mr. and Mrs. Davis," she says, stepping forward and extending her hand. "It's nice to meet you." I can tell she's nervous, but I'm so fucking proud of her for not running away. We'll face this together, just like we have every other speed bump that's been set in our path. My parents shake her hand, each giving her a gracious smile, but they're obviously a little confused. I never let the women I sleep with meet them, so I'm sure they have questions.

I clear my throat as Dia steps back toward me, clearly needing to feel my closeness. "Why don't you guys sit down?" I say. They walk quietly to the couch as I turn to my wife, trying my best to reassure her. "They're the best people I know," I whisper so only she can hear me. "I promise this will be okay. Please trust me."

She stands there for several moments, nervously chewing on her bottom lip before she gives me a small nod of agreement. "Alright. Let me go put some shorts on, though."

I blow out a breath in relief, quickly kissing her forehead before she takes off down the hall and I turn to where my parents are sitting in the living room.

"Honey, we didn't mean to interrupt," my mom whispers. "We didn't know you brought jersey chasers back here now. We'd have called." She isn't using the term in a mean way. The woman doesn't have a malicious bone in her body. That's just what we've always called my hook-ups...because that's what they were.

I look behind me to make sure Dia didn't hear that before I turn back, lowering my voice. "She's not a jersey chaser," I tell them. "I love her. I'll explain everything." My mom's eyes light up just as my wife re-enters the room, now wearing her own clothes. I take her hand, lacing our fingers together as she looks up and gives me the best smile she can muster. When she nods, I know that's the green light to tell them whatever I need to.

So, I tell them everything.

I tell them how I knew Dia was different the very second I laid eyes on her. About how we ended up at the chapel in Vegas, and how we thought we'd be able to get our marriage annulled the next day. I tell them how we have to share a legal residence for six weeks before we can file divorce papers. And I tell them that despite the fact that we care very deeply for each other, our marriage may not last much longer. I purposely leave out the reasons behind why Dia is set against trying, because that's her story to tell, not mine. She may never feel comfortable enough to tell my parents about her upbringing, and that's okay. I certainly would never pressure her to.

I finish talking and look to my wife, because making sure she's alright is my first priority. When I see that her expression is a little more relaxed and confident than before, I squeeze her hand before looking to my parents. My dad has a small smile tipping up one corner of his lips. My mom has a shocked hand over her mouth and her eyes are full of unshed tears.

Shit.

"Mom, are you oka—"

"Welcome to the family, sweet girl," she says, standing

and walking over to Dia before wrapping her in a tight hug. I let go of her hand, smirking as she stands stone solid for a second, clearly not knowing how to behave at first. I wait with bated breath, until she finally reaches up, returning the embrace.

"Thank you," Dia whispers. I'm sure she's surprised by the reaction, but I can also see some emotion in her eyes.

My dad stands, shaking my hand and pulling me in for a hug before turning to the women. "Alright, Carrie," he says to my mom. "Let the poor girl breathe."

She pulls back, sniffling as she slaps his chest. "You leave me alone, Sam. I always wanted a daughter. Don't you dare ruin this for me." I don't miss the excited little twinkle in Dia's eyes as my dad leans in for a quick hug before letting my mom swoop back in.

That went exactly how I thought it would go on my parents' end. They've always been supportive and under-standing of all the crazy decisions Benton and I have made. But what I *am* surprised by is how my wife reacted to the whole encounter. I expected her to run, or at the very least, clam up until they left and retreat to the guest room for the day to process things alone. She's definitely a little shell-shocked, but otherwise, she looks happy.

"Are you guys hungry?" Dia asks. "I made pancakes. There's plenty for everyone."

My mom and dad happily accept, glad that I'm no longer kicking them out. I text Blaze to cancel our work-out, briefly explaining why and promising more details later. When I enter the kitchen to find the three most important people in my life co-existing like they're completely comfortable, I hope this locks in another missing puzzle piece for Dia. I want her to know she can have the love she's always longed for. That she's always deserved. Her parents are missing out on being a part of her life, but mine won't take it for granted. They'll treat her as one of their own, no matter where our marriage ends up. And that's something I'll be eternally grateful to them for.

We eat our breakfast, making dinner plans for later this evening. I'm surprised when Dia agrees to a shopping trip with my mom tomorrow morning so they can get something to wear to Benton's game. I asked her to go with me to support my brother, reassuring her that we'd be with a group so nobody would suspect anything, but her answer was non-committal. I guess she's cool with it now.

Two hours later, my parents take off to the hotel, my mom having already exchanged numbers with Dia so they can text about tomorrow. When I shut the door and turn to her, the last thing I expect is for her to run my way, launching herself into my arms with a sigh. I hold her as she hugs me tightly, relief radiating from her small body as she buries her face into my neck. When she looks up, all I see is a happiness I've only hoped for in her eyes.

"They're amazing," she says. "Thank you."

I shake my head. "Don't thank me, baby. That was all you. You're impossible not to love."

I hope she understands what I mean. That I'm not only talking about my parents. Because I love her with my whole entire heart. And even if it scares her, it's only a matter of time before I can't hold those three words back anymore.

THIRTY
DIA

I GET in the driver's seat of Dalton's Audi, rubbing my hands together like a little gremlin. I fucking love this car. It's similar to Blaze's, but it's a newer model and is completely blacked out instead of Candy Apple Red. Now that I don't have the extra cash to rent a vehicle, I've either been walking or taking an Uber. But today, Dalton insisted I take one of his cars. He let me choose, and of course, I chose the R8. I reminded him that I almost drove Blaze's through his house a few months ago, but he said he doesn't give a shit about the car as long as I don't get hurt. Then he tossed me the keys, gave me a kiss and a tap on the ass, and told me to have fun.

The distance from the apartment to the dance studio is short, so I drive slowly, cranking the music as I nod my head to the beat. It's uncharacteristically warm and sunny today, so I just have a cropped sweatshirt over my sports bra. It's nice to not need a coat. I can't wait for my first Boston spring.

I pull behind the building, parking in the almost empty lot. I don't have to worry about Bella noticing me driving

Dalton's car because she's always here before me and Carlo insists on making sure I get out of the lot safely before pulling to the door to usher her into his SUV. But honestly, I don't really care if she notices. She and I have become so much closer since I moved here and it is starting to feel wrong keeping her and Mav out of the loop. So, if it comes up, I won't hide it.

"Hey, Carlo!" I greet Bella's bodyguard, giving him a fist bump on my way into the studio. Bella was extra giddy on the phone yesterday when she asked me to meet her here, and I'm wondering why. I wouldn't be surprised if Maverick proposed, but I doubt she'd wait to tell any of us. She's the type to just blurt it over the phone.

"What's up, Diamond?" he says, throwing me off. Carlo is cool, but he's usually very formal. It's always *'Miss Spencer'*. Never Diamond or Dia. As much as I hate people using my full first name, because it usually means we're having a serious moment, I'm pretty sure I love it coming from Bella's burly bodyguard. "She's inside waiting for you," he says, smiling brightly as he opens the door for me.

I'm light on my feet, his good mood rubbing off on me. Well, that and the way Dalton twisted me up like a pretzel while he fucked my brains out before he left for the practice facility this morning. *That* certainly wasn't the worst way to start the day.

I round the corner, hanging back to watch Bella as she dances by herself. The song isn't familiar, but it's definitely her voice. It's unmistakable. She's wearing pink spandex shorts and a very long gray and white Blizzard hoodie. I'd be willing to bet it belongs to her boyfriend. It's funny how we all wear their clothes whenever we can, although I'm not as able to be open like they are. But you bet your ass the first thing I do when I get home is strip off my shirt and put on Dalton's.

She turns, catching my shadow in the corner and halting her movements. "Dia?" she asks, squinting.

"Sorry," I say. "I was stalking. What song is that?" I walk into the room, stopping by where she's set her bag on the floor.

"It's my new single," she says proudly. "Well, not yet. I recorded it before my break so we could release it as part of my big comeback. I'm not technically working, but we're planning for the next tour." She's smiling and bouncing on her tiptoes like an absolute weirdo. I'm a little confused why this is exciting her so much.

"Have you had any Red Bull today, Bells?" I ask, half joking, half not.

"Nope," she answers, still bouncing.

"You okay?"

"Yep." More bouncing.

"Bella, what's going—"

"Come on tour with me!" she yells like she just can't hold the words inside her tiny body anymore. "Be my new dancer!"

I stand there, confused for a second, but then everything starts to make sense. I can't believe this is happening.

"You want to pay me to dance?" I whisper.

"Yes!" she squeals. "I played the video I took of us for my choreographer, Sammi. We just found out that one of my dancers is pregnant by one of my other dancers. It's a whole thing, which I'll explain later," she rushes out, "but we have an opening and I *need* it to be you. Please, Dia."

I'm stunned silent. All my life, I was told that girls like me don't grow up to be professional dancers. My parents made sure I knew that I wasn't destined for anything special. But now, I realize that they were just holding me down. If it weren't for their negativity and gaslighting, I'd have been long gone, leaving them behind to deal with their messes on their own. All the nights I went to bed discouraged, thinking I wasn't good enough to pursue my passion...it was all wasted time. I want to be angry with my mom and dad for not giving me the support I needed as a child, but I refuse to spend another ounce of emotion on them. Moving forward, I'm living the life I always dreamed about. And I have my new family here in Boston to thank for it. They've shown me more love and encouragement in the handful of weeks that I've been here than my parents have in my whole life.

I nod my head rapidly, smiling through my tears. "Yes! Definitely!" I tell her.

"Oh my God! I'm so excited!" Bella squeals, jumping on me. She hugs me way tighter than such a small person should be able to, swaying me back and forth as I cry-laugh on her shoulder. She pulls back. "We're going to have so much fun! And you get to keep the stuff you wear on tour when it's over. Last year, I wore my sequined Versace jumpsuit around the house for a week straight just because I could." I can definitely see Bella, washing the dishes in head-to-toe sparkles. That's very on-brand for her.

She sets me up with the information I'll need to sign my contract, informing me of the very hefty signing bonus I'll get when my paperwork is all taken care of. We lace up our shoes and she shows me some of the choreography for her new song, which is absolutely amazing.

When we part ways, promising to meet up again next week, I head to the car and immediately rifle through my purse for my phone, connecting it to the Bluetooth. Usually, when something good happens in my life, Mads is my first and only call. But without even thinking, I pull up another contact, hitting the *Call* button on the steering wheel as I pull onto the road.

"How much is it going to cost me?" Dalton says in greeting.

"What?" I reply, caught off guard.

"Whatever...or *whoever* you hit with my car."

I roll my eyes. "You're such an asshole. I didn't crash," I say with a laugh. "But guess what!"

"What, baby?" he replies.

I bounce in my seat, too excited to sit still as I wait at a red light. "Bella asked me to join her next tour as a backup dancer!"

"What?" he chokes. "That's fucking amazing! I'm so proud of you!"

"Thank you." I shake my head, still in disbelief. "I couldn't have done any of this without you, Dalton. Seriously. Thank you."

"No way, babe. You did this all by yourself. I was just lucky enough to have a front row seat to your comeback."

This man. He's given me so much and he doesn't even realize it. Maybe I did do some of this on my own, but I would've never had the courage to break out of the life that was holding me down if it weren't for him throwing me over his shoulder in Vegas. Although I thought it was the worst possible situation when we were told we'd need to stay married for longer than we expected, I'm truly thankful that things worked out the way they did. With Dalton behind me, I've had the courage to take the life I've always wanted.

"Hurry home, Wifey. We'll order from Donatello's and get naked so I can congratulate you properly."

"Okay, be right there," I say, still high on my good news. "I love you!" I freeze, not knowing where that just came from. I vowed I'd never say those words to a man again. But they just came out before I could stop them. "I...uhh," I stutter, not sure how to recover.

"I love you, too," he says. "Drive safe, baby."

THIRTY-ONE
DALTON

I WALK IN THE DOOR, *exhausted from a hard workout. The only thing on my mind is finding Dia and wrapping her in my arms while we lounge on the couch together. I take off my shoes, kicking them out of the way, and set my keys on the table in the entryway. The house is uncharacteristically quiet for this time of day. Usually, she's either dancing around with the music blasting, or I'll hear the shower running from the primary bathroom.*

"Dia?" I yell, pausing to listen for a reply.

I round the corner, checking the kitchen. It's a little late for her to be having breakfast, but not completely uncommon for her to be sitting at the table with a bowl of cereal while she scrolls on her phone. When I see that the room is empty, I turn, walking back toward the hallway. "Wifey! You home?" I try again. I check the bedroom first, pushing the door open to find it dark and quiet. The bed is made and it looks like nobody has been here in a while.

I peek into the bathroom, already knowing that it's empty, as well. I start to panic when I think that she may have walked to the dance studio by herself. I know my wife is a strong, independent woman, but that doesn't mean that I want her all alone walking the busy streets of Boston. I keep telling her to take my car, but she puts up a pretty good fight every time I offer.

I get more and more anxious with every empty room I encounter. Thinking maybe I missed something, I return to the living room, but she's still nowhere in sight. Out of the corner of my eye, I see a piece of paper on the sofa table. I guess she did leave without telling me her plans for the day, but at least there's a note. A wave of relief washes over me as I walk over to it, picking it up and reading it.

My heart sinks in my chest as I clutch the paper in my hand. I fall to my knees, gripping my hair and letting out an agonizing cry as the signed divorce papers flutter to the floor beside me.

She's gone.

I WAKE up in a cold sweat, my pulse pounding like a drum between my ears. I reach over to Dia's side of the bed, finding it empty and cold. I immediately sit up, panic taking over every one of my senses as I quickly move from the bed and run down the hall. Unlike in the nightmare I just had, I find my wife sitting on the couch, phone in hand, like everything is right in the world.

And it is. For now.

Today marks six weeks since we legally moved in together. We are officially allowed to file for a divorce. I know there's no way in hell that it'll be me making that move, because it's the furthest thing from what I want. The time Dia and I have spent together just solidified that I want to be married to her for the rest of my life.

It's been almost a week since her little slip up on the

phone. I know she didn't mean to say she loved me right then, but I don't believe for a second that she didn't mean the words when she said them. And I definitely meant them when I said them back. It felt like a million pounds had lifted off my chest when I finally got to let them out. The fact that she said them first made me feel like the luckiest man to ever walk this planet. But I know that scared her. That's why I haven't said them again or even addressed the situation. When she wants to talk about it, she will.

I've been counting down the days until today. Not because I wanted it to come, but because I was dreading it. I've had nightmares almost every night this week about her leaving me, and I wake up every time to her still here. But what happens now that she's free to go?

"Morning, baby. You're up early today," I say, sitting down next to her and pressing my lips to her warm cheek. She smiles in response, setting her phone down so she can turn and kiss me properly. I take it in, enjoying the moment as she opens her mouth, allowing me to push my tongue inside. I swallow her desperate moans as she grips onto my t-shirt to keep me close. I love when she's like this. It's these moments where I can feel what she feels, even if she has trouble saying it out loud sometimes. I feel my body relax a little, because these certainly don't seem like the actions of a woman who has her running shoes laced up and is headed out the door. As a matter of fact, she seems even more clingy this morning than she normally is.

Zero complaints out of me for that.

"Morning," she says, pulling away. But it doesn't feel right not having some type of physical connection to her, so I grab her by the hips and pull her so she's straddling my lap. I'm not trying to make things sexual. I just want her as close as possible right now. I know that we'll eventually need to talk about what's going to happen going forward, but I'm trying to process what this could mean for us.

I've been in my own head all week, trying to slow down time and make this day not come at all. I was imagining the worst. Me coming out here to her dressed and ready to end our marriage. And what would that mean for us? Does getting divorced mean that there's no hope for us in the future? Or is it the marriage alone that scares her? These are all questions I want to ask, but right now, it feels like we're living in a house of cards. One wrong move, and the whole thing could collapse with us inside.

"What are your plans for the day?" I ask her. I'm half expecting her to remind me that we need to go back to the courthouse, but she's acting as if she doesn't even realize what day it is. Or maybe I'm just making a bigger deal out of it than it actually is.

"Not sure," she replies. "We could go to the Mr. Burger drive-through and eat in the parking lot at the beach. I kind of want to get out of here for a little bit, but I also want to keep you to myself." She pops a shoulder. "That seems like a good way to do it."

I smile at her. "You're right. That's the best idea I've ever heard." Maybe I am overthinking this whole thing. We've been getting along so well, and now that I know that she loves me back, maybe we're just going to bypass this whole day and treat it like any other one. I'll admit though, it's hard not to have everything playing in the back of my mind. But as long as she's here, I'll be right next to her.

I'm sure it would freak her out if I said it out loud, but I've been putting a lot of thought into what the future will look like if she decides to give us a real shot at marriage. My wheels have been turning for weeks and I've got a lot of big changes on the horizon, depending on what Dia does this week. But I want to prove to her that I'm all in on this. I was the day I married her, and I will be until the day I die.

I stand from the couch, taking her with me as I walk toward the bedroom. She throws her head back in a care-free laugh as I give her heart-shaped ass a squeeze, and I can't help but admire the way she's grown since she's been here. Even if she leaves, as much pain as it would bring me, I'll eventually be able to breathe knowing that she's stronger and more confident than ever. I'll be proud to watch her stand on her own two feet, even if I have to do it from far away.

"Let's take a shower and we'll get out of here," I tell her, setting her on the counter in the bathroom while I turn on the tap. I take her in as steam fills the room and I'm reminded of our first night here. She was nervous and rigid as I washed her tired body with no intentions of taking anything physical from her. I didn't even want to that night, which was certainly off-brand for the old Dalton. But, as soon as I became her husband, it's like I had a direct line to her subconscious. I knew exactly what she needed, and I just somehow had the ability to give it. It's not something she was used to, and her discomfort was painfully obvious when she realized it wasn't a sexual connection I was after. But here we are now, six weeks later, and we've made it part of our daily routine. It's become a part of her healing, and I'll never be able to thank her enough for choosing me to be the one she let into the heart she swore she'd keep closed.

All I've ever wanted was her love and trust. And now that I have it, I'm praying to God that she doesn't take it all away.

THIRTY-TWO
DALTON

MY HANDS SHAKE with anticipation as I grip the steering wheel. Dia sits beside me in the passenger seat, taking in the expensive homes as we pass by. This neighborhood is the safest in the area, with a good school system and around-the-clock security. But it also has a quiet and quaint feel to it. It's nothing like the busy city street where my apartment is located. That place is great for a bachelor pad. But this? It's the place you can only dream to live when you want to set down roots and raise a family.

When I gave the realtor a list of things I was looking for a few weeks ago, I certainly wasn't expecting her to get back to me so fast. I honestly thought I'd end up having to build a custom home to make sure it checked all the boxes, taking months or even years to complete. But somehow, as it has so many times in the last couple of months, fate stepped in and dropped perfection right into my lap.

I steal a glance at Dia. It's been nearly two weeks since our six-week period ran out, and I know we probably should have discussed everything by now, but she hasn't brought it up and neither have I. I'll admit I haven't because the thought of her leaving terrifies me. Everything between us is going so well. Our daily routines have stayed the same. Taking turns making breakfast before showering together. Sometimes when I'm an extra good boy, she drops to her knees and starts my day with her heavenly mouth. I go to the practice facility, and she takes off to meet Bella at the studio or Mads at the café or shopping center. Then, we spend our weeknights at home, wrapped up in one other on the couch. On the weekends, we get creative with our adventures. Sometimes we return to our secluded booth at Club Liquid. Sometimes we put on wigs and fake mustaches so we can sneak into a movie theater unnoticed. Talking about putting an end to all of this definitely isn't high on my to-do list.

I know what I'm about to do could go either very well, or it could blow up in my face, but I really need Dia to know that I'm still completely in on being married to her. I want to build a life with her, and we can't do that in my bachelor pad. There are so many things she wants out of life, and I want to give them all to her. But I also understand that this may completely scare the shit out of her. I know there's still a part of her that thinks I'll abandon her like her parents did, but she couldn't be more wrong. Even if I wanted to, I am bound to this woman. I feel it in my soul. She's my other half, and I'm lucky enough to have found her in this great big world full of people. So, no matter what feelings get stirred up from her past when I show her what our future could look like, we'll get through it together.

I pull through the gate, parking the car and running around to open her door. She's been particularly sassy today, and I can't say it isn't turning me on a little. But that melts into confusion as I go through all the steps to make sure she's able to get into the house, even when I'm not here. I program both of our fingerprints into the lock on the door and hold my breath as I swing it open to reveal my wife's dream house.

The night she came to me, promising to let me love and care for her, I asked what she wanted for her future. I wasn't expecting much out of her because I knew she wasn't used to opening up to people like that. But, once she started talking, it's like she just couldn't stop. The excitement in her voice as she described the house she dreamed of living in set me on a mission, right then and there. I was going to find it for her. And if I couldn't find it, I'd build it.

At first, I didn't know where our relationship would go. So, the house was less about us, and more about her having a life she deserved. Whether or not I would be living in it with her wasn't my concern. Of course, I'd hoped we'd be able to share it, but if she decided to kick me to the curb, I still wanted her to have this.

I'm in awe as I look around at the beautiful interior of the entryway. When the realtor sent over the photos and told me that this place had everything I asked for, I knew I didn't want to see it for the first time in person without Dia. It just didn't seem right to come here and not have her to experience it with. So, I bought it, sight unseen, and here we are.

We both stand there, taking in our surroundings. From here, I can see the large living room, complete with the fireplace she wanted. I was able to purchase all of the furniture and have it ready to go earlier this week, so if she wants to, we can pack up the boxes at my apartment and move in right away. Off to our right, there's a large kitchen for her to host her friends. There's even a big island in the middle of the room for all of her wine bottles to be put while she dances like a crazy person in her pajamas. The mental image of that makes me smile as she takes a few steps forward, trying to see more.

"Who lives here?" she asks, her voice breathy as she looks up the marble staircase.

I walk up behind her, snaking my arms around her waist and pulling her into me. The scent of her minty shampoo overtakes my senses, calming my raging nerves.

"We do," I tell her.

She stands there for a moment, and I feel her body go rigid before she freezes completely. I give her some time to process everything, letting go of her so she knows she's not being held down, but keeping my front pressed against her back. She takes two quick steps away from me before whipping around, her brows pulled together in confusion. "What?"

She looks a little nervous, but I want her to understand what this house is, and what it could mean for us. "I know it's a lot, but please let me show you around. Let me show you why you're here."

Thankfully, she trusts me enough to go along with what I'm asking. I take her hand, leading her from room to room, reminding her of everything she told me she wanted that night. The realtor was completely right. Every single thing on that list is included in this house. It's almost like it was waiting here for us to find each other, get married, fall in love, and start a life.

When we finish on the first and second floor, we go back through the kitchen and I open the French doors to the backyard. Although it's still chilly out and nothing is open for the warm weather, the pool is completely visible, as is the waterfall that sits off to the side. It isn't running, but I can envision her laying on a lounger in her sexiest bikini, or if I'm lucky, nothing at all, reading her smutty romance books while she waits for me to come home from practice. I fantasize about nights alone out here, making love to her in the water, the sound of the waterfall mixing with her moans as I make her come, over and over. These are all thoughts that have run through my head a million times, but they're all so real now that we're standing here.

"It's the house from my dreams," she whispers. I can't really make out the emotions that she's feeling from the sound of her voice, but I know there's an internal battle waging on inside her.

"What are you thinking?" I ask. If she's having mixed emotions about this, I want to talk them out. I know it was impulsive to buy the house, let alone bring her here when we haven't discussed our long-term future, so I don't expect her to just be all smiles and jump to move in right away. I actually anticipated her giving some pushback, but when I went to tell the realtor that it was too soon, it just didn't feel right. I knew this place was made for Dia. There was no other explanation.

"I need to get out of here," she says, turning and running back through the doors. I rush in behind her just in time to see her bump into the kitchen counter, the contents of her bag scattering across the floor. She drops down, trying her best to gather it all up as quickly as she can, shoving her phone into her back pocket and stuffing more items into her purse.

I walk over, kneeling beside her and reaching for a piece of paper that's lying face-down in front of me. "Hey," I say softly. "I know this is a lot, but let's talk about it. I don't want us to—"

I'm cut off when I notice the way she's nervously looking at the paper in my hand. My brows knit in confusion as I reluctantly flip it over and read it silently. It takes my brain a minute to register what this is, but when it does, panic and anger flow through me like an electric current.

"No," I whisper, shaking my head rapidly. I look down at it again, hoping that the large, bold text on the top of the document has somehow magically changed and I'm not holding divorce papers in my hand. "Dia, please don't do this. I love you," I choke out. I feel so desperate right now. If I wasn't already on my knees, I'd drop down to beg her to stay.

She stares at me like a deer in headlights, her big brown eyes filling with tears. She squeezes them shut, bringing a hand over her mouth as her face twists with emotion. I think maybe she's going to open up to me. Tell me why she's still so scared of giving this marriage a shot, but she stays silent.

I reach out for her hand, needing some sort of connection, but she tries to back away, landing on her ass before I can even touch her. She stands quickly before taking another step backward. "I'm sorry, Dalton," she says as tears stream down her beautiful face.

I shuffle toward her, still on my knees. "*Please*," I plead. "Please don't leave me." I reach out again, but she puts her hands out in front of her to keep me at a distance.

"*Elvis*," she whispers, halting me completely.

And then, she's out the front door.

I scramble to my feet, running after her while frantically patting my pockets to find my keys. But as I hear the door to my Audi slam shut, the engine roaring to life, I realize I must've left them in the car in my excitement to get Dia into the house. I hit the porch just in time to see her fly down the driveway and out of sight, taking every piece of my soul with her.

"Fuck!" I yell, gripping my hair as my whole body trembles. I let my emotions take control as tears roll down my cheeks, soaking my skin. I feel like my heart has been ripped out of my chest. I gasp for breath, feeling truly scared that this is it for us. My knees wobble violently before giving out and I drop to the hard wood of the wrap-around porch where I envisioned Dia rocking our babies on a warm, summer evening. Now, the memory of the future I had dreamed about is nothing but a painful reminder that I couldn't do enough to make her change her mind.

I was stupid for thinking she was ready for any of this. I've been pushing too hard, right from that very first night, even though she warned me that she'd break me if I got too close. And now she's gone, leaving me here with a piece of paper that proves she was never fully mine to begin with.

I want answers from her so badly. Did she ever really let me in? Or did I break through her walls, only to find a heart that was padlocked without a key the whole time?

I know I need to let her do this alone. She needs time to figure all of this out without me. So, I reach into my pocket, calling the only person I can think of that knows what it's like to feel as broken as I am right now. I may not know his story, but I can tell that something *or someone* changed him into the man he is today.

It rings twice before he greets me. "Hello?"

"Hey," I say. "Can you come get me?"

Not even ten minutes later, I open the door of my quarterback's Tesla. I hesitate, stopping to take one more look at the house before I lower myself into the front seat.

"Let's get you out of here," Tanner says as he pulls around and heads back toward the road. I take another look in the rearview, watching every dream I had of my future with Dia disappear as the house gets further and further away.

We ride in silence all the way to Tanner's house. It's in a secluded area, up on a hill with an epic view of the Boston skyline. I've been here a few times before, but he usually doesn't offer to host events for the team. He'll pay the big bucks to rent a hall or ballroom, but it's rare that he invites people into his space. I'm glad we're here though, because I couldn't stay at the new house, and everything in my apartment reminds me of Dia. I can't go back there until I know what's going on.

After she grand theft autoed my Audi, I told myself I'd give her some time. She's used to doing things on her own. And although I promised she'd never have to do it again, I know this is one of those times where she needs to make decisions about what happens next without me putting extra pressure on her. So, I deleted my car's app from my phone. That way, I'm not tempted to watch the GPS as she drives.

We come to the end of Tanner's long driveway, and he

pulls his car into the open garage door as it shuts behind us. I follow him silently as we enter the house. My body feels like I just got hit repeatedly by a monster linebacker. Every one of my muscles is tense with anxiety as my brain goes a thousand miles a minute, conjuring up every possible bad outcome of this situation.

I want to kick my own ass for not waiting to show Dia the house. I guess I just got comfortable these past two weeks, knowing she was free to leave, but didn't. Little did I know, she was considering it the whole time if she went through with having divorce papers drawn up without telling me. I want to be angry about it, but do I even have a right to be? She told me before I married her that after that night, we were done. I should be thankful I got another two months with her. I gained her trust, showed her what she was worth, and I know she loves me. Even if she hadn't slipped and said it on the phone, her actions speak loudly. Starting with the night she ran into *my arms* when her parents broke her heart. She could've gone to Mads, or suffered in silence like she's used to doing, but she didn't. Instead, she showed up at my door, knowing I'd do everything I could do stop her pain. That's all I've ever wanted to do.

Tanner leads me to the basement, where he has a completely stocked wet bar set up in the corner. He opens a small refrigerator, sliding a beer across the wooden counter to me before pouring himself a glass of whiskey. "Alright," he says before pausing to throw back half the glass at once. "What happened?"

I tell him everything. From the moment I laid eyes on Dia, to the wedding in Vegas, to finally feeling like I had broken down her walls, only to have her run away from me. He lets me speak, listening intently and never interrupting. When I'm finally finished, he leans forward onto the bar top and blows out a breath.

"The summer before my senior year of college, I had a," he pauses, looking for the right word, "*thing* with my best friend's younger sister. It started as just physical, but feelings got involved on both of our parts. Knowing that I'd be entering the draft and she had dreams of her own, I pushed her away." He looks down, sadness in his expression as he swirls the amber liquid in his glass. "I should've fought for her, but I thought I was doing the right thing. It was the biggest mistake of my fucking life. A mistake I've lived with since I walked away from her as she begged me not to. Her cries still haunt my dreams." He looks up at me. "Fight for her, Davis. Give her the time she needs right now, but when she's ready, do whatever it takes to get her back."

I try to protest the tears that threaten to fill my eyes, but I feel so fucking broken. I keep trying to reach for some semblance of hope, but the folded-up piece of paper in my pocket right now feels like a boulder, pulling me under the surface as I try to keep my head above water.

I know Tanner is right, though. Dia needs time, but there's no fucking way I'll let her walk away from this marriage without a fight. I love her too much to just lay down and let that happen. If she decides in the end that she wants to leave, I can't force her to stay. But I'll definitely go down swinging.

"Thanks, Tan. For coming to get me. For telling me all of that. Just…for everything."

He gives a tight nod. "Of course, man. We're brothers."

We sit there for a while, talking as we drink. Eventually, my body lets me know that the day has taken its toll, my muscles aching from the stress. As I go to call for a ride, Tanner stops me. "Just stay here. For as long as you need."

I'm way too tired to turn down his offer, thanking him before he shows me to the guest suite, which is somehow bigger than my whole fucking apartment. It has its own kitchen, bathroom, and bedroom. It's a pretty perfect place to think about all of this while giving Dia the space she needs. I'll go back to my apartment eventually, but I just can't tonight. It's too much.

I brush my teeth before stripping down to my boxers and sliding under the covers, into an empty bed for the first time in weeks. I miss her so goddamn much. I feel like my chest is caving in as I struggle to breathe. I fight back every emotion that's battling inside me, closing my eyes, hoping that she's okay. And that maybe she's missing me, too.

Just as I'm about to drift off, my phone dings on the bedside table, lighting up the room. I pick it up, seeing a notification from the security camera system I had installed in the new house. I pull up the app, seeing Dia as she places her finger on the lock to the front door and pushes it open. The camera switches to the one in the entryway, triggered by her movement. I should stop watching. I should be thankful she has somewhere safe to stay and give her some privacy. But my eyes stay glued to the screen as she walks around the house. And when she heads toward the basement, that she didn't get a chance to see earlier, I know there's nothing that could drag me away.

THIRTY-THREE
DIA

I DROVE around for hours trying to make sense of things. I half expected to be pulled over and arrested for driving a stolen car. Or at the very least, I figured he'd call or text, telling me to bring it back. But, as always, Dalton knew what I needed. There's way too much going on in my head to talk about any of it right now.

That's why, instead of going to Mads' house, I find myself punching *1123* into the keypad next to the same gate I drove out of earlier today. I'm relieved when I see that everything has been locked up and all the lights are off, indicating that Dalton has probably left. I walk up to the door, pressing my finger to the lock, waiting for it to blink green before I turn the doorknob and let myself in. The contents of my bag have been picked up from the floor and set carefully on the table in the entryway. I walk over slowly, going through it, noticing immediately that there's one thing missing.

I had the divorce papers drawn up the day after our six-week period was up. I reminded myself that this was the plan all along. I had a good job now, dancing for Bella.

I wouldn't have to worry about mooching off of Dalton anymore. I could start my new life in Boston, standing on my own two feet and relying on myself like I have since I was a kid. That's what I wanted.

But with every hour that passed, and me still not giving Dalton the papers, things just got more confusing in my mind. I promised myself every morning when I woke up that I'd do it, but we'd fall into our normal daily routine, and I just couldn't. I didn't want to let it go. And that, right there, scares the shit out of me.

I've spent my whole life relying on the wrong people for my own happiness. My parents would reel me in, acting like they loved and cared for me, just to let me down again. It was the same way with Josh. As long as I was giving him what he wanted, it was good. But as soon as I voiced my hope for our future, he threw me away like I wasn't worth wasting his life on. By the time Dalton found me, I was damaged beyond repair. I was afraid that the moment I let him in, even a little bit, he'd leave. But he didn't. He just kept trying to get me to see that I could trust him.

He's shown me so many times over that he isn't like them. But here I am, still struggling to believe that I can have it all. That I can have a life with someone who loves me while keeping my strength and independence. I know I have to figure this out, because being stuck in limbo like this is hurting us both. I just need some time to work through it.

I take another walk around the house, this time appreciating the way it fits every single part of the dream I had for my future home. I can see myself enjoying a girls' night in with Mads and Bella in the kitchen, drinking wine and laughing obnoxiously until our guys had to drag us to bed. I let myself imagine Dalton pulling me in to dance while we cook breakfast, looking at me in that adoring way he always does. I walk up the stairs, swinging open the bedroom door, thinking of the way he'd press me against the mattress as he made love to me. Every part of this hurts. But it's not until I make my way down to the basement that I get overwhelmed with emotion.

I flip on the light switch, illuminating a completely finished dance studio. The light-colored maple flooring under my feet shines brightly as I step further into the room. Mirrors stretch along the length of the front and back walls, with a barre installed the entire way across. In the front corner, there's a high-tech stereo system, with speakers mounted around the room. And in the back, there's a purple velvet couch with a large coffee table. In the center of it lays a white box with a big silver bow decorating the top. I can't stop myself from walking over and plucking the small envelope from it. Pulling out the card, tears fill my eyes as I recognize his handwriting.

> Dia,
> The last eight weeks have been more than I could've ever imagined. I've won a Heisman trophy and a Super Bowl ring, but my greatest accomplishment in life is you. Thank you for making all my dreams come true. Hopefully, I can do the same for you. Starting with this.
> I love you.
>
> Your husband,
> Dalton

Tears blur my vision as I pull the lid from the box, finding several pairs of brand-new dance shoes, all in my size. I sit on the couch, trying to keep myself from falling apart as I remove my sneakers and pull on the pink canvas ballet shoes. I look down, realizing that it's been a long time since I was able to own a new pair like this. The padding in the bottom feels like a cloud on the soles of my feet compared to the old, worn-out pair that I have.

I stand, walking over to the stereo system, pairing it to my phone. I've never felt more at home than I do in this studio, and if I never get a chance to come here again, I want to know what it's like to have danced in a place that was made just for me. I don't even look at the song I'm choosing. I just hit *Shuffle* and set my phone down, moving to the center of the room.

Unstable by Justin Bieber and The Kid LAROI comes from the speakers as I move, closing my eyes and letting myself go wherever the music takes me. The melody flows through me, carrying me around the floor effortlessly. I spin and jump, covering the entirety of the room with my steps. I imagine Dalton watching in the mirror as he looks on from the couch, mesmerized by me.

I dance for him. Trying my hardest to apologize for all the ways I've hurt him in the only way I know how. And when the lyrics hit too close to home, making me feel too much, I fall to my knees. I let the tears I've been fighting flow freely as every emotion I've been avoiding crashes into me. I cry for what seems like hours, until I can barely breathe, and my eyes are almost swollen shut. I scream into the empty room and plead for forgiveness, even though I know nobody can hear me. I curse my parents out loud for turning me into a scared, weak woman who can't accept love from a man who has done everything he

can to prove that he's not going anywhere. And I cry for
the little girl who deserved better than the life she was
given.

Then, I make a promise to myself to do some serious
soul searching. To find a way to let go of my past for good
and take the future I deserve.

THIRTY-FOUR
DALTON

I WAKE up alone in my bed, my head pounding violently. I'm hungover as fuck and probably in need of about two gallons of water. But after Mads stopped by to get Dia's clothes yesterday, I had to get shitfaced. I honestly don't think I can get through this any other way. At least not right now.

I miss my wife. This apartment feels like a prison without her here. I wander around like I'm lost, going from room to room, trying to feel her. To smell her. Anything to remind me that she was real, and that she was mine. The first night I stayed here without her, I fell asleep on the living room floor, wrapped in her favorite cashmere blanket. I woke up stiff and aching, still clinging to the soft fabric as if she were inside it. But she wasn't. She was gone, and I was alone. I almost caved and called her so many times, but I'm trying to honor the promise we made. She used her safe word, and I need to give her time.

It's been three days since she took off in my car, leaving me to consider that her future may not include me. Mads drove it here, planning to leave it and have Blaze pick her up, but I told her to take the Audi back to Dia for now. Even if it's not for long, she's still my wife and I don't want her walking around Boston when she doesn't have to.

I couldn't hold back from asking how she's doing, now that she's staying with Mads and Blaze. I know she needs time, but I'd give anything to hold her hand through this. Part of me hoped that Mads would tell me Dia was doing okay, but the other part of me was hoping she's been as miserable as I have. She told me she hasn't talked much, but that her usual M.O. is to shut down while she processes her feelings. Mads promised me that she'd be there when Dia was ready to talk or be comforted. If it can't be me with her, her best friend is the only other person I'd trust to make sure she isn't going through this alone.

It killed me to watch her break down in the dance studio the other night. The security cameras don't have sound, but the image of her in so much pain had me up and out of bed, pacing the floors in Tanner's guest suite, fighting the overwhelming urge to go to her. But I know my wife. And I know that she needs to do this without me. When she figures it out and is ready to talk, I'll be waiting. I just hope the answers she finds don't mean the end for us.

My phone rings from next to me on the bed, the sound making the pounding in my head even worse. My instinct is to ignore it, but what if it's Dia? That has me sitting up, trying to focus my burning eyes on the caller ID.

Fuck.

One thing about Carrie Davis. If she calls once and I don't answer, the rapid-fire texts and callbacks begin immediately. Especially during the offseason when she believes she should be our main priority. Otherwise, we're subject to a retelling of our birth stories, in their entirety. Benton was lucky enough to have an epidural involved in his. But me? Twenty-eight hours of hard labor with no drugs. And something about an episiotomy, whatever that is.

"Hey, Mom," I say, my voice full of gravel. *Good fucking God, I need water.*

"Hi, honey!" she greets me back. "I tried texting Dia a few times because I was going to order a shirt that she said she liked while we were out shopping, but I wasn't sure what color she'd want. Is she home?"

Shit. I didn't want to tell anyone in my family what was going on until I knew whether or not we were staying together. I know they're already attached to her and I didn't want to put anyone through what I'm going through while I wait for Dia to work it out. I also didn't want them worrying about me. I honestly just want to be left alone until I have answers from my wife. But I absolutely refuse to outright lie to my mother.

I take a deep breath in through my nose, blowing slowly from my mouth, trying my best to quell the nausea. It doesn't work, but I go on anyway. "Dia left. She's staying with her best friend, Blaze's girlfriend, while she decides what's next for us. I fucked up, Mom," I say, defeat evident in my tone.

"Oh, baby," she says softly. "What happened?"

I fight back tears, which seems to be happening a lot lately. I've never been an overly emotional guy, but this situation is new for me and it's hard. I've never loved anyone before, especially not in the way that I love Dia. And knowing that she's out there, also going through pain and heartbreak, is almost too much to bear.

"Dia didn't have a good childhood," I begin. "I don't want to get into all the details, because it's her story to tell, but her parents weren't like you guys. They provided the bare minimum for her until she was able to start taking care of herself as a teenager. So, when she told me what her dream house looked like, I went on a mission to find it. I wasn't expecting it to happen so fast, but the realtor found it a few weeks ago. The only thing I had to do to make it perfect for her was have them install some mirrors and a stereo system in the basement. Otherwise, it was the exact house she described. I offered the owner fifty-thousand dollars above asking price to be out in a week and they jumped at it."

She exhales slowly, and I know she's about to hit me with a truth bomb. "If you knew she was considering divorce at the end of your time together, why did you buy a house?"

Because hindsight is twenty-twenty and I'm a fucking idiot, Mom.

I squeeze the bridge of my nose between two fingers. "I just wanted to give her everything. At first, I didn't care if we moved in right away, or if we were married at all. If she wanted the divorce, I was going to sign it over to her. But when she didn't come to me with the paperwork after two weeks, I thought we were moving in a positive direction. It was dumb, but I was desperate to show her how important she is to me. I love her so much…and now she's gone," I choke out.

"Sweet boy," my mom says, and I can tell by her voice that she's trying not to cry. As always, she's being strong for me when I can't be strong for myself. The same way she did when I tore my ACL my junior year of college. It was the Big Ten Championship game and although the season was basically over, I was worried my recovery would fuck with my chances of being drafted high.

"That girl loves you. She may not say it, but I can see it in the way she looks at you. And the way she talks about you when you're not around. And the way she leaned into you when we showed up unannounced that day. You're her comfort, Dalton. I'm sure that's a scary realization for a girl who has been on her own for so long."

I know she's right. Dia has told me several times that she's afraid of becoming dependent on me. But I don't know how to show her that she can still take care of herself and keep me in her life. The only other option is letting her go and hoping she sees it for herself.

"What do I do?" I ask, desperate for an answer.

She takes a moment, considering her words before speaking again. "Exactly what you're doing, my love. Give her the time and space she needs. As tempting as it is to contact her, she won't be able to give you an explanation of how she's feeling until she sorts through it all. She was never planning on falling in love with you. And now that she has, it's a whole new set of feelings. Just like you did with me, you threw that girl's whole world off its axis in the very best way. She'll come back to you, Dalton. Just give her time."

Tears spill over as I blink, exhaling a shaky breath. Dia is everything to me. So, whatever she needs to find her way back to me, I'll give her.

"Thanks, Mom. I love you."

"I love you, too, honey. It's going to be okay."

We say our goodbyes, and I get out of bed to hydrate. I should probably eat, too, since I haven't had much of an appetite in the past few days. I've been surviving on a diet of Sam Adams and whatever whiskey in my cabinet will finish me off every night so I can bear sleeping alone.

I make my way to the kitchen, reaching into the refrigerator for one of my prepared meals for the week. I warm the chicken and rice in the microwave before squeezing on some fresh lemon juice. I'm pleasantly surprised when I take the first bite and, for the first time in three days, don't feel like I'm going to puke. I guess that's a good sign. The last thing I want is for Dia to have even more guilt if we happen to cross paths and I look like death. Our best friends live in the same house, where she's also staying. Depending on how much time she needs, it's very possible that we would see each other.

The thought is both comforting and terrifying. I want to text and let her know I'm thinking of her. Ask if she's okay. Literally anything to let her know I still care. But I know better, so I try to think of things to do that'll keep my mind off of this whole situation.

I clean up my mess, still feeling well enough for some physical activity. I grab my hand wraps from my gym bag, heading downstairs where my heavy bag hangs from the ceiling. I carefully remove my wedding ring, setting it on top of the stack of PR boxes I still haven't sorted through before winding the wraps around my wrists and through my fingers. When they're secure, I walk over to the bag, forcing myself to push every thought from my mind. I start easy, throwing some jabs while focusing on my breathing. I feel like I haven't worked out in years, when it's really only been less than a week. I fight through the fatigue, throwing harder hooks and uppercuts while bobbing and weaving, trying my best to stay quick on my feet. My lungs burn and I'm dripping sweat, but it feels good to get my aggression out.

When I'm completely gassed out, I lean forward, resting on the bag while I try to slow my breathing. I'm exhausted again, but at least I got my blood flowing and don't feel like I'll need to get hammered in order to get a full night of sleep. I sit on the stool in the corner of the room, removing the wraps and flexing my fingers. The indentation from my ring makes my chest squeeze tightly. I hate the way my hand looks without it. I can't imagine what it'll feel like if I end up having to take it off for good.

I head toward the boxes, taking the ring and sliding it down my finger. My chest loosens slightly, and I let out a relieved breath. As I go to pick up my wraps, an address label on a medium-sized box catches my eye. It's from the hotel we spent our wedding night at. I don't even have to open it to know what's inside, but I do it anyway. I tear off the tape and pull back the flaps. The first thing I see is my black tuxedo t-shirt. Dia said it was ridiculous, but I didn't miss the way she smiled every time I asked how I looked.

I set the shirt aside, reaching back in the box and pulling out her wedding dress. It's all wrinkled and there's a rip in the tulle, but as I clutch it in my hands, memories hit me like a freight train. The defeat in her eyes when she told me her ex said that she wasn't wife material. How she stole my breath as she walked down the aisle toward me. I knew right then and there that my purpose in this world was to love her. The only thing I've seen since that moment was her. She's all that matters.

And I'll do whatever it takes to make her happy. Even if it breaks me completely in the end.

THIRTY-FIVE
DIA

"I HAVE SOME FOOD FOR YOU," Mads says softly through the door. When I don't answer, just like I haven't for the past four days, she speaks again. "D, you have to eat. I'm coming in."

"It's locked," I say, just as I hear a faint *pop* and the door swings open. My best friend stands there, food tray in one hand, bobby pin being wielded like a sword in the other. "Come on in," I mumble, turning my back toward her and pulling the covers over my head. The smell of her mom's homemade soup fills the room and my stomach lets out an embarrassingly loud growl as I slap my hand over it like I can muffle the sound.

"Either you eat this on your own or I'll have Blaze hold your mouth open while I pour it in. Choose wisely," she says. I honestly can't tell if she's kidding, so I pull the covers down just enough that she comes into view.

Shit. She's being serious.

I sit up, wincing at the pain in my back from laying here like a potato for the last ninety-six hours. I've only gotten up to use the bathroom and drink water. Yesterday, I went downstairs and tried some crackers, but I couldn't keep them down. Today is a new day and Diane's soup is usually the cure for everything, so it's worth a try.

"Since I know *exactly* where Blaze's fingers have been, I'll do it myself," I say, taking the steaming bowl from her and setting it in my lap.

"Good choice," she says. "He got pretty creative this morning."

I scoff. "Gross."

She gives me a sympathetic smile, sitting on the end of the bed. "You okay?"

I take a small spoonful, blowing on the hot liquid before giving it a try. My stomach roils a little, but I think I can handle more if I go slow. "I don't know," I reply. "Being away from him feels awful. The longer I lay here, the less my reason for running makes sense. I wish I wasn't like this," I whisper.

"I wasn't completely positive before, but you love him." It's not a question. She's stating a fact that at this point, is painfully obvious. I've been a wreck for the past four days.

"Yeah."

She straightens her back, turning to face me. "Can I ask you a question and you promise to answer it?"

Here we go. She's about to tear me apart. But I deserve it. "I promise."

"You understand that your parents were bad people before they even had you, right? That's why you've never met a single family member of theirs in your whole life." She looks at me, waiting for confirmation.

"Yes," I say, not sure where she's going with this.

"And you understand that Small Dick Josh is now on his second marriage at age twenty-five...an unhappy one by the way, if we're going off of his wife's vague Facebook posts about how men suck. So, you were never the issue in that relationship."

"Okayyyyyyyy," I say, knowing there's more coming.

"So, why do you keep punishing yourself for their bad choices? I've known you almost our whole lives and I've never hurt you. My parents think of you as their own daughter. You're strong, funny, beautiful, resilient, and so many other things that make you impossible not to love. You've never been the problem. And this whole thing with Dalton should prove that to you." My heart beats faster in my chest at the sound of his name. She reaches over and takes the bowl, setting it on the nightstand before scooting up next to me. "He's seen you at your most vulnerable points. He's watched you fight yourself...fight *him*. And he's still here. He knows everything about you, and the only thing he wants is to build a future with you. To give you the love that you should've had a long time ago. Let him love you, Dia. Start your life over with him and trust him to make this one everything you've ever dreamed of. You're enough. *More* than enough. You deserve happiness and so does he."

I lean into her, resting my head on her shoulder. "I miss him so much," I say, tears filling my eyes.

"What did you tell me when I left Blaze behind in Boston after Brady lied about me?" I don't answer because I know exactly what I said to her, but now I need to hear her say it to me. "Go get him. You can and will have *both* a wonderful life with a man who would do anything for you, *and* still be a bad bitch that can take care of herself. You don't have to choose."

She reaches over for the soup, handing it back to me before kissing my forehead and walking toward the door. "Just think about it," she says, smiling at me before pulling the door shut. She definitely had a lot of good points. I *do* deserve good things. It's not my fault that I was treated the way I was. And Dalton has shown me how lovable I am with his actions and his words.

I need to talk to him. As I pick up my phone, it rings in my hand. Carrie's name comes up on the screen along with a selfie we took at Benton's hockey game. We're both wearing Davis jerseys with his number 10 on the front and back. I remember Dalton complaining all night that I wore his brother's jersey before I wore his.

I broke her son's heart, so I may as well face the music. "Hello," I say, quietly.

"Hi, sweetie," she replies. "How are you doing?"

I take a breath, getting my emotions in check before I speak. "Carrie, I'm so sorry. I never wanted to hurt Dalton. I—"

"Dia, I'm calling to check on *you*. Dalton is a big boy. He'll be okay."

I freeze because my mom has never once called to see how I'm doing. Even after everything I did for her. She knew I was growing up too fast, stressing about adult problems when I was just a kid. But she never, ever stopped to make sure I was okay. She'd call to make sure I was making payments on her restitution, or that there was enough money in my bank account to cover the checks she wrote when she went on her spending sprees or when my dad had gambled all their bill money away. But calling just to check on me? Not a single time.

I realize then that family isn't who you're born to. Family can be found in the least likely of places. This time, it happened to be inside a Vegas wedding chapel. Marrying Dalton gave me a whole new family. One that cares about *me*.

"I'm good," I tell her, feeling surer about my future than I ever have. My muscles relax and I take a deep breath for the first time in days. "Really good, actually."

"Oh, that makes me feel so much better. I was worried about you," she says, and I can almost see her sitting back in her chair, a look of relief melting over her expression.

"I have to go, Carrie," I blurt. "I have somewhere to be. But maybe we can get together soon and hang out."

"Sure, honey. Take care of yourself," she says.

"I will," I reply, a smile blooming across my lips. "And thank you for calling."

"Have a good day, Dia."

I hang up the phone, immediately pulling up the text app.

> DIA: Can we talk?

> DALTON: Of course. Now? I can call you.

> DIA: I was hoping we could do it in person. At the house, maybe? It'll give us some privacy.

> DALTON: How about tonight? 7 pm?

> DIA: Yeah. Can you bring the divorce papers?

It takes a minute for him to respond, but as I'm pulling clothes out of my suitcase so I can shower, my phone dings again.

DALTON: OK

I head to the bathroom, with clarity and hope for my future for the first time in my life.

THIRTY-SIX
DALTON

I SIT on the couch in the new house, immediately standing again because I can't stay still. I check my phone to see that it's six-fifty. I continue pacing, practically wearing a hole in the area rug as I shuffle my feet across it. I'm anxious as fuck. My hands won't stop shaking and I've gone over every possible scenario in my head since I got here an hour ago.

I look over to the coffee table, the divorce papers staring at me like a giant monster waiting to jump out and get me. When Dia asked me to bring them, my fucking heart sank to my stomach. I don't know what I'll do if she asks me to sign them tonight. I may as well take the still-beating organ out of my chest and hand it over to her if she leaves me, because I'll never love anyone this way again. If it's not her, it's nobody.

I try to block out the negative thoughts just as I look out the window, watching the gate swing open slowly and the headlights of my Audi come into view. I take some deep breaths, trying to calm myself now that she's here.

I walk to the door, pulling it open as she makes her

way up the steps. My instinct is to reach for her. To pull her in and inhale her scent. To kiss her so thoroughly that she feels my love flowing out of me and into her. But I don't know where she's at, so I just step out of the way, letting her in.

"Hey," I say. My body shivers with nervous energy. Fuck, this sucks. I feel like we've become strangers over the past few days.

"Hi," she replies. I shouldn't, but I take a little comfort in the way she looks so tired. Has she been unable to sleep through the night like me? She's wearing makeup, but dark circles peek out from under her eyes.

"Want to go sit?" I ask, motioning toward the living room. She gives a small nod and I follow her, trying my best not to get caught while I breathe deeply, searching for any hint of her minty shampoo. She sits on the couch, so I mirror her, keeping enough space between us so that I'm not tempted to pull her into my arms. But *fuck*. It's hard being here with her and not touching her. She looks fucking beautiful in her simple gray crewneck and black leggings. Her long, black hair frames her flawless face as she looks at me, and I wish I could read her mind.

"Dalton, I—"

"Hold on," I blurt, cutting her off. "Before you say anything, I just have to get some things out. I might not be able to say them if I don't do it now. Is that okay?"

She nods her head, allowing me to start. "I'm sorry, Dia. I pushed you so hard, even when you kept telling me you weren't ready. I wanted so badly to gain your trust, not realizing that I was dismissing your feelings and wishes in the process." I look up, seeing her beautiful brown eyes staring back at me, giving me the strength to continue. "I was selfish. But I swear it came from a good place. I just wanted to show you that I was here, no matter what. That you could fall with me and I would catch you every time. And if you decide you don't want me anymore, I'll still be here, loving you from afar until my last breath. I just want you to be happy." I do my best to steel my expression as I reach into my pocket, pulling out the small blue box and opening it before handing it to her.

Her brows furrow in confusion as she locks her eyes on the large diamond. "I thought you sold it," she whispers.

"I did," I tell her. "I got halfway home that night and turned back around. It felt so wrong. That ring belongs to you. Even if you don't wear it and it sits in your jewelry box forever, you'll always have something to remind you of the time you were loved so fiercely by a man who would choose you a hundred times over, even knowing it would break him in the end." I hope she doesn't ask about the check I left on the counter that night. After I left the jeweler the second time, I stopped by the bank and had a hundred grand put on a traveler's check so she wouldn't know that it came from my account. I knew she needed the money to feel like she had the freedom to take care of herself here in Boston.

A single tear slips down her cheek as she sets the box on the table and picks up the divorce papers. My heart rate speeds up, and it takes everything in me not to get on my knees and beg her to stay. But I don't want to stop her from whatever decision she's about to make, so I fist my hands in my lap, waiting for her to speak.

But she doesn't. She doesn't take her eyes off of me as she holds the paper between us, tearing it down the middle. I'm frozen in place, unsure of how to react. Before I can ask her what this means, she puts me out of my misery.

"Since that very first night, you've only ever wanted to show me what being loved felt like. And I'll admit that it was foreign…and *scary*. I was terrified that I'd never be able to give you the life that *you* deserved. To be a wife that you could be proud of. That one day, you'd wake up and realize I wasn't enough, and you'd leave me. And I wouldn't know how to go back to the way I was before. I've had a lot of people come and go from my life. But I know I couldn't survive loving you and losing you, Dalton." Her tears flow freely as I reach out for her, unable to stay away any longer.

"I'm not going anywhere, baby. Ever," I say, wrapping her tightly in my arms as she sobs. I breathe a sigh of relief at the feel of her, back where she belongs. I'm never letting her go again.

She pulls back, looking up at me. "I love you. More than I ever thought I was capable of."

"I love you so much, Diamond Davis. And I'll spend the rest of my life reminding you so you never forget how perfect you are."

I cup her face in my hand, lowering my lips to hers. The kiss starts tentatively, like we've been away from each other for years instead of days. I explore her mouth, dragging my tongue along her plump lower lip as she opens, inviting me to lick inside. I can't hold myself back any longer, feeling like I'll die if I don't kiss and touch her in a way that tells her exactly how I've felt since she ran away from me.

"Baby," I whisper against her lips. "I love you so fucking much, but I need to show you what it was like. I need you to understand. Can I?" I'm practically begging her, but the urge to do this is overwhelming. She nods her head, and this is normally where I'd ask for her to say it out loud, but I don't want any more words. We can say everything with our actions.

I lay her back on the couch, covering her body with mine as I place unhurried kisses all over her jaw and neck. My hands, that can't seem to decide on one single part of her body, slide up her shirt, stopping to squeeze her hips before skating over her stomach and up to her tits. My lips move back to her mouth and the pressure on every part of her increases. I'm kissing her harder, grinding into her harder, and when I pull the cup of her bra down, exposing one hard peak, I give it a firm pinch that elicits a groan from deep in her throat.

"I missed this fucking body so much," I whisper as I pull her shirt over her head and throw it over the back of the couch. I don't even bother taking the time to unclasp her black lace bra. Instead, I grab firmly between the cups and pull until it tears away from her. She gasps in surprise, staring at me with wide eyes, but I don't give her a chance to speak before sucking one perfect, pink nipple into my mouth. Her satisfied moans fill the room as I move back and forth between them, laving her tits with slow strokes of my tongue. Her hips push up into me, telling me she needs more, but she's not getting it yet. I pin her down with my body, just barely grinding my cock, that's probably leaking through my jeans at this point, against her core.

"Is your little pussy aching, baby?" I coo. "Do you want me?"

She squeezes her eyes shut, clearly being overtaken by need. "Y-yes," she stutters. "Dalton, please."

Her begging spurs me on as I sit up, pulling her pants and thong down in one fluid motion. She spreads her legs as far as the couch will allow and I just about abandon my plan all together. Her pussy glistens with her arousal, and I start to feel lightheaded with the need to bury my nose between her legs and inhale her scent.

I reach back, pulling my shirt over my head and tossing it onto the floor. I feel like a god when her breathing becomes more rapid at the sight of my bare chest and abs. She reaches out to touch me, but I grab her wrists, pinning them both to the armrest above her head. "No," I tell her. Her eyebrows furrow in confusion, but she keeps her arms in place like a good girl while I stand to pull off my pants, boxer briefs, and socks at an agonizingly slow pace.

Instead of laying back over her, I move her legs, sitting on the other end of the couch. "Straddle me," I tell her. She scrambles up, thinking I'm finally giving her what she wants, but she's so far from any semblance of pleasure, it's not even funny. She throws one smooth leg over my thighs and settles her knees on each side of my hips. When she lowers, pressing her dripping heat against my hard shaft, I almost cave and slide in right there. It would be so easy, but she needs to feel this. *We* need to feel this.

I let her grind down on me for a bit, her juices coating my cock as she does. I can feel the muscles tightening in her body as pleasure starts to gather in her core, but every time she tries to pick up speed, I grip onto her hips. I'm only allowing her to move enough so that her orgasm feels like it's building miles away, far from her reach.

"I need you," she breathes. "I—I can't...please fuck me." She's already barely making sense, doing whatever she can to get me to give in.

I lift her up, grabbing the base of my cock and slowly lowering her down. She sighs in relief as I fill her, her cunt stretching around me. She's so tight, I feel like it's been forever since I've been inside her.

"Fuck," I choke out. "You're strangling me." My vision starts to blur, but when she lifts her hips to ride me, I hold her down so she can't move.

"Dalton, please," she whines. "I need to move."

I continue holding her still as her body tries to thrash against me. She's shaking her head rapidly, trying to tell me she can't handle it anymore. But she knows her safe word. She'll use it if she needs to. Until then, we're going to experience this together.

I bring my hand up, pushing my thumb into her mouth. "Suck," I order. She takes it between her plump lips, swirling her tongue around the tip before I pull it out with a *pop*. Without a word, I reach down and rub barely there circles around her clit. I'm applying almost no pressure, but I can feel how hard and swollen it is against the pad of my thumb. She cries out in frustration when I pull away for a moment, waiting for any buildup from her orgasm to subside. I still have one hand gripping her hips, preventing her from moving as I bring the other one back down and rub her again.

I build her up slowly, adding more pressure against her aching bundle of nerves. She's growing wetter by the second as I feel her inner walls start to clench around me. Pulling my thumb away again, I shove my hips up into her, feeling my head press against her G-spot, but still holding her tightly to me so she can't get the friction her body is begging for.

"W-what are you doing?" she asks, barely able to get the words out. There's anguish in her voice, and as much as I want to give her everything she wants, the sound of her pain right now spurs me on.

"Does it hurt?" I ask, trying my best to keep my voice even. I'm about two seconds away from fucking her into oblivion, and it's taking all of my self-control to keep her still on top of me. "Are you desperate right now?"

"Y-yes," she whimpers, her head lolling to the side as her body shakes in agony. She tries again to move her hips, but I dig my fingers in harder. There's no way I'm not leaving marks right now, but we need this in order to heal.

I run the pad of my thumb along the spot where we're joined, gathering her arousal, and returning to massage her clit that is swelling more and more every time I edge her. Her nails dig into my skin as I allow her to get even closer this time before pulling away once more, ruining the orgasm that she was almost able to grasp. Her head drops forward as small, involuntary tremors ripple through her body.

"Look at me, Dia," I order. She obeys, slowly bringing her hooded brown eyes to mine. She looks dejected and exhausted from trying to fight me. "Every time you leave, *this* is how it feels. When you shut me out instead of talking to me, it tortures us both. It kills us *both*. No more," I say, grabbing the back of her neck and pressing our foreheads together. "Tell me you won't run again."

Tears fall from her eyes as her body slumps forward onto my chest. "I promise. I won't run again."

The words are music to my ears as I pull out, flipping us over so I'm on top of her. One of her feet is on the floor, while I pull the other one over my shoulder and push back into her. The last string of my self-control snaps and I thrust wildly into her, fucking her like I need it to live. Because I do. I need every part of Dia Davis to be mine. Her hands shoot out to my abs, her nails digging half-moon shaped marks into my skin. I hope she does it hard enough to draw blood and scar me forever.

"I love you so much," I growl, fucking into her like a wild animal. I'm going so fast and hard, that the couch begins to move along the floor with every punch of my hips.

"I love you, too," she says on a gasp as I feel her walls start to close in tightly around me.

I pick up my pace, needing to feel her come more than I need my next breath. "That's it, baby. Choke my cock. Come for me," I tell her. It only takes one more thrust before she's soaking the cushion under us. She cries out, but I don't let up until I'm sure she's completely spent. It isn't until I know she's given me everything that I let myself go, emptying into her with a groan.

We lay there as I soften inside her, breathing heavy and dripping with sweat, but I can't leave her warmth yet. I could stay here forever if she'd let me. And the thought of her full of my cum makes my possessive side want to hold it in as long as I can. I know she's on birth control, but I want this woman carrying my children as soon as she'll allow it. I'm done waiting for forever with her. I want to start right now.

I bring my lips down to her, kissing her with all the love and passion I have. "I can't believe you're mine," I whisper against her mouth, feeling the corners of her lips turn up into a smile.

"Til' death do us part, hubby," she says. "You sure you can handle me that long?"

I roll my eyes. "I was made to handle you, Wifey," I say, dropping a kiss to the tip of her nose before reluctantly pulling out and watching as my cum leaks out of her and pools into the wet spot under her ass. I cringe.

"We're going to need a new couch. We fucked this one up."

"Worth it," she says with a dick drunk smile as I pull her up, tossing her over my shoulder and walking toward the bathroom to shower while she laughs, half-heartedly punching my back, pretending to want me to put her down.

And she's right, it was definitely worth it.

THIRTY-SEVEN
DIA

IT'S BEEN two days since Dalton and I had our talk. I finally feel like I'm free of my past. It was never really my fault that the people in my life treated me the way they did. The only thing I did wrong was put my trust in the hands of the wrong people. People who didn't treat it like a gift, the way my husband does. And although it took me a long time to put the puzzle pieces together, once I did, it was like a switch had been flipped. All along, I felt like I didn't deserve love and wasn't capable of giving it. That every time I came close to it, I somehow messed it up. But now, I see what real love and trust looks like. Dalton has shown me that I am worthy of more than my parents made me think I was. That I can accept love and help while still being strong and independent. He's shown me that I have so much to offer the people around me, starting with being the best wife I can be to him. I don't think I'll ever truly be able to thank him for opening my eyes simply by standing beside me while I figured all of this out.

We decided to invite everyone over to the new house today. I only talked to Mads for a moment the other night, telling her I would fill her in on everything when I saw her. As we left it, she has no idea that Dalton and I are staying together, so we get to break the news to everyone at once.

"Baby, have you seen my wedding ring? I left it on the counter and now it's not there," Dalton says from the top of the stairs. He's fresh from the shower, with only a towel slung loosely around his waist, and if I wasn't down here cleaning like a nut job, I would definitely be up there on my knees in front of him. Something about the way the excess water drips down his abs makes me turn into a different person. But I have the rest of my life to enjoy that. Because right now, company is coming.

"It's on your dresser," I reply. I've been moving things around and cleaning up all morning, even though you could literally go through this place with a white glove and it would still look brand new. I've never owned a home that I could be proud of, so I want everything to be perfect. This will be the first of many get-togethers at our new house, and the thought makes me so happy. I grew up with nothing. We moved around so much, my parents constantly being evicted due to nonpayment, that I never really knew what it felt like to be secure in one place. But now I have everything I've ever wanted, and so much more.

The doorbell rings and Dalton rushes down the stairs, almost biting it on the very last step. I try to hold in my laugh, but fail miserably, bending down with my hands on my knees as I cackle at his expense.

"God, you're fucking brutal," he says under his breath

as he reaches for the doorknob and pulls it open. Tanner stands on the other side, and I have to admit that I'm kind of surprised to see him, considering he's been in and out of town for what seems like the last two months or so. But I'm glad he's here because our group wouldn't feel complete without him.

"Hey, man," Dalton greets him, giving him one of those weird bro hug, back pat things. "Glad you could make it."

"I wouldn't miss it," he says, handing Dalton a bottle of champagne that looks like it cost more than the entire outfit I'm wearing right now, shoes included, which my very impulsive husband bought for me, so you know the price tag was steep. Tanner looks over at me before looking back at Dalton. "Everything good?" he asks, and I wonder exactly what he knows about the last week. Not that it matters, because I have a feeling he knows more about love and heartbreak than all of us combined.

"Yeah," Dalton says, looking over at me and winking. I swear, this man's objective in life is to ruin every single pair of panties I have. Those dimples alone have me ready to throw this six-foot-four professional quarterback right out my door so I can take my hot-as-fuck husband for another ride. As if he can read my mind, he turns to me and mouths *'bad girl'*. I roll my eyes as if I wasn't fantasizing about sitting on his face, before motioning to Tanner to head into the kitchen. Dalton gives me a little pat on the ass as he follows behind me, which does nothing to lessen the ache that's blooming between my legs. I step far away from him, trying to collect myself as he grabs three beers out of the fridge, handing one to each of us.

"So," Dalton says, focusing on Tanner, "Where have you been lately?"

He looks like a deer and headlights at first, but is saved

from having to answer by another ring of the doorbell. My husband darts out of the room, and moments later, I hear Mads and Blaze as they step into the entryway. For some reason, I feel my nerves kick up. Maybe it's because I didn't tell her immediately after the other night. I was just so wrapped up in things with Dalton, that I didn't have time to call her with all of the details. I'm sure I'll be paying for that one later, but at least I have some ammunition. All I have to do is remind her that she was canoodling with her boss-turned-boyfriend without informing me just a few months ago. I know she'll be happy for me, no matter what. All my best friend has ever wanted is for me to be happy.

We all fall into a comfortable conversation about the upcoming NFL draft, when the doorbell rings again. I know it's Bella and Maverick because they're the last ones we're expecting. We broke the news to Dalton's parents when they called him last night. They were both completely ecstatic and so upset that they would have to miss our little housewarming party today, but promised to get here as soon as they could. Now that hockey playoffs are in full swing, they've been traveling to watch Benton play as much as they can. I love how tight their family is and I am so thankful to be a part of it now.

Once we have everyone gathered in the kitchen, I can barely contain myself as I walk over to Dalton and take his hand in mine. He looks down at me, giving me a supportive smile before we turn to our friends.

"We have something to tell you," I say. A collective gasp fills the room. Mads' hand covers her mouth, and her eyes immediately fill with tears. "For those of you who don't know, Dalton and I got married in Vegas. I wouldn't call it an accident, but I guess it wasn't really on purpose, either." I look at him as he shakes his head in mock annoyance, making me laugh. "It was a fight to get to this point, mostly on my part, but we've realized that we love each other so much. And we're staying together. Welcome to our new home," I say, tears spilling over as I smile proudly at them. Saying the words felt a million times better than I could've ever imagined. Dalton leans down and kisses my forehead as Mads jumps up, rounding the counter and wrapping me in the tightest hug I think I've ever gotten from her. They each take turns hugging and congratulating us, and at this moment, my life finally feels complete. I have a husband who adores me, a best friend who would do absolutely anything for me, a newly found family that I trust with everything I have, an upcoming job that is literally a dream come true, and a future that I am truly excited for. The battle was long and hard, but thanks to the man beside me, I've finally won. I've let go of the darkness of my past and all I see are bright skies ahead.

"Hey, guys?" Maverick says, breaking me from my thoughts as he peeks into the living room. "Why don't you have a couch?"

I can't help the laugh that bursts out of me as I look over at Dalton who has a smug look on his face. I point at him, giving him my best stern look, one that says *don't you dare*, before he doubles over with laughter, too.

"Oh, ew!" Mads says, realizing what's going on. "You guys are gross."

"What?" Blaze asks, obviously still oblivious.

Mads grabs his hand, yanking him out of the chair he's sitting in. "Just don't sit...*anywhere*," she says, looking around at all the seating options in the house. We haven't christened them all, but we're working on it. I can't even tell you with one hundred percent certainty that the new couch we're having delivered won't suffer the same fate as the last one, but I *can* tell you that marriage is the most fun I've had in a long time.

Here's to many more years of love and laughter with the husband I never wanted, but couldn't live without.

THIRTY-EIGHT
DALTON
ONE YEAR LATER

"DUDE, I'm so fucking nervous. Why am I so nervous?" I say to Maverick as I pace the hallway. It's the first night of Bella's tour, which means it is also Dia's first night as one of her dancers. They've spent the last four months rehearsing pretty much around the clock. That's probably a little bit dramatic, but every minute I'm not spending with my wife feels like an eternity.

Thankfully, we just kicked off another offseason, so Mav and I are able to travel around the country with the girls on the US leg of the tour. We'll have to say goodbye once they leave for Europe because the Blizzard will be starting OTAs, which means I'm soaking up every last second we have until then. Dia and I haven't spent more than two nights away from each other since we got back together and the thought of being apart makes my stomach churn with anxiety. But, knowing that she'll be out there living her dream makes it all worth it.

Maverick pulls his head out of the trash can, where he definitely just yakked up his entire dinner, looking back at me with a terrified look on his face. "I don't know," he groans. "I'm nervous, too." He takes a few deep breaths, making sure his stomach is okay, but whips around when the dressing room door opens behind us.

"You good, babe?" Bella says, giving her boyfriend a sympathetic look. "Did you puke again?" She cringes for a moment, but schools her expression as he sheepishly nods. She walks over to him, wrapping her arms around his waist and leading him into the room. He looks like a four-year-old with a tummy ache as he follows her with puppy eyes to the couch.

I enter the room, my eyes immediately locking on my wife. Her back is to me, but I would know that ass anywhere. She looks hot as hell in a pair of baggy cargo pants and a cropped tank top with slashes along the back. Her red bra peeks out from under one of the straps and I have an overwhelming urge to rip it off of her while I fuck her in the bathroom down the hall.

Nobody goes from nervous to horny quicker than I do. Especially when Dia is around.

I do my best to hide the half-chub I'm rocking as I walk over and wrap my arms around her waist from behind. She jumps, but relaxes when she realizes it's me, leaning her back into my chest. I drop my lips to her ear so only she can hear. "You look edible, Wifey. And I'm a very hungry boy," I growl, subtly grinding my dick into her. "I can't wait to fuck this tight ass when we get back to the hotel."

She turns around, a look of shock on her face as she peeks to see if anyone is close enough to us to hear me. Everyone in the room is going about their business, definitely not paying attention to what we have going on in our little corner.

"Mmmmm," she purrs. "That sounds like the best way

to work off the post-show adrenaline. I can't wait to have you inside me."

"Fuuuuck, baby," I groan. "I love you so much."

"I love you, too," she says, giving me a chaste kiss and pulling away before this thing turns into something extremely indecent. Good thing she stopped it because I definitely wasn't going to. All these people can watch me bend her over and own her, for all I care.

The door opens and a man with a headset tells the group that they have five minutes before they need to head toward the stage. Dia's expression changes and I can tell that the nerves have kicked in.

"Hey," I say. "You are amazing. You earned your spot on this tour and you are going to kill it out there. I am so fucking proud to call you my wife." I swipe my thumb across the single tear that falls down her cheek, bringing it to my mouth. I don't know why that was my first instinct, but I want to taste her, and this is the only way I can right now. I want to take a part of her with me while she's on stage.

She looks at me with pure love and adoration before lifting her chin and giving me a tight nod. "I can do this. I can do *anything*." I can't help but smile at the changes that she's made in the last year. How she's grown. I never thought she would say those words. Even though I believed them, I was afraid she was too broken to see how strong and amazing she really is. I am in awe of this woman, and I still can't believe that she chose me to share her life with.

"Okay," Bella says with a clap. "Hands in!"

We all reach to the center of the group, stacking our hands on top of one another as she counts. "One, two, three!"

"Family!" We all yell, in unison. I look over to see a bright smile stretching across Dia's face. She deserves all of this and more.

The group heads toward the part of the stage they'll enter from while Maverick and I walk to where we'll be watching the show. Bella offered for us to sit in the wings, but we both agreed that we wanted to experience this thing just like the rest of the fans. We paid full price for front row seats, and I already know it'll be worth every single penny.

The supporting acts do an amazing job of getting the crowd ready for our girls. We try our best not to dance around like teenagers because there are just as many cameras pointed at us as there are at the stage right now. We're trying to uphold our reputations as big, tough football players, but I'll admit that this pop music really makes me want to move.

The lights dim and the crowd goes absolutely nuts as Bella comes into view. The band plays the first notes of her biggest hit, making the screams go up about a million decibels. I look over to see a giant smile on Maverick's face as he watches his girlfriend in her element. But my attention snaps back to the stage as soon as the beat drops and the dancers run out to surround her. I can't take my eyes off my wife as she hits every move with absolute precision. Her giant diamond ring glints against the spotlight, making my dick stir to life behind my zipper. Nothing makes me harder than the thought of being her husband.

I've seen Dia dance before in her studio at home, and I've caught a few rehearsals for this tour when they didn't interfere with practices and games, but there's nothing like seeing her on stage in front of this crowd. The energy in the room is electric, and I know she's feeding off of it as she dances. This is the dream she's wanted all her life, and I'm so lucky to be here as she takes it.

Diamond Davis is a force to be reckoned with in this world. And I've enjoyed every single second of loving her through all of the hard times and the good times that brought her here to this moment. The best decision I ever made was throwing her over my shoulder and walking into that chapel in Vegas. She may have thought it was crazy, but I knew right then that my heart belonged to her. If I'm honest, I think I knew from the moment I laid eyes on her that she was it for me.

Because even though she might not realize it, *she's* my dream come true.

EPILOGUE

DIA

ONE YEAR LATER

"OKAY!" I yell, loud enough for everyone to hear me. "Before we open these doors, I wanted to take a minute to thank all of you for being here. I never thought I would have all of this, but with your love and support, I'm here."

I look over at Mads, who knows first-hand the struggles that I went through growing up. She gives me a proud smile as I continue.

"When I was a kid, I didn't have much. Being able to dance freely, even at a very young age, wasn't always a possibility. Whether it was family stuff or not having the money for lessons, there was always something standing in the way of me achieving my dreams. There are so many kids out there who hope for the same things I did, and what we're doing here will give them a chance to go as far as their little imaginations will take them."

I cradle my growing belly, looking over at my husband with pure adoration and love. "All I've ever wanted was to provide a place for future dancers to learn and grow without having to worry about anything else. With the donations from my very generous friends and family, we've put together several scholarships for dancers who may not have otherwise had the means to achieve their goals. Everyone here, no matter where they come from, will have an opportunity to dance with us. One day, maybe my daughter will lace up a pair of pointe shoes right here in this very room. That means the world to me. So, thank you."

'I love you,' Dalton mouths, blowing me a kiss. There's no mistaking the pride in his eyes as he watches me take another one of my dreams and make it a reality.

I smile as I walk over to the door, flipping the sign to say 'Open' before turning the lock. "Diamond Dreams Dance Studio is officially open for business!"

The room erupts into cheers as I run over to Dalton, wrapping my arms around his waist. He kisses my forehead, giving me that same loving look he's been wearing since the night I married him. I turn to watch as people flood in through the doors, looking around at all of the special things we have set up for our grand opening. We have different costumes for kids to try on in one corner, which most of the little girls flock to right away. We laugh as some of the smaller ones struggle to step into the pink tutus we have set out.

Dalton puts his hand on my stomach, leaning down to whisper in my ear. "I can't wait to watch our little one dance with her mama," he says. My eyes fill with tears at the thought of my daughter being able to do whatever it is that she wants without anyone telling her that she isn't good enough. I will always build her up and support her, no matter what she chooses to do in her life. The sky will be the limit for her, and she'll know, without a single doubt, that her parents love her fiercely.

When I saw those two pink lines six months ago, I'll admit that I was terrified. I wasn't raised in a stable home with anyone to care for me. I faced all of my struggles alone and there were times when I felt so broken, that I didn't think I'd ever get to a point of true happiness. I was afraid that I wasn't given enough of an example to be a good mother to my own child. But Dalton reminded me that I am not my past. The things that happened to me back then do not have to define the way I continue in this life.

I vowed right then that I would do everything I could to be the best mother this world has ever seen. I'm sure there will be plenty of struggles, and there will be times that I have no idea what the fuck I'm doing, but I'll never leave my child or make her feel like she has to do anything alone. We'll always be in her corner.

I may not have started out with a lot of love in my life, but now I have more than I could ever imagine. The past two years have changed me in every possible way, and I'm so proud of how far I've come. I went from a scared, self-doubting shell of a girl to a strong, confident woman who knows her worth. And anytime I slip up and start to forget, Dalton makes sure to remind me that I am every bit of the bad bitch I've always tried to be.

No amount of time in this life will be enough with him, but I'm perfectly happy starting with forever.

ACKNOWLEDGMENTS

My husband - I couldn't have written Dalton without knowing the lengths a man would go to for the woman he loves. You've been that for me since we were teenagers; always going to the ends of the Earth to show me how amazing I am and that I can do anything. You will always be the ultimate book boyfriend and the reason I'm able to create these men that live and breathe for their girls. I love you infinity.

My mom - I'm still trying my best to see what the line is that'll make you yell at me for being too spicy. We know it's not a belt around the neck with Blaze or butt stuff in the hotel room with Maverick, but how about now? Any of Dalton's antics strike your fancy? I'm just kidding...I know I could write anything and you'd support it with your whole heart, just like you always have. I couldn't do any of this without you. Also, I hope Dalton was *funny enough* for you.

Breanne - We did it again! Our first full-length book together and I honestly can't find the words to tell you how happy I am that we're on this journey, creating such amazing memories. You're the best sister, friend, editor, artist, comic relief on the days I'm stressing myself the fuck out, and everything else you've been to me in the last two decades. I love you! Thank you a million times over.

Hannah Gray - I really can't express how thankful I am to have you. This is my third book and even though I never thought I'd get here, you always believed that I would. You push me to be the best author I can be, and you remind me to take it easy on myself when my anxiety tells me I'm not enough. We may joke about how out of control our daily voice messages are (and that's definitely an accurate depiction lol), but they're exactly what I need some days to remember that this *should* be fun and relaxing. I'm beyond thankful for the amazing friendship we've built. I love you!

Lexi James - Even though being in different time zones makes me feel like we live on separate planets sometimes, I take so much comfort in knowing that you're only a voice message away. There are days when I'm stuck on how to move forward, but talking through it with you has always been the best way to get my thoughts together. I absolutely wouldn't be doing any of this without you beside me.

Jaime Rayyan - I don't even know how tf we got here. One minute, you were suggesting some tweaks to Maverick's story as a beta reader and now I literally can't get through a single day without our weird texts and voice messages... and of course, our Daily Dose of Bosa. Dalton and Dia's story wouldn't be half of what it is without you and I am so thankful for this crazy little friendship we've built.

Amanda Mudgett - Where do I even begin? You're the captain of my cheerleading team and I know if I'm struggling with anything, you've got my back. Even if it's just you telling me for the millionth time that my books don't suck, every word is so important to my process. I love you to the moon!

My beta readers, Jenn, Nicole, Ashley, Maggie, Meghan, Andie: I can't thank you enough for all of the care you put into helping me create these books. I'm beyond grateful that you're all so open and honest with me because your input has 100% made these stories what they are. I appreciate you all more than you'll ever know.

My ARC team - You took a chance on a baby author and I'll never be able to express what that means to me. I love you all and can't wait to see what we accomplish next!

Autumn and Wordsmith Publicity - Thank you for always going above and beyond for your authors. I couldn't have done any of this without you!

The Bookstagram/BookTok girlies - You make me feel like a rockstar every day. Your comments, reviews, and edits keep me going on the days that I let the negativity creep in. I always know I have a safe, soft place to land with the bookish community. Thank you.

My readers - You are the reason I do this. Your positive words make me want to sit at my computer and continue creating. There aren't enough *thank you*s in this world to accurately measure how grateful I am. I'll never take it for granted.

ABOUT THE AUTHOR

C.L. Rose is a wife and mother of two. She lives in Northeast Ohio with her husband, son, daughter, and dog, Tank. When she isn't writing, you can find her reading in front of a space heater, wrapped in a thick blanket, probably complaining that she's cold.

authorclrose.com

MORE FROM THE BOSTON BLIZZARD SERIES

Hot Route

The Stunt: A Boston Blizzard Novella

QB Keeper - Summer 2024

Printed in Great Britain
by Amazon